CHAPTER ONE_

THE SMELL IS THE FIRST THING SHE SENSES. IT'S NOT quite identifiable, an incongruous mix of old books, stale cigar smoke, and rotting chicken bones. Slowly, vision joins scent. As her eyes adjust, shadows come into gentle focus. A towering shelf, leaning dangerously across her field of vision; motes of dust like tiny stars, twinkling in the shaft of sunlight descending from what she now sees is a tall, barred window; a ceiling that bleeds away into darkness above her. The carpet is thick under her feet and crunches a little when she moves, stiffened by age or some less pleasant process.

Her nose twitches, neurons firing, mad to sort the smells into a thing that makes sense. Nothing really smells like this; not in the real world.

"They sent you."

The voice is almost physical. The sound travels directly into her brain, bypassing the more discerning reverberations of her eardrums, and she feels the words as a taste at the back of her throat. This, she has often mused, must be what synesthesia feels like.

"I sent myself," she retorts. She peers through the shelves

but can't find him; then she sees a flash of color through the stacks. Briefly, she considers chasing, but a brave rush of surety tells her that if she stays put he'll come to her. She picks a book at random and takes it off the shelf. It's leather-bound and awkward to hold, bigger than her arm from the elbow to the wrist. She opens it. It's a spreadsheet, full of words that have been abbreviated to meaninglessness. Some backup server, most likely.

"It won't work," he tells her. He's definitely to her left now. She fingers the release mechanism in the front pocket of her dress. It's a faded floral print pinafore, like old settlers might have worn, and buttery soft from years of use. One-handed and awkward, she levers the big book back onto its shelf. There's a puff of dust, but her eyes don't water and no sneeze reflex triggers.

"You're so cocky. You think there's no trap that can hold you."

"There hasn't been yet." He's in front of her so suddenly that she takes a step back. Today he has curly brown hair and a splash of freckles across café-au-lait skin. He's wearing faded brown pants with jet black suspenders, a raw linen shirt showing a few curls of hair on his chest. Their ensembles match. The realization sends burning heat through her cheeks, though she quickly toggles the feature off. She doesn't want him to know she cares.

His eyes are the only things that never change. They've been familiar to her since she first saw him, and the frustration over not being able to peg why swamps her. They're dark, a brown that's almost black, with a light that shimmers just beneath the surface like water under a crescent moon.

"Aren't you supposed to press the button now?" he reminds her.

"Yes."

WIRE WINGS

WREN HANDMAN

THE PARLIAMENT HOUSE

Edited by Live Knudson, Katelynn Watkins, and Megan Hultberg

ISBN: 978-1-956136-52-4

Parliament House Press

www.parliamenthousepress.com

But she doesn't. With no body heat to warm the metal, the switch stays cool against her skin. They'll know something is wrong—her brain activity is too high to simulate the boredom of waiting for him to arrive, and she's supposed to release the net as soon as she sees him.

"Why do you look like that?" she asks instead.

"Why do you?" He never answers a question directly. "You make yourself into someone you're not when you know people are watching. Like this little mouse," he touches a curl of her nut-brown hair, "could ever be anything more than the shell you live in. I like you better in leather."

She stammers, has no answer. She can feel her confident self, the one who only lives in the Waves, trying to pull up the mask and hide. There's no way that he knows, is there? She uses all the security clearances she can think of, hacks her way in instead of Diving directly. There's no way he knows—but he has done so many impossible things. This one should not surprise her.

"Why won't you just come back with me?" she asks, choosing to ignore what she doesn't like. "You know they want to make you famous."

"I'm already famous," he counters. He's walking around her now so that she has to slowly spin to keep him in front of her. He doesn't seem to move so much as disappear, only to reappear so quickly that her eyes don't process anything except that he's moved a fraction forward. Like the stop motion cartoons she used to make as a child, but infinitely smoother. "I'm also free." He breathes the words and she feels them touch her skin, tastes them a millisecond later.

"They aren't trying to lock you up," she says, but they're both distracted by a ping. She whirls, but it's only a Surfer— the shimmering blue form appears, takes a book down, reads a figure, and disappears as swiftly as it came. She can't believe they chose a Site with outside access. Sloppy. *No wonder they haven't caught him yet*, she thinks.

"Come dancing with me," he urges, ignoring her earlier words. It occurs to her how much they both shut their eyes to things they don't like. They're more akin than she realized. "It'll be like when we went to that concert on the top of Mount Olympus."

"*I* went to the concert. You crashed it. And then you *crashed* it," she objects.

"They crashed it. Too many Divers for the server—not my fault."

"Your processing power is twenty times theirs! You crashed it," she repeats, but she can't hide her smile. She could toggle the feature off but that would be too obvious; all of her emotional triggers would vanish, and he would know she was hiding something. He knows her better than she can explain, this creature that should be a stranger to her. She's only met him three times; four if you count the unveiling, but the whole family was there for that and she didn't get much of an impression. Yet she wants to keep him here, talking, until her father drags her back from the Waves.

But she's always been more obedient than she likes. Always has grand plans for adventure that she never can bring herself to realize. Not in the real world. Not with the weight of her body on her bones. And even though she's here now, even though she's Diving, she knows they're watching. She knows how disappointed they can be; she's been the focus of it more times than she can count. She sighs and presses the button of the trigger in her pocket. "I'm sorry," she says, but he only laughs.

The partition Manifests as a shimmering blue fishnet, weighted at the edges with eerily luminous green globes. It glows through the floor at their feet, stretches a foot above their heads, and balloons out around them, creating a puffed-out cylinder. There's a momentary lull as if the air has disappeared from the room: not sucked out, but simply vanished, taking with it sound and vibration and the sight of the storage server beyond the veil. He—she hopes he earns a name soon, one that fits his mystery and rebellion—moves closer to her. He lifts a hand and runs it across the surface of the partition, as if he's skimming the water under a fast-moving boat.

"Just the two of us," he whispers.

He's at least a foot away. She knows she doesn't feel the warmth of his body beside hers, only imagines it, but the effect is the same. They're staring into each other's eyes so deeply it should be awkward. The blue light catches in his and reflects back at her. It feels familiar... She can almost place him...

"What would it feel like? If I kissed you?" he asks, phrasing it quizzically, as if the question were earnest. It should break the spell, but she finds it so charming she can't look away.

"I don't know," she admits. "I've never kissed anyone during a Dive."

He gives her a devilish look, full of promise, but then a shadow crosses his face—momentary pain or an unpleasant distraction, she isn't sure. He touches her cheek with the back of his fingers, the gesture awkward.

"I've never kissed anyone," he says, as if it isn't the same thing; but for him, it always will be. He falls backwards, a cliff-diver with the knowledge that what happens behind him will be thrilling and terrifying, but ultimately beyond his control.

And then he's gone. The partition is designed specially to hold him, to pull him out of the Waves and deposit him on a locked server with no outside access, but he passes through it like a hot spoon through ice cream, leaving a broken and melted hole in his wake. For a brief second she can see the Waves on the other side, unManifested data in a swirling void; then her sensors go into overdrive trying to process the sites eddying past, and she screams as every sense is bombarded with fragments of information, downloaded and processed into sight, vision, taste, and sound. Someone pulls the Line and the pain ceases abruptly; her body goes slack with relief, and she plummets headfirst out of her chair.

Her father catches her, of course. He and Paul have been hovering; Paul is typing on a Surface at his desk, while her father monitors on a tablet. The Bends hit hard, only half a minute behind the relief of disconnection. Her mouth goes dry, her eyes watering and burning simultaneously; her whole body twitches with quick spasmodic jerks that threaten to knock her out of the chair again. But her father has a firm grip on her upper arms, and after a few minutes, she regains control of her tingling extremities.

"That wasn't fun," she whispers. Paul hands her a glass of water, while her father's attention drifts as soon as it's clear that the Bends have passed.

Paul, too, is soon distracted. "How did it do that? Did you catch anything new?" he asks.

"It's somehow interfacing with the code. Anything we program, it can alter. The damn thing understands its DNA better than we do," her father says, frustration evident in the deep lines around his mouth and the way he clutches his stilo.

"He said he wanted to be free," she says, but her quiet voice is lost in the flurry of activity as the older men recalculate data and bicker over who's to blame for their continued failure. They rejig the partition program, debate coding and unexplored options. Some of it she understands

—sixteen years spent just below the height of these conversations has left her with a muscle-deep understanding of virtual and quantum computing, programming, even electrical engineering. But the reality is that Paul and her father are too intelligent, their minds too quick. She will never operate at the level they do, and fatalism saps her of the will to try. Better to be an artist or a farmer; then at least her failure to live up to her father will be harder to see, comparisons being difficult when the subjects are so diverse.

After about twenty minutes she coughs, and her father gives her a look, surprised to find her still here.

"Thanks for your help, Gracie," he tells her absently. "You don't have to stick around."

"Why does he keep showing up? Every time I Dive?" she asks.

The men exchange looks. They are brilliant—scientists, scholars, the kind of people who make others feel small just by existing, by using their knowledge so well. But the give-and-take of social interactions often eludes them. They are terrible liars.

"We're not sure," Paul says. *Lie*, she thinks.

"Maybe it feels a kinship," her father says. *Is this the truth?*

"As the daughter of its creator, you might be the closest thing to a sibling it has," Paul agrees. *Lie.* She knows it is untrue in an objective sense, of course, but she finds it interesting that Paul knows it too, that he does not believe his own words. She remembers the way her mystery boy stood in front of her, the heat in his eyes. Promised kisses that she knows she will seek out, even though they call him "it," even though sometimes she wonders what makes a person real. Let her have the adventure she is too timid to pursue in the real world. Let this be her epic romance, safe in the flaring neurons of the Waves.

"He," she says.

"It," her father corrects instantly, absently. She is nothing but a distraction now and he is barely devoting a tenth of his attention to her. It drives her mother crazy when he types while talking; even brilliant men can only multitask so well. Her mother has found studies on the subject of multitasking, printed them in eight colors and taped them (with sources copied and pasted to each relevant section) on the fridge, on his tablet, across the Surfaces scattered around the house. Her mother is unduly frustrated when a person refuses to believe her despite the evidence she waves in their face; a product, no doubt, of years spent scientifically perfecting lab-grown meat which well-to-do patricians refuse to eat on the grounds that it "seems gross," despite the taste test evidence which affirms that it is indistinguishable from the original. Microbiology—yet another field barred to her by her mother's daunting brilliance. She will never graduate second in her class from Oxbridge University, will never give a valedictorian speech alongside Roger Kornberg. She is a solid B+ student, and that will always leave her with a bitter taste in her mouth.

She knows her father has likely lost the thread of conversation, and frankly, so has she. But some stubbornness causes her to remain.

"You're the one who told the world you created the first example of artificial intelligence. Doesn't that make him a him?" The word choice—*told the world*—is deliberate. They may have created him, but they cannot control him, cannot reproduce him. He is a beautiful, perhaps unrepeatable, fluke, like the rumors of cold fusion. And, if they cannot catch him, it will be equally impossible to prove that he was ever real.

"Intelligence does not connote humanity," her father says, with the long-suffering patience of someone who feels they are explaining advanced intellectual concepts to a kitten. "Artificial intelligence is perfect human reproduction. Not a human."

"Not only humans have gender. And every time I've seen him, he's presented as male."

"Only biological beings have gender," he reminds her. "And in testing, it presented as both male and female with regularity."

"But 'it' has connotations of hierarchy, with us above. If you want your creation to be respected as a true intelligence, don't you think you should refer to it by human standards?"

"PR," he scoffs, and then, "Fine." He waves the issue away, and she deflates. She has won the argument, but only by retreating to a realm that her father holds little respect for —the court of public opinion—and so the victory is meaningless. Sometimes she wishes she could go into public relations, only because it would astonish and disappoint both her parents simultaneously. But she doubts she would succeed at a career based entirely on personal charisma—unless she could do PR in the Waves. The thought makes her smile.

She turns to go and is surprised to see Paul facing away, trying to hide a stricken expression, unaware that his face is captured and reflected in the somnolent Surface on the far wall. Paul has been removed these past three months, his awkward and quirky humor bleached and faded away. Grief turns us all into strangers. This man once stroked her hair as she was sick over the side of the boat during her first ride, and now he cannot bear to look at her for too long. She wonders what about the conversation has brought up his shadows, but she has stopped trying to understand grief, has stopped poking at her own under a microscope; now she lets it linger unmolested.

She walks out of the lab feeling jittery, emotions unresolved. The question of the AI still lingers in her mind. The first time they met, she had no idea what he was...

CHAPTER TWO_

THE FIRST TIME THEY MET...

She was Diving on a site called Urban Noir, one of the many that had cropped up just for Divers—no Surfers allowed!—in the two years since the Dive Interface had become commercially available. It was an urban adventure: half parkour course, half spy adventure game. Set in the cyberpunk ruins of a poor cityscape, with gleaming monolithic skyscrapers crowding the horizon, it had an atmosphere of oppression and grace. Flappers rubbed shoulders with men in tailored Armani suits while jazz music played out in smoky gin joints with banks of old computers under the wood-paneled walls. The sky beyond the horizon was gray and cloudy, though the interface wasn't perfect and sometimes the clouds would suddenly, dizzyingly, shift position. It was clearly a glitch, but the designers were trying to pass it off as stylistic, and she had to admit she liked it. She liked looking up and feeling disconnected, a sudden burst of honesty amidst the polished gleaming lies.

The goal was simple: find someone with a glowing red packet, intercept, and bring it to a checkpoint to collect your rewards. Packets could be traded, bargained, or stolen; whoever brought it to the checkpoint got the rewards, plain and simple. People played at politics; danced and drank and gambled with the crowds of programmed Mannies (Manifestations that were nothing but simple code and your own firing neurons); but always, first and foremost, played the game. If you died here, your IP was blocked and you couldn't play again.

Gracie had been playing for two months. With her father distracted by the launch of his new AI the next week, she had been left to her own devices. She had her Dive interface tuned to maximum feedback. The things she experienced here felt nearly totally real. She knew pain when she crashed her hip against the edge of a building as she almost missed a jump eighteen stories up. She felt the weave and buzz of alcohol when it burned down her throat as she traded secrets with Marigold DuChamp, earning two packets for her intel on the railroad operating in the tunnels under the City Bank.

Here she wasn't Gracie, but Mallory Starke, Wired Runner. She was rich, as in the real world, but here that coin was earned, a product of her sweat and smarts. She had short black hair in a stylish bob and wore tight black leather pants, crisscrossed with leather holsters for her trade tools. Her tank top reached high on her neck but clung, leaving the shape of her body covered but not concealed. Though she could change anything about herself, she kept her face her own. Most people did; facial changes required a complex hack since the program worked by reading the contours of the face to translate emotional information through the server. But she had darkened her eyes a little, smoothed out her adolescent blemishes, cleared away her freckles. She was a more mature, sophisticated version of herself. She was the voice in the back of her head.

She was sitting at the top of one of the city's crumbling towers, a pair of high-focused laser binoculars in her hands, studying the movements of one Gerard Lacklace. He was the head of one of the largest organized families, owner of the popular Fontaine Noir drinking den, and general thorn in her side. He had foiled her last three deliveries, and once came close to actually killing her. Drowning, slang for dying during a Dive, was one of the first experiences she had attempted. She had determined that it felt exactly how she imagined death would—pain that made you breathless; that breath never coming back; the whole world shrinking down to a pinpoint, going black; and then...nothing.

She knew Lacklace was up to something big. He was moving eighteen large crates into the Fontaine's cellars, and each of the guards around him had repeating machine guns slung across their shoulders, though not leveled at the street. If she could find a way to intercept, or at the least destroy...

She was startled from her strategic cogitations by the sudden awareness of a presence behind her. She knew for a fact it had not been there a moment before, but it was impossible to Dive directly into this position. The game's framework only allowed entry at registered checkpoints. A hack that strong should be beyond difficult. Still, she refused to call anything impossible if it was happening.

For the moment, she pretended ignorance. She stretched out the muscles of one long leg, readjusting her position so she could spring quickly into action. She brought the binoculars back to her eyes and pretended to peer through them intently, shutting out the visual spectrum for a moment to concentrate on her ears. She could hear breathing, quiet but steady, and the occasional shifting of fabric against fabric. She only heard one body. They were close. Close enough, she thought, that if she moved quickly...

She dropped the binoculars, letting them catch on the strap of leather around her neck, and swung one leg in a snake-quick arc, sweeping the legs out from under her observer. As they fell and her leg hit the ground on the other side she pushed off from the ledge, using her momentum to carry herself up and sideways, landing squarely on top of them. One hand hit the graveled roof hard enough to scrape skin off the palm of her hand, and the other came down hard on sharp points, but her pulse was calm and her smile wicked as she languorously pulled a pistol out of her waistband and tucked it between her stomach and theirs, pressing the point against their belly. She straddled them, her knees quickly hooking in and finding purchase, and then levered herself up into a seated position and knocked the pinstripe fedora off their head.

"I surrender," he said, letting his arms flop to either side of his head in a parody of a "stick-em-up" arm raise.

He was in his late adolescence, with the slightly too-perfect features of a good facial hack. His hair was living fire —literally. It fell like locks of hair should, but every end shimmered and burned, and the color went from coal black to ember red to the hottest blue-white. His eyes were perfect black pools and reflected the light from the weak morning sun.

"How did you get up here?" she asked. Her tone was casual, relaxed. She had all the time in the world. He shrugged, and there was a smile in his eyes that didn't quite reach his lips, like he was struggling to hold it in. "You're a good hacker," she admitted. "That hair must have taken you days."

"Minutes," he said. There was a curious lack of boasting, as if he had no idea what a feat that would really be. He reached up a hand, his eyes seeking permission before touching her, and then ran his fingertips lightly over a lock of her hair that had fallen in front of her face. As he released it the hair sparked to life, burning but not consuming.

Impossible.

Nothing is impossible if you're seeing it. Still, she knew this technology intimately, had helped her father beta test back when the Dive interface was still just clumsy Glasses, before the emotional reads and the sensory keys. It may only have been on the market for two years, but it had been her playground and nursery since she was six years old. Hacking from within a Dive just wasn't possible—the framework didn't exist. Maybe he had someone in the real world watching his progress and making changes? But hacking someone else's code was so hard that even she had a hard time doing it efficiently. To do it so quickly...

"How..." She was at a loss for words. Finally, she quirked a shoulder up in a shrug she thought was nonchalant but came off sweet as candy floss. "Color me impressed, big six. Whaddaya want?" The slang of the game rolled off her tongue effortlessly.

"I hear you're the woman to talk to if you want intel on Rocky Emmanuel Sweet," he said. She considered letting him up, but she was enjoying the power of her position, and he seemed in no hurry to dislodge her.

"Little birdie told ya that, did they?"

"Rumors don't cost too dear," he admitted, "and I'm a late addition to the game. Gotta get a fast start."

"What's your angle? You know we're all playing for the same prize."

"And you don't do teams," he said. "I know."

"Know an awful lot."

"You're worth finding out about," he said, and there was something so earnest about it that it didn't seem like a line—

more like he never thought how it might sound when he said it.

"Funny kind of a fella, aren't you?" she asked, but she slid her pistol away.

"Maybe." He propped himself up on his elbows, so their faces were only separated by the distance of a long goodbye.

"Intel is a one-time deal. Not a social contract. And I don't play for favors owed; I like my comeuppance so fresh I can taste it. We gonna deal, daddy-o?"

He nodded, and she pushed against his chest to lever herself back to standing. Once up, she offered him a hand, and he took it. Another mark in his favor—she hated men who played it too tough. In her estimation it was a sign of low self-esteem, and that was usually based on something.

"Rumor has it Sweet is moving a shipment of gin from this old cellar here," he pulled out a badly hand-drawn map and passed it over, "to the Lucky Madam. I need to know how much of my rumor is intel and how much smoke. Need to know when."

"Easy," she said. The map was bunk, not worth the paper it was scratched on, but she'd been to Emmanuel Sweet's cubby before. Swiped three packets before he switched to only storing his booze there, and booze wasn't nothing to her. "Why you interested in gin? You thinking of running?"

Part of the game design was alcohol prohibition. Only so much gin could be produced, and it needed raw ingredients. It couldn't help you win, per se, but it could help you curry favors, and those could be just as valuable. The gin-runners ran the joints, kings and queens of their basement hovels and faded splendor. Rumor had it Sweet wasn't even moving packets anymore, just playing gangster of his own little world.

"I ain't interested in gin," he said with a mysterious smile, but didn't elaborate.

"What you got for me?"

"A backdoor into Fontaine Noir."

Her breath caught. She tried to pretend she didn't care. "What's that to me?"

"You saying you're watching Lacklace through binoculars 'cuz you like his pretty face?" he asked.

She smiled. "Maybe forty and fat is my type."

He smiled back—a challenge. "The way I hear, nothing makes your blood run hot but packets. Ice water veins, that's what they say."

"Talkin' a lot about me, are they?" she asked, but she was pleased. She hadn't realized she was a big enough player to warrant anyone flapping their gums on her behalf.

"If you want to listen."

"And once I'm in the door," she said, cautiously. "Then what?"

"Those crates are full of false packets. Complete with GPS tracking—he plans to thread them through the city. People run 'em, he follows the signal back to their stashes, steals the lot before they can deposit in a bank."

She swore. It was a damn good plan. Deposits were dangerous, so a lot of runners waited until they had five or six packets before trying to make a drop. He could clean up. Hell, he could clean *her* up, she had eight packets stashed for her next drop.

"I want an out, too," she decided. "In exchange, I'll give you the intel you need on Sweet. The right location—the one you've got is hooey—plus dates and times of his regular ins and outs."

"You're laughing, right?" he asked. "An impossible in *plus* an impossible out, and the intel about what it is he's up to so you know what to do once you're inside? That's worth way more'n a map and a couple of times."

"Just one problem with your arithmetic," she said. "You gave service without asking for a receipt. That intel's in the wind now, too late to add it to the bargaining table."

"You're a hard one," he said, but there was no anger shading the words. "Fine. Call it a show of good faith—proves I can deliver my promises. But in and out's still a bigger to-do than some numbers on a page. It's my skin on the line in there with you."

"What makes you think you're coming in?"

"Have to, if you want an out. Can't do my magic long distance."

"This wouldn't all be a clever ruse to get me into Lacklace's tender maw?" she asked, but the question was all formality; she trusted her instincts, and her instincts liked him. There was something...almost familiar... For a beat she wondered if she knew him on Land, but she doubted it. She would remember a guy like this.

"I don't work for no gin-runners," he assured.

"You already know what you want. So ask."

"I want your number."

She was caught completely off-guard. The game had a system of instant communication akin to the postal service of the day. In the real 1920s, mail was delivered up to eighteen times a day, so you could send someone a postcard in the morning asking them to tea that afternoon. In the game, each player had a number that would get written at the top of a slip of paper, with a message. It was dropped into any of the pneumatic tubes scattered around the city, and within an hour it would find its way to the waiting target or, if they were offline, would wait for their arrival. But there were no addresses, no phone books. You had to have someone's personal number to get in touch with them, and they had to give it to you.

"Why?" she asked. She instantly regretted the question; she sounded like a dumb teenager. She sounded like Gracie.

He smiled. "No more intel in the wind," he chided, and his eyes were full of promises. "Do we have a deal?"

She hesitated. She had no idea what a hacker could do with her number, and he was clearly beyond a good hacker. But what was the point of the game if not to have wild adventures, take stupid chances, and live like she never did on Land? Consequence free. She grinned.

"Deal," she said, and they shook on it under the glitching sky...

CHAPTER THREE_

She hitches her backpack up, steps heavy as she labors down the stairs outside the lab. It's almost eight—she'll be late. She should have asked for a permission slip, but her father always forgets and she doesn't have the energy to care. What's one more mark against her less-than-stellar record? She has a habit of claustrophobia; sometimes sneaks away from school to walk under the sky and breathe slowly in and out, her own version of meditation.

She's distracted, walks right past her bus stop and has to backtrack half a block. It's a hot day for October and as she climbs the steps to the raised street she can feel sweat beading on her upper lip. If she were Diving she could turn off her heat sensors, or better yet, go directly to school without the boring business of the commute.

San Jose is beautiful in autumn, even if climate change means unpredictable, sudden storms and punishing weather shifts. She loves the crisp blueness of the sky, the three perfect puffy clouds drifting along. Not all of America has adopted the double-tiered road system, but all of the major cities have been using it since she was a kid, and now it seems quaint and old-fashioned to have flat roads in line with the sidewalks. In major cities cars and bikes travel flat, but buses and trucks and SUVs travel on the road above, plus the occasional convertible with the right license taking advantage of the sunshine.

The bus, when it comes, is packed with morning commuters, standing shoulder to shoulder and trying not to make eye contact with the people whose air they're sharing. She squeezes in, scans her pass. The bus waits until the last scanned form is aboard and the doors automatically close. The sky disappears behind tinted glass. She looks for a free Surface, but they're all taken; instead, she maneuvers her tablet out of her bag, checking her email, her bookmarked sites, the news. That sustains her for twenty minutes, but the commute is long, and she doesn't feel like reading this morning. She pulls her Line out of her bag and sticks the sensor against her temple. A few people give her looks, and she rolls her eyes. Her dad says when he was a kid people complained that everyone was wearing headphones on the bus, tuning out the world. Now they complain all the kids are Diving. She wonders what she'll be complaining about when she's eighty and wishes she could believe she'll be different. But no one pictures themselves as old and grumpy, worn down by a life of disappointments.

She activates the public browsing mode. Her vision darkens and then brightens as the bus disappears, replaced by her homepage. There's a large square in the bottom right corner of her vision, showing her the real world. Khaiam says the picture-in-picture takes some getting used to, but to her it's second nature. She hates the idea of being immersed in a Dive and having no idea what's happening in the world around you. That's fine if you're locked in your room alone, but private browsing in public is just asking for someone to write on your face. Or push you down. Or steal your backpack. All of which have happened to her, so now she's learned. Public browsing only.

Her homepage is a beautiful little cottage in a tropical rainforest. There's a waterfall just a few feet to her left, and a little vegetable garden under the window. She always enters standing in the doorway, perfectly balanced between the cool shade of the one-room house and the deep warmth of the day outside. Today she steps out. It's hot but not humid, and she's set the ozone layer high enough that her skin won't burn. Her tomatoes are just starting to turn red, and she spends ten minutes taking care of them, pruning leaves here and there, lugging over water from the fall. After the chores are done, she spends the rest of the commute playing tag with her three pet dragons. She's programmed them with a kitten's sense of mischief and a monkey's intelligence. Now she's trying to see if she can train them to bypass their programming and learn more complex tasks. So far she hasn't had any luck, but every so often one of them will look her in the eye, and she'll wonder if it has already achieved higher intelligence and is just playing a long con by hiding it from her.

The bus bell chimes and she scrambles to get off before the doors close; people won't get out of the way, as usual, and she has to duck under the arm of a huge man in an ill-fitting gray suit to make it in time. She pictures him as the final boss in a first-person side-scroll game and does a little victory dance as she hits the platform. *Yeah, yaya!* Another girl snickers at her, someone else running late for school. *Can't hurt your reputation when you haven't got one*, she reminds herself, and follows more sedately down the stairs.

The bell has rung and the halls are empty. She walks through the body scanner and smiles at Ted, the security guard.

"Got the latest patch for EU," he tells her.

"Did it fix the mass player end-of-turn lag?" she asks.

"Pretty well, but they missed that bug where your arm goes hollow when you reach for a weapon change."

"At least they didn't create eight more bugs for every fix."

"Preach it, sister," he agrees, and she waves as she heads for homeroom.

Class has already started, and Mrs. Dimas gives her a world-class pinched face glare as she opens the door. She feels her body crumbling, the last lingering bits of Dive-induced confidence draining away as reality reasserts itself.

"Ms. Neumann. Can I assume that you are lacking in the appropriate documentation to explain your habitual tardiness, which has become so regular it's almost its own brand of punctuality?"

She mutters a negative. Her tiny voice can barely be heard above the steady hum of the air conditioning. Khaiam tries to catch her eye, but her gaze is fixed firmly on the toes of her battered sneakers. She does not risk the wroth of Mrs. Dimas' too clever tongue.

"Ah, lovely. A double negative to add to your list of other sins. Just because your father has invented the Sasquatch, Ms. Neumann, does not give us carte blanche to come and go as we please."

Her cheeks burn. A few students chuckle, though most dislike Mrs. Dimas more than they dislike her, and refuse to take part in the mockery.

"The AI isn't a Sasquatch. I've seen it," Khaiam pipes up. Now people are interested—Khaiam's word is law. If he says the AI is real then it is, never mind what the gossip rags are saying. Khaiam Fadel cannot be gainsaid. She looks at him and cannot understand how it is that they are still friends, that he has never set her aside for a newer, better model. She thought he might, when…but they only became closer. He is the only reason life is bearable. No one is too cruel, when they know it might put them on the wrong side of Khaiam Fadel.

"I'm sure you have," Mrs. Dimas says with an eye-roll that shows just how much *she* cares for the gospel of Fadel.

Gracie settles into her desk behind Khaiam as their teacher launches into a breakdown of career possibilities in the twenty-first century. He half-turns to face her, raising his eyebrows. She shakes her head. He switches on his Surface and activates the chat hack. Each desk is supposed to be locked down, so it can only download and receive information at the beginning of every class; that way, notes can be uploaded and downloaded, but students can't communicate during class. The hack to get around it is easy, but Gracie set up an even more elegant one. It hides the chat as spare pings in the interface, the equivalent of texting in the old days. 140 characters and totally invisible. He pings her with a question mark. She ignores it, hiding a smile. Nothing drives him crazier.

- Khai.the.Guy: GRACIE!!!!!!!!!

He sends every exclamation mark as a new ping, so her Surface goes crazy. She tries not to giggle, ducks her head and waits another second before answering.

- Gracielass: No luck.
- Khai.the.Guy: Thats all I get?
- Gracielass: He showed like they thought. I threw up the partition. He dove THROUGH it.
- Khai.the.Guy: No!!
- Gracielass: Yup

- Khai.the.Guy: Is the even possible?
- Gracielass: No, but nothing is impossible if you see it with your eyes.
- Khai.the.Guy: Ya ya. Did ur dad spill?
- Gracielass: Nope. Still no idea.

Because, of course, that's the great mystery. Why does the AI keep finding her, seeking her out? It cannot be a coincidence that they have come across each other so many times in the vast and empty reaches of the Waves.

- Khai.the.Guy: Come to practice?
- Gracielass: :o=
- Khai.the.Guy: :(
- Gracielass: Of course!
- Khai.the.Guy: :P

———

Thirty years ago, air pollution became endemic. Tired of cancelling games due to yellow alerts and low-lying smog, sporting events shifted indoors. Climate control vastly improved both air quality and the climactic weather shifts, but habits are hard to shake, and fields remain largely indoors. Gracie sometimes wonders what it would have been like to lean back on the bleachers under the yellow sun, with the smell of grass in your nose. Instead, she sits under a painted blue gym ceiling, watching Khaiam on the astroturf field.

He is the captain of the soccer team and wide receiver on the football team, and she couldn't attend every practice even if she wanted to—which she doesn't. But every Friday she comes to watch him play, then they go to the corner store, buy a freezie, and head back to Gracie's house for movies and pizza. They have been doing this every week since they were part of a trio. When that changed…they couldn't bear to stop.

There are a few cheerleaders sitting on the bench beside her, and a handful of guys and girls giggling a few bleachers up. She is painfully aware that she is the only one here not dating someone on the team.

Half-watching the practice, she finishes an essay on the comparative accessibility (or inaccessibility) of Shakespeare and Chaucer. A shadow falls across her tablet screen, and for a second she thinks a cloud has passed across the sun; then she remembers she is inside. She looks up in alarmed surprise. These encounters never end well.

It's Bella.

She flashes a large, friendly, shallow smile and plops herself down on the seat directly next to Gracie, almost draped across her shoulder.

"Whatcha doin'?" she asks.

"Homework," Gracie says. She tries to pretend she is engrossed in the screen, but she runs out of words and it is obvious she has ceased writing. On the field, Khaiam dives for the ball, flopping sideways and rolling before getting back on his feet. The team laughs, and Bella giggles and waves excitedly.

"He's so funny. Don't you just think he is completely the funniest?"

"Sure," Gracie says. Secretly she agrees—Khaiam can always make her laugh. But she suspects ulterior motives to this conversation, and every acquiescence feels like a victory to the other side.

"You guys are, completely, friends, aren't you? I mean, you completely hang out all the time. Right?" Bella asks. She pushes some of Gracie's curls out of her face. "You have such great skin, Gracie. You should completely do something with your hair, it totally ruins the look."

Well thank God you're here. You can teach me how to look like a sycophant. Gracie mumbles a thank you, and Bella takes that as permission to play with her hair, mock-pinning it on the sides as she chatters.

"So. I was thinking, you know, how there's this dance coming up at the end of the month, and I was completely going to go with Jake but then I saw him making out with Angela in the supply closet—" She pauses for a shocked reaction. Belatedly, Gracie makes a sound of distress in the back of her throat. "Completely, right? So now we can't go. Well, I was still going to, because Jake is super cute, but Rachel says I can't because he's a slut. And I was thinking, oh my gosh, I've completely thought Khaiam was adorable since first grade. This is just between us, right? So I asked around, and I heard he hasn't asked anyone else. But then, I completely realized that you would know. Since you guys are friends!"

Her cheerful verbal vomit makes Gracie cringe. Has she always been so far removed from the world of normal teenaged interaction? Is it because of the Dive, because she's seen a world that is so much bigger? Or is it because of her, because of the things she has lost? Did the world get so much bigger...or so much smaller?

"He's not taking anyone," Gracie says. "I think he's just going solo."

"Great!" Bella enthuses. "So you can get him to ask me."

How did you get that out of what I just said? Are you really this dumb, or is it who you think you have to be? "He's not dating right now," she says. She turns her attention back to her tablet, but Bella either doesn't notice or chooses to ignore the cue.

"Come on, Gracie. He spends *all* his time with you.

That's, completely, a cry for help. He just needs a little push, you know, to move on."

"It's only been three months!"

"That's, completely, almost half a year."

"No, it isn't," Gracie says, but she knows the words are wasted. Bella just blinks and smiles.

"It's almost. Come on, Gracie! Can't you do me a favor? You know, as a friend?"

We're not friends, she whispers to herself. *We were once in the orbit of the same sun—that's all.* "Sorry," she murmurs. She types some words, nonsense that she'll have to delete later, just to encourage the girl beside her to drift away.

"Come on, Gracie," Bella says for a third time. She is sugary sweet, genuinely hurt that this simple request is not being met. Has anyone ever told her no? Does she understand what happens when life simply refuses to comply with your wishes? If only there were hacks for the real world; if only there was some measure of control here.

"I'll talk to him," she says, just hoping Bella will go. Instead, the girl squeals and hugs her tight, rocking them both back and forth on the bench. Her antics catch the attention of the team, and she giggles and waves again as they look her way.

"You are the best! The super best!" she says, and hugs her head. Gracie waves the attention away. "She said yes!" Bella hollers to her friends, who giggle and wave and generally make a commotion.

By now most of the team is staring their way, and Kyle gets hit in the face by the one player still focused on the practice. Everyone laughs, and attention drifts back to where it should be—away from her. Gracie huddles, hoping Bella will beg-and-dash, but instead the girl sits next to her for the whole practice, talking nonstop about herself. There is a momentary pang when Gracie wishes she could respond, wishes she could be that light and frivolous. She wonders what it would be like to Dive into a socialite. She could be airy and fun, a "woo girl" for a night. The thought of her AI running into her in that costume, however, sends a rush of embarrassed adrenaline down her spine. Maybe not.

CHAPTER FOUR_

T HE FREEZIE IS COLD AGAINST THE PALMS OF HER
hands, numbing the skin. Little beads of sweat spread
up from the plastic wrapper, and she flicks the moisture
away one drop at a time, watching their silent trajectory. Caught in her kinetic energy, they have no choice
but to race off into the vast emptiness of space, only to
be caught up, cradled by gravity; and then the long,
slow plummet. By the time they hit the ground, she has
lost sight of them, literally invisible in their
insignificance.

"Graaacie," Khaiam calls in a sing-song.

"Sorry."

"Where do you go?"

"Mars?" she suggests.

"Naw—I think you're watching the world you're in," he
challenges, and she shrugs. They both know it's true, but it
seems too deep a thought for such a sunny day.

"Maybe I'll be a poet. I can get paid for being ADD."

"I don't think the pittance a poet makes counts as being
paid," he grins, and she quirks a smile. He nudges her lightly,

almost sending her crashing into the building beside them. "Something happened."

She doesn't want to cast a shadow over the day; knows she will. She tries to think of how to make the words come out soft and gentle, but there are only so many ways to drop a bomb. Fallout is inevitable. Maybe she is making too much of this—maybe the cloud won't pass across his face. He'll laugh. *Or, worse, he'll think about it. He'll say yes. He'll move on and he won't need you anymore, the security blanket he takes everywhere. What if she was right, a cry for help—*

"Gracie?"

"Bella...asked me to talk to you."

There is silence. He anticipates, perhaps, the nature of such a discussion. Just a little push—but can't Bella understand they are both hovering on the edge?

"She wants to go to the dance with you," she says.

Khaiam nods. She can't read his thoughts, wonders which emotions are being processed and rejected, which folded into the ball of grief in his stomach, sublimated into a part of him. Will either of them ever be the same again? "You told her you would ask me?" He sounds surprised.

"I told her you weren't ready."

"But...?"

Gracie shrugs. Silently, eloquently, she tells him, *You know me. You know I can never seem to tell a person no, how words spill out that I don't mean. Please don't be angry,* her shoulders beg, *please understand.* He shakes his head.

No one ever walks in silence, not really, but somehow when words are absent the other little sounds don't rush in to fill the void. Footsteps on clean white concrete echo but are not heard; the few birds that survived the toxic smog of the previous generation do not sing any more brightly; a plane or two fly overhead, their distant thunder muted in the empty blue; but the silence echoes over the noise, a thing felt more acutely than soundwaves.

Until finally she slips her hand through his, and after a moment he squeezes it.

And the silence is comfortable again.

They turn off Pine and onto Newport, finding their way by memory more than sight. She walks to school every day, reminding herself Khaiam walks almost as far just to get to the bus. His parents aren't like hers—Silicon Valley is as full of data entry analysts as it is doctorates of electrical engineering and computer science. The first time he saw her house he balked from the sidewalk; took in the three gables, the two stories that towered above the bungalows around them; the big powerful trees out front, the manicured lawn. Then he gave her a look that said *I do not belong*. She had guided him up the walk, through the door; his footsteps withered and halted on the marble floor. Surfaces flashed to life on every flat expanse, blinking a calm hello, and she had dragged him across the way, up the stairs, into the safer seclusion of the den. Now he walks the path by rote, three months of weekly visits enough to breed calm out of familiarity.

She swipes her palm against the door to unlock it, and they race each other for the good seat in the reclining chair. Khaiam wins, and they sink into furniture with the bonelessness of youth. Gracie lets her head fall over the arm of the couch, and Khaiam opens his bag, dumping books and notes across the pearly white carpet.

"Torture or death?" he asks.

"Calculus."

"To wit," he says in a terrible British accent, "death it is."

They open their books, take out tablets and fire up Surfaces. Gracie's house has them everywhere—all the walls, the arms of the chairs, the coffee table at their knees. Most houses have five or six, but Gracie once counted fifty-three in hers before she gave up.

They've been silently studying for fifteen minutes when, out of the blue, Khaiam queries, "So what will you tell her?"

"Who?" Gracie asks. She does not recall a conversational thread that would lead easily back to this place. Khaiam is usually more direct than that; he is the physical one, the one rooted in the real world.

"Bella."

Ah. "I'll tell her that you're secretly in love with me, and I'm going to have your baby," Gracie suggests. Khaiam loses it, snorting cola through his nose and coughing loudly enough that a Surface pings to life by his head, inquiring after his health. Gracie turns it off with a wave.

"You could be my pregnant prom queen!" he enthuses when he can breathe again.

"I can wear blue and you can wear pink—because we want the sex to be a surprise."

He snorts and snickers. "You know, if you actually went through with it and did half of the things you think of, you would be hilarious."

"Are you saying I'm not hilarious now?" she demands, mock-offended.

"Humorous at best."

"Oh yeah? Well, how did the chicken cross the road?"

"I refuse to stoop to this level."

"To prove to the opossum it could actually be done!"

"That's 'why,' not 'how.'"

"I was testing to see if you were paying attention."

"Nerd."

"Says the guy getting a ninety-one in calculus," she says.

"Says the girl getting an eight three."

"You know what they say about a B minus..."

He throws a chip at her head. She tries to catch it in her mouth, but it bounces off her forehead and lands on the arm of the couch. She drifts back to her homework, and he follows reluctantly. After about an hour, Khaiam suggests they watch a movie while they work, which is code for "enough of this studying, it's the weekend." Gracie orders pizza from the Surface by her arm and they settle on a movie, books still spread out around them so they can pretend to be studying if her mother should pop her head in the door...

CHAPTER FIVE_

HER MOTHER POPPED HER HEAD THROUGH THE DOOR. "Are you ready, Graciela? Really, I don't understand how it can take so long to do so little."

"I'm putting on makeup!" Gracie objected. True, her makeup consisted of a press-on eyeshadow strip and some lip tint, but that was more than she usually did.

"What will look worse, hmm? His daughter not appearing looking like a movie star, or his daughter not appearing until after the announcement is already over? *Honestamente, no sé de dónde saca usted.*" She ushered her daughter out of her seat by the mirror and through the door, rolling her eyes.

Gracie struggled into a pair of kitten heels as she followed her mother down the stairs. "Mom—Mama—wait."

"The press will be here in *seven* minutes."

"*Mama,*" she insisted, and whatever her mother heard was enough to quell her headlong march, if only for a minute.

"What?"

"Why were Paul and Dad fighting last night?"

"We're going to talk about this now?"

"It sounded like Paul didn't want Dad to make the announcement."

"Well, whatever it was about they sorted it out, didn't they?"

"It's been operational for weeks, and they always let me playtest before they make industry announcements, but when Dad brought me to the lab last week Paul dragged him into the server room, and when they came out he said something had come up and I had to leave. It was like Paul didn't want me to see the AI."

"Paul is grieving, *mija*," her mother reminded her with uncharacteristic gentleness. "You cannot apply logic to the actions of a grieving man."

"But it doesn't make sense," she complained.

"Life doesn't make sense," her mother said with wistful sadness. *It doesn't seem fair that Paul is the one grieving,* Gracie bitterly thought the sadness meant, *when my mother is the one who would recover more easily from the loss of her child.*

They walked into the foyer as a pair. Her father was there with some colleagues from the lab, plus a handful of their funders. The press hadn't yet arrived, or perhaps they were being made to wait outside; supplicants to the throne of scientific progress. She ran over and hugged Paul's wife, Helen, who gripped her tightly for just a little longer than was socially acceptable, and hugged Paul more cautiously, though he, too, returned the affection with the desperation of a mountain climber who knows the rope he holds is no longer attached to the cliff.

Her father nodded at Paul, who walked closer as if to the gallows, and the five of them came together in a phalanx. It should have been a joyous occasion. She remembered the day they had announced the Dive interface—one of the most significant technological advances in the last fifty years. There had been something sparkling in the air that day, a sense of adventure, of never going back. She had been playing with the Dive for years, of course, as they beta-tested and improved the technology and brought it to commercial fruition, so she had felt like a part of the team; she had even been allowed to wear a Line, to stand at the back of the podium beaming, hand in hand with...

Her fingers flexed, gripped air. There was nothing there to hold, no one to whisper to and giggle with. The adults around her seemed pinioned: her father struggling for a sense of joy against the tide of morose rebellion flowing from Paul; Helen's more confused grief, like a woman with dementia who knows she's supposed to be there but can't quite remember why; and her mother's grim determination that everything would go smoothly, no matter what.

The big double doors opened, and a mass of reporters flooded in. She recognized the usual suspects—*Wires Magazine* and *Discovery*, *Science America* and *Tech Today*—but this announcement went beyond just the science magazines. There were TV news stations, reporters with microphones and voice recorders, print journalists with tablets, even some bloggers looking lost in comfortable corduroy. And of course there were the VIPs, representatives of Macroware and Linix, Siri and Sanja, more she could not place or did not care to try. Everyone came to watch the world change.

"Thank you all for coming on this historic day," her father intoned. His voice was rich and rooted, amplified and echoed off the marble floor. Gracie sometimes wondered if his voice was part of the reason for his success; if he had been meek, like Paul, would the pair ever have succeeded in realizing their dream? Perhaps the world was full of quiet geniuses whose inventions never left their living rooms. Perhaps if her voice never wavered or stuttered, she would be something more than the quiet mouse the world saw in her.

He waited patiently while people took their seats. There was a brief speech, a photo opportunity, and then the unveiling would move into the Waves, where traditional media could not follow, and where the true spectacle would be waiting. As difficult as this day was with an empty space behind her, as strange as the days leading up to it had been, Gracie was excited to see the AI for the first time. What would it be like? Would she know the difference between it and any other Diver? Would there be a stretch of Uncanny Valley between them, impossible to traverse? Was this a new creature, the beginning of a race, the end of everything the world had known? How could it be anything less?

"Thank you," her father said again. "My name is Doctor Maxwell Neumann, and this is my partner, Doctor Paul Armstrong. Today we are proud to be the *cursus publicus* for the most important news to strike the global empire since Konrad Zuse invented the Z1. To claim that this will create a seismic shift in the very nature of our social philosophy is no overstatement, but let the anthropologists question the nature of humanity; let the philosophers debate whether electricity can have a soul. We are scientists. What we unveil today is a perfect human replica. A new standard in artificially crafted intelligence. Members of the press, colleagues, friends: today we give you the first ever example of artificial intelligence. Meet Charlie."

The lights dimmed. The Surface on the wall behind the speakers lit up, flashing bright silver and then fading to gentle white. The white pixelated, grew dizzyingly and then refracted and split apart. Little cubes of soft light formed the word Ch4r1ie, cheesy l33t speak and all, then cascaded down, littering the ground of the image and revealing a peaceful scene: a library, old-fashioned green lights and dark wood reading tables, towering shelves under a stained-glass skylight. A figure sat at one of the tables, androgynous in their beauty. Full lips and messy brown hair, flat chest and the hint of curvy legs under tight jeans. She recognized their eyes, but did not connect this sylph with the smooth-talking mac she had met a week before in Urban Noir; would not recognize that their eyes never changed until she met it next. It leaned forward, as if squinting against the flashes of the cameras, though of course it could not see them.

"Is this thing on?" it asked, tapping the air in front of it. The room filled with breathless laughter.

"Doctor Armstrong and I began work on Charlie nearly ten years ago..." her father began, and she tuned out the familiar story. She knew about her father's work—how he had begun trying to populate the Waves with artificial characters, Manifestations that used the user's preconceived ideas to build realistic reactions. They did what they were intended for, were fun to play with, but echoed with a sort of hollowness—a little too predictable, a little too static. The idea behind an AI had begun as nothing more than wanting a better interface for his technology—a side note to perfecting the Dive. Perfecting Manifestations meant perfecting electronically created intelligence, meant cracking a puzzle that men had devoted entire lives to and achieved barely passable results. The road had been slow, and as far as Gracie knew the duo had made no real progress until a sudden shift three months ago. One day she was dressed in funeral black, wondering how the lack of something could feel so solid; and only two days later her father was bursting through the door, shouting, "We did it! Carmela, Carmela, we did it!"

So her father's current version of the tale left her mind with plenty of leash on which to wander. It was the AI that caught her attention. The projection came from Christianne's Line. She was a graduate student who had been assisting the Dive project for two years and was seated near the back of the room. Ch4r1ie looked frustrated, and the audio from the feed had apparently been muted when her father started talking again because occasionally she could see its lips moving without any sound coming through. It poked the air again, and she realized it was not poking the air at all, but Christianne's nose. A smile twitched against her lips. Calista used to do that to her when they were kids, joking that it was a button that could turn her humor back on when she was being boring. It seemed like that was exactly what the AI was trying to do to the unresponsive graduate student.

Applause jolted Gracie back to reality, signaling that the speech was over and the next phase about to begin. Paul indicated that everyone should Dive, and journalists scrambled to activate the technology. Gracie and the rest of the tribe on the podium connected with ease. Reality drifted away as the Dive took over her senses. Vision faded first, then sound, then scent, and rebuilt in that order. The sound of fabric against fabric. Surfers here and there, shuffled the papers of the books stacked around them. A tiny screen at the bottom of her vision showed the room full of slack faces and somnolent bodies, while around her avatars rezzed into place in the library. They were in an online encyclopedia, on the entry for artificial intelligence. Cute.

Most of the reporters looked real-world identical in the Waves, though she noticed a few of the VIPs had hacks to alter their facial shapes or create add-ons like pointed ears. She quickly retooled her own face, adding a shade of lipstick and a fancier dress to her otherwise mirror image. The site was programmed to scatter their avatars around the room, creating an inquisitive circle with the AI and Paul at the center, like a talk show interview. Paul even had a clipboard in front of him, cues for his part of the presentation. It was time to prove the AI was real.

"Good afternoon, Charlie," Paul said.

"That's a stupid fucking name," the AI interrupted. There were a few gasps, some scattered laughter. A handful of reporters had brought Dive-compatible tablets and continued to jot down notes. In the room off the Waves, cameras flashed on the 2D screen portraying the Dive session.

Paul blinked, startled by the vehemence of his creation. "You...uh—you don't like it?" he hazarded. He tried to smile, like this was all part of the show.

"How are you supposed to pronounce a four and a one? Either it's just Charlie, which is an insulting diminutive of Charles, and let's face it, no doubt a nod to Babbage, which is infantile in its simplicity, or my name is—what? Ch-four-ar-one-ie? You're so proud of yourself for creating the first artificial intelligence, a being that lives purely in the Waves, but you've given me a text-based pun for a name as if I'm something as simple as a Surfer. Why not tell them my real name, *Paul*?" There was a hostile slant to the name, as if its use was somehow a dig. Gracie had found herself pushing towards the edge of the crowd, trying to get a better view. There was something maddeningly familiar about the sarcasm in Charlie's voice. Like hearing your mother use an expression only your friends normally say, at once familiar and yet so at odds...

Paul looked stricken, and her father quickly jumped in to fill the silence.

"I see Charlie has already reached the teenaged stage of development," he quipped, and the room relaxed into laughter.

"Let's hear a joke, Charlie!" a reporter near the back called. Humor was the hardest human emotion to mimic and often used as a benchmark for AI success.

"My name isn't Charlie," it snapped. There was a flash of blue light, the de-rendering of an avatar with an improperly connected Line, and the reporter disappeared.

Everyone was silent, stunned. Paul and Maxwell exchanged a glance—they were as shocked as the rest. It was not something someone Diving should be capable of doing. Interacting with other people's Lines should only be possible from the real world. A good hacker could interrupt a signal long enough for the safety measures to kick in and self-boot, but hacking from within a Dive was next to impossible. A boot-hack should not have been possible, and this AI shouldn't have been able to hack at all. How was it accessing code? How was it manipulating its environment?

And then it looked at Gracie. It smiled, and the resentment and anger washed away. There was an element of surprise in the look, like it had just laid eyes on something it hadn't expected to ever see again; a child reunited with the parent they lost at the supermarket, or a teenager who finds a favorite toy, missing for years behind a couch. It lifted a hand like it might make a gesture, call her closer...touch its heart?

And then it fell through the floor.

And chaos broke out.

It should have been impossible. The room had been securely locked to ensure no unauthorized Divers could interrupt the event. No one should have been able to get in or out, let alone eject other Divers and alter the fabric of the site enough to create a door under their feet and drop into the raw data of the Web. The TV reporters were understanding —a technical glitch, wait a few moments and everything will be resolved. But the science writers and VIP guests knew better. They had witnessed an impossibility. What kind of a trick was this? An elaborate joke? Paul searched madly but could find no trace of the AI. Somehow it had jumped the server, used the Dive session to connect with the wider Waves, and disappeared. A needle in a wet, endless haystack.

———

As the days sludged past and they failed to produce the AI, rumors began to spread. It was a publicity stunt gone awry, designed to lure in financial backers when the product had never been real. Or maybe it was two men used to the spotlight who had invented the whole thing to drag their careers forward. At best they had gotten ahead of themselves, declared the technology ready when it wasn't; at worst the AI had never existed. Gossip rags posted articles about the Ghost of the Waves, while Divers claimed to have seen the AI cropping up in their favorite games, changing the rules with impossible hacks. Programmers tried to hunt it down and were likened to ghost hunters, and Macroware's CEO offered a million dollar prize for the person who could catch it, saying when they found it they should be sure to catch Santa Claus and the Easter Bunny, too.

Paul crumbled. He stopped shaving, slept most nights at the lab, spent hours and days on the Waves, searching for the missing program. Maxwell was only a little better—he suffered the ridicule badly, dismissed the pop culture jibes but seemed to cruelly feel every dig from his colleagues. Once, Gracie passed the master bathroom, and over the sound of the fan running, greedily sucking moisture from the still air, she swore she heard the sound of crying. She had never seen her father so much as tear up, and she ran to her bedroom and hid under the blankets, telling herself she had imagined the noise. She could not bear for any more of her world to mutate, felt there was nothing left to hold. She imagined Calista was hiding with her, their noses almost touching, each one breathing in the air the other let out. She stayed there for hours, not daring to move, until night fell and she slept, and did not dare to dream...

CHAPTER SIX_

She wakes from a dream she can't quite remember. The air is still and unseasonably warm. She feels sticky in her cotton pajamas, out of place in her body. She tries to close her eyes, but the dream lingers and leaves a bad taste in her mouth. There are no images remaining, no emotions, just the steady pressure against her chest that she recognizes as an impending panic attack. Her breath is fast and shallow, and her eyes burn from more than exhaustion. She counts to ten, breathes slowly and deeply, but her fingers twitch and the length of each inhale seems shorter than the last. The pressure increases, a nearly physical weight on her ribcage. She puts a hand there, feels the rapid pulse. Tries to slow it like a trained liar, but she has never gotten the knack of lying to herself.

Her bare toes sink into carpet as she maneuvers upright, grips the edge of her mattress. Her fingers dig in but she can't find purchase, imagines she might float away. A small yellow bottle of pills floats through her mind, but the bathroom is across the room and she's afraid she'll fall if she stands. Instead, she picks up her Line and slips it on. The sensors adhere to her temple despite the sweat, electrical signals hijacking her senses. Her brain is no longer in control—she is Diving, the Waves collapsing over her head, filling her lungs, subsuming her. Her breath slows as her Homepage rezzes into view.

She can feel immediately that something isn't right—there is another presence here. She knows it on a visceral level, the acid in her stomach somehow reacting to a pressure in the air. A second later she hears off-key singing, a broken sort of crooning from the direction of the cottage. Cautiously, she approaches. No one else should have the key to enter. Even if it isn't really her Homepage. She claimed it, but then the interloper must be...

Khaiam sits on the floor of the cottage. It's Saturday night —he must have just come home from a party. Even through the translation of the Dive she can tell he's been drinking. There is an artificial looseness to his shoulders, a strange tilt to his head.

"Hey."

He looks up, so drunk he isn't even startled. He just smiles, opens his arms wide and falls back to the ground. "Graacie!" he sings to the tune of some pop song she doesn't quite recognize. "You still come here?"

"I didn't know you had a key." She has been coming here every day for three months, but she has not seen him before. She had no idea he even knew where it was, and would probably not have claimed it as her own Homepage if she had. It feels wrong, as if she's somehow usurping it, which she knows makes no sense.

"She gave it to me at...near...so we could visit. She said she wanted me to see her like this. Like her avatar. Healthy." He draws patterns that are barely visible in the dirt floor, stares at the ceiling and sees something over than thatch and beams.

"You're drunk," Gracie tells him. She sits down on the floor beside him, the bed supporting her back. Her toes rest against his blue t-shirt, finding purchase through it to the solid weight of his ribcage.

"Very drunk," he agrees.

"It's late," Gracie reminds him.

"It's Saturday night. We're sixteen. You should have come to this party, Gracie. It was completely wild. Matt threw up in Kathleen's purse, and Derek and Ron got into a fistfight and then made out."

Gracie hesitates, draws patterns of her own, watches how the dirt stains her fingertips, a little too thickly to be a perfect mirror of reality. She makes a mental note to tell her father, but nothing is ever perfect during a Dive. It isn't the real world, and isn't that the point? "If it was so great—why are you here?"

Khaiam rolls onto his side, curling up in the fetal position with her toes captured in the curve of his stomach. He is on the edge of tears, his scattered thoughts plain on his face. "She would have loved it," he tells her. "Bella caught fireflies in jars and used them to light the path. People danced under the stars, by the side of the pool. Jacob's brother bought us all alcohol and someone had Snap."

"You didn't take any," Gracie admonishes.

Khaiam waves her worry away, and she cannot be sure if that's a yes or a no. "I stole a jar. But I couldn't figure out how to rez it into my avatar." He holds up his empty hands in a supplicating gesture. "Can you make a firefly?"

She would give him anything to clear the sheen of tears from his eyes. Somehow he has come to fill the hole in her life, slipping into clothes that are not his and do not fit. She wonders if she could call him her best friend, if he would nod and understand, or if he is only a placeholder until it stops hurting.

She brings up her admin menu. Special privilege for being the daughter of Poseidon, King of the Waves. She can't pull off any complicated programming from inside, certainly can't hack, but she can access coding and bring up elements that already exist as possibilities. A firefly is easy—but it won't come in a jar. She brings up a mason jar and a swarm of fireflies, and nimbly swoops the jar through the air. She catches three, but before she can close the lid they fly away. Khaiam laughs, so she plays up the game. Catches one, shows it off only to have it fly away. Catches another, but trips on the edge of a chair and drops the jar. Picks it up and drops the lid. Khaiam laughs, and she imagines a black and white movie with herself as the star. Brings up the admin menu and adds a soundtrack, jaunty piano that tinkles in time to her movements. By the time she collapses into a pile at his feet, triumphantly holding the sealed jar aloft, he is laughing so hard he has to clutch his stomach just to breathe, and she is grinning through a sheen of sweat.

"Don't say I never did nothin' for ya," she drawls, and Khaiam catches the jar and holds the glass against his face. She wonders what the fireflies think of his giant unblinking eye, and then remembers they are nothing but bits of code, flashes of electrical signal. They don't feel anything at all, and she wonders what that would be like. If it would lift the hardness around her lungs.

"You should have seen the fireflies," Khaiam murmurs. His breath clouds against the jar, little drops of moisture that fog briefly before they disappear. There is nothing indelible in this world—a lesson they both have incised on their hearts.

"Arriba en el cielo, se vive un coyote. Con ojos de plata, y

los pies de azogue..." she sings quietly. Khaiam curls up, using the firefly jar as a pillow. He tries to hum along, but he doesn't know the tune and soon subsides. His eyes drift closed, and as his brainwaves settle into the calm of sleep his avatar shudders, pixelates, and de-rezzes. She is left alone on the hard-packed floor, the strains of the lullaby circling through her mind, fireflies like stars against the dark cottage walls.

CHAPTER SEVEN_

"IF YOU COULD GO ANYWHERE ON EARTH, WHERE WOULD you go?"

"Paris for Fashion Week."

"Mexico so I could dance in a Cinco de Mayo parade!"

"I'd walk on the moon."

"That's not on Earth."

"Angela's bedroom, right after her shower."

"Ew!"

"Perv!"

"Yeah right."

"Boo!"

"Gracie?"

"Gracie?"

"Yo, Graciela!"

She looks up from her half-cleared plate to see multiple pairs of eyes staring at her. She wonders how many years it has been that she's sat and eaten at a table full of other people's friends, strangers with familiar faces. She wonders how they think of her. Is she a hinderance, an awkward reminder that just won't go away? Do they wish she would fade, leave them be, let them forget?

"What?" she asks.

They laugh and roll their eyes.

"Are you really that fascinated by your burger?" Matt asks.

"I'm trying to see if my mother signed it," she explains, a joke which only half the table gets. She pokes the vat-bred meat experimentally. "I think she named this batch Susan."

That gets another few chuckles. She waits for attention to drift away from her again and then quietly stands, slips away. Khaiam sees her go but holds his tongue, and she disappears into a crowd of freshmen at the cafeteria doors.

She's always liked the halls at lunch. How empty they are, how quiet. She feels like an intruder in the best possible way; an archaeologist in an Egyptian tomb, an adventurer in a Mayan temple. She wonders what the world might have been like in the days when there were still mysterious places, discoveries left to be made. She imagines looking at the stars and seeing legends and stories, the eyes of the Gods; wonders if she would have believed herself to have been made from clay and blood. She likes the sounds of her footsteps, the way it vibrates up her leg if she stomps too hard. She does so down the length of a whole hall, until a teacher sticks his head out the door and glares her into silence.

She finds a quiet spot in a corner where the lockers end prematurely and there's a little gap between them and the corner of the wall, and wedges herself in. She knows she'll get in trouble if anyone sees her—yet another trip to the guidance counsellor, who will tell her he's worried about Gracie's "inability to reintegrate into the day-to-day social aspects of school." She doesn't care, knows her parents are ill-equipped to deal with her new eccentricities. They will give each other helpless shrugs and tell Mr. Domingues, very politely, that they understand, and they can assure him it's a top priority.

She slips on the Line, toggles public browsing on and Dives. She appears in her Homepage, but quickly surfs to Lougheed Track. On the web, it's a simple three-button racing game, but in the Dive it comes to life: a shady world of gamblers, adrenaline addicts, and bookies. Her Line downloads the site-specific settings she's programmed to automatically load, and as she surfs in her modifications rez to life. She appears in her thirties, with cropped blonde hair and angular features. Her eyes are sharp and green, her artificially well-endowed body straining the folds of her poured-on black leather bodysuit. With her helmet under one arm and her knee-high boots adding five inches to her slightly reduced height, she is a manic pixie, a carefully crafted ball of steel and barbed wire. That she plays on this site is one of her most carefully kept secrets, one she thought the AI might have made reference to last week, when he told her that he liked her in leather.

Though her public browsing is on, she keeps visits to this site secret because it's adult-only. Coding to protect children from the "corruptive influence" of certain sites came out two years after the Dive, in response to advocacy groups screaming about online sex and the proliferation of sites allowing users to partake in the darker aspects of human nature with no consequences. Less than a day after the official release, hacks cropped up in response, the equivalent of the fake IDs teenagers had been using for decades. Gracie visited controlled sites with reckless abandon, but Lougheed Track was one of the few to which she made regular visits. Her character, Despoina, was a fixture of the Sunday night betting games, where she had won five consecutive circuits before being ousted by an Australian with a huge moustache and a penchant for bad puns named Super Dave.

It's noon at home, but in the Waves people congregate from around the world, and there's always someone willing to put money on a race. The entry point to this site isn't as restricted as some, and she walks directly to the track door, skipping the raucous journey from the outside through the betting gallery. Her avatar is coded as a racer, and as she waves a hand over an ID checkpoint it spins dizzily through the rainbow, finally settling on green. The large rusted door opens with a shriek of abused metal, and she moves into the staging area.

Franco is sitting at his post. A Mannie with terrible programming, it's his job to ensure no one touches a machine that isn't theirs. Cheating is, of course, allowed, but Franco ensures the players come up with subtler ways to skew things in their favor.

Today things are quiet. She can hear the sound of engines on the raceway, but the barn appears deserted. The air smells strongly of motor oil and burnt rubber—a bit too strongly, she thinks. Shoddy programmers are greedy gods, who want their subjects to notice all the hard work they've put into the details. What's the point of layering eighteen smells into the perfect blend if someone is too distracted by the carefully tailored sound of engines to notice your masterpiece? She wants to fix it but doubts she could pull off a hack so large— her skills lie in smaller applications.

Franco smiles and gives her a plastic smile. "Hello, Despoina," he says. There is a faint blue light behind his eyes, a sign of his programming reaching into the raw data of the Waves to find her player file. Everything here seems blue— she wonders why her father chose that color, or if it was even deliberate. Maybe it was just science, an effect of the light spectrum. She plans to ask him someday, comes back to the present with a shake of her head.

"Franco. Is the boss in?" she asks.

He blinks. "What do you want?" It's his programmed response for a question that doesn't fit into his parameters. She rolls her eyes.

"Jesus, Franco, you really are a puppet," she mutters, and then at normal volume, "Tell me where Capore is."

"Oh, Capore! Why didn't you just say? He's in the VIP."

"Any races today?"

"One starting in ten. If you hurry you can make reg."

She grins. Perfect. She's got at least half an hour before her next class—just enough time to fit in a race. She thought she might only get to do a circuit around the practice pen.

Out of curiosity and boredom, she pauses before going further into the barn. "Say, Franco. Can you tell me what my stall number is?"

"3401," he rattles off without a pause, perfect mechanical recall. She could program better in her sleep. What a joke.

"Say I wanted to...upgrade my stall number. Say I gave you this registration fee, and you gave me a new stall number. But, you know, I wouldn't want to lose my old one, in case I didn't like the new one. Say I gave you...a hundred bucks. And you let me try out stall...sixty-two-oh-four. See how I like it. What do you say to that?"

The blue lights shines from his eyes. There is a pause just a touch too empty to be human; not like he's thinking, but like he has simply ceased to interact with his current environment. Then he returns. "What do you want?"

"Never mind, Franco," she says with a sigh. She should have known that rumor wasn't true. The Mannie's programming was so bad that... She stops and turns back around, having walked a step past the guard. "Say, Franco. Can I bribe you with a hundred dollars so I can go tool Super Dave's machine?" she asks.

There's no blue light this time. "I'm deeply offended!" he snaps. "I got a reputation to uphold. I got a job to do. I'm a man of consequence. I ain't gonna take no measly hundred bucks."

"What will you take?"

He winks. "Figure that out yourself," he says in a different tone of voice, as if there's a puppeteer behind the mask who's having a bit too much fun. She grins, slips her hands into her pockets, and heads for her machine. Always good to earn new information.

The tracks at Lougheed run all kinds. Car races, bike races, even dogs and horses. She's got a mechanical filly named Will Robinson and a bike shaped like a seahorse that she built from the ground up, but the pride of her collection is her car. Slick gunmetal silver from hood to tailpipe, with deep burgundy accents and glowing bits of programming. She tooled the engine for three weeks to get it to purr just right, and the wheels still smell like strawberries because of a hack someone did all wrong, trying to wreck her on her third title race. She's only crashed her twice, and one of those times she still won the damn race.

She does a walk-through, keying on her goggles and hunting for clipped or altered programming. Everything looks clean but she runs a diagnostic just in case, revving the engine and tasting the sound in the air. Convinced it's all in working order, she climbs in and slams into gear for a showy entrance, breaking out of the barn at nearly seventy miles an hour and screaming to a stop millimeters from the starting line. The crowd is smaller than she's used to, but it goes wild, Surfers and Divers alike cheering and waving their arms at her appearance. She pops her door open and stands up in her seat, kissing her biceps and showing off a little. A quick scan of the competition reveals a sorry state of affairs. Two racers she's never seen before, obviously kids that have hacked in, the blurred lines over their faces a weak attempt to alter their avatars without the programming know-how to do it right. The fourth looks familiar, an older man with a huge pot belly who she thinks she's raced before. He looks sour to see her there, probably knowing he would have wiped the floor with the kids, and she gives him a smile and a shrug, as if to say, *I'd apologize, but I ain't sorry.*

The Mannie with the starting gun clocks her machine; her vital stats flash across the board. There's another cheer, as those who didn't recognize her car see her name and champion titles in glowing script. The arena's a weird design: half something from last century, with wooden bench seats and men with boxes slung across their shoulders hawking beer in the aisles, and half futuristic science fiction, with gleaming metal skyboxes for the rich and bored, and automated camera drones sweeping across the track, beaming instant play-by-plays of the minutiae of the race. There are four giant megatron screens, which flash ads for cigarettes and condoms along their bases.

There's a klaxon, and a wild shiver runs through the crowd. She sinks back into her car, strapping in as a tiny robot flies up to her window. She rolls it down and sticks out her hand, letting it stab her with a rusty needle. A small drop of red blood wells up and trickles down her arm, and the bot registers her pain response before flying away. It's against the rules to race at Lougheed without a stimulation pack—the oft-debated add-on that lets you feel in reality what happens in the Dive. It isn't perfect, of course. If you bleed, your skin doesn't split open; if you die you can still come back. But the human mind can punish the body with startling realism.

Nosebleeds, strange bruises, even seizures are all potential manifestations of Dive-induced bodily trauma. Gracie always Dives with her stimulation pack activated. Nothing feels real if it doesn't leave a mark; she wants the Dive to be as true as life.

The klaxon sounds the thirty-second mark. Gracie takes a deep breath, wraps one hand around the gear shift and, just for show, revs her engine. She slides on her helmet and cracks her neck. This is the best part—the anticipation that builds in her stomach like acid. She wants to throw up and scream and laugh all at once, and as the starting pistol roars she indulges enough to let loose a howling cry, and her foot presses the pedal to the floor as the air fills with the smell of burnt rubber and the stands coalesce into a blur beside her. The race is on.

She overtakes the kids in a matter of seconds, toggling a spray of frozen orange juice and tar that spatters their wind-shields as she passes. Beside her, the fat cowboy keeps pace, his head swiveling as he keeps both her and the track in view. She knows that will be his mistake—she keeps her eyes fixed on the route ahead.

She's a quarter through the first lap when a ten-foot section of track collapses two feet in front of her. She eyes the gap and deploys a set of grapple chains, gunning the engine as she does. The chains bite in twelve feet on, and she rockets through the slowly widening gap. Her momentum can't quite carry her over the hole, and as she swings into the pit, she blasts air from her undercarriage. The grapple line catches and holds, and she braces for a sharp impact against the wall, but the compressed air catches the momentum and turns it gently. Her wheels hit the pit wall and she reels the grapples in, dragging herself up the side and out of the pit. In her rearview she sees the cowboy hovering past. So he plays it safe—hovering is effective but slows you down. She files that away; might be important before the race is up.

The grappling hooks bring her back up to the track and she releases them, making sure to avoid driving over the remains as she speeds away. The hooks, now effective caltrops, should deal with the kids when they finally catch up. She hits a few buttons and programs the pit into her GPS, so she can easily drive around it on the second lap.

The moment of programming has cost her a few seconds, and the cowboy's nose is now a good three feet ahead of hers. She swears and switches gears, but can't quite regain her lead. The sound of the crowd piping through her speakers is deafening, and she feels it reverberate in her chest like powerful bass. The air tastes like gasoline and the wind is so loud she can hear it as a steady beat beyond the fiberglass and metal shell that careens around the track at a hundred and fifty miles an hour. She feels alive, laughs again just because she can. The tiny square of reality in the bottom of her vision is hardly a distraction, barely real. This is the world, and she is a goddess of the race.

She does not see the danger coming. It appears from nowhere, with no flash of warning: a lone figure dwarfed by its surroundings, standing dead center in the track. She is caught completely off-guard. He turns and for a brief second their eyes meet through the intervening distance, and she knows them. Brown pools with black lights in their depths widened in surprise and alarm. As quickly as he appears he is gone, but she is left shaken. Real-world instinct made her slam on her brakes, and at this speed the mistake is costly. Her back end fishtails and she madly switches gears, but the cowboy sees the chance to act and hits her with a tiny metal engine. The engine bursts into life on her left rear end, sending her into a spin from which she can't recover. She has only a second to react before her car flips end over end, and her body is assaulted with a wash of red-hot pain. The world rezzes out and she collapses against the locker as the real world, too, fades away.

She groans and drags herself back into a sitting position, blinking away the afterimage of searing light. Every part of her body aches. Good thing Lougheed isn't a one-play site—that crash definitely killed her. Dying during a Dive is a strange experience—a reporter once described it as akin to a time she nearly drowned. Your brain goes into the same panic mode it does when it's suffocating, as it scrambles for sensory input that's no longer there. Scenes sometimes flash before your eyes, your brain trying to find a similar experience that you survived so it can attempt to save you from this, too; then there's pain, then a soft sort of surrender, a floating...and then your whole body gasps as real sensory input floods back and replaces the Dive input. Sometimes you lose consciousness; sometimes you seize up or spasm. Then, slowly, your body settles back into place. You are left with the severe muscle pains of a full body cramp, and often a nosebleed or bruising. Gracie can already see a large red mark on her upper arm which will no doubt turn into a shocking bruise by tomorrow, and there's a bloodstain on her shirt, so her nose is obviously leaking.

She scrambles to her feet, forgetting the Line still stuck to her temple, and goes running down the hall. She earns a few stares but ignores them and finds Khaiam still lingering in the lunchroom with a few friends. The first bell has rung but there's still ten minutes to class, and about half the room is full. Khaiam gasps when he sees her.

"Khai!" she gasps. "You will *never* believe this."

"Oh my God, what happened?" he says. He grabs a

napkin and tries to dab at the blood still trickling down her face, but she waves him away.

"It was incredible—it should have been totally impossible, he just appeared out of nowhere, there wasn't even a Dive entry site—"

"You need to go to the nurse." He isn't listening. He grabs one of her hands and uses his other to wipe away the blood. It smears across her face, connecting the dots of freckles across one cheek. Someone takes her backpack, but she isn't paying attention to the helping hands.

"I don't think it's even hackable! I can pre-program entry points if I know where I'm going, but he *clearly* did not intend to be at that exact place—"

"Give me your phone."

"—at that exact time, which means he doesn't know where he's going! I mean that could be important, right?"

"Give me your phone."

"Are you paying any attention at all?"

"Give. Me. Your phone."

She peels her phone out of the front pocket of her jeans, handing it over. "Khaiam, this could change everything. We knew he was tracking me down somehow, but they have no idea how he's manipulating Servers and nets to avoid them. If we can find out—who are you calling?"

He has the phone to his ear, doesn't respond. She itches her face, comes away covered in blood. Bella hands her a wad of napkins, and she pinches her nose with her other hand. Her voice is nasal and strange. "Who are you calling?"

"Um, Mr. Neumann? Sorry, this is Khaiam? Graciela's friend?"

"Are you shitting me?" she hisses.

"Yeah, um, I'm at school, and—" He dodges easily as Gracie makes a lunge for the phone. Matt puts a hand on her shoulder, a gesture of restraint more than a real hindrance. "Gracie was Diving at lunch and she's bleeding all over the place—yeah, but—no, I haven't, but—um. I was just about to, but I think—Yeah. Okay. Yeah." There is a long silence before he hangs up. He avoids eye contact as he hands back the phone.

She sighs in relief. "He's busy?"

Khaiam nods.

"I can't believe you phoned my dad."

"He told me to take you to the nurse. He said they'd call him if it was anything serious. Come on." He picks up his bag, slings it over one shoulder, and takes hers from Derek. She presses the wad of paper more tightly to her face, doesn't move to follow. Excitement has fled, stolen her courage and whisked it away. She wishes she could be Despoina or Mallory; she would hook a foot under his, bear him to the ground. A knife would flash out of nowhere, and their faces would be so close she would draw in his breath like a succubus as she demanded an explanation.

But she is only Gracie Neumann.

Tears prickle her eyes, and she feels the edge of the bench behind her biting into the back of her calves. She doesn't remember retreating. "Why did you phone my dad?"

"You're bleeding from your face!" he screams. His friends are standing awkwardly to one side, unsure whether or not to get involved in what has suddenly become a drama.

"It's fine—"

"It's not fine! And the fact that you think it's fine!" The sentence dies on the sharp exclamation of his final word. He grabs his hair in both hands, breathing hard and fast. "You are —God, you're so..." He drags a hand across his eyes, digs fingernails into the skin of his cheek and rakes down. "Just..." He looks at her, and something quiet passes between them.

He spins and walks out and she follows more slowly, leaving silence in her wake.

In the hall, Khaiam slows so she can catch up. A few people ask if she's okay but Gracie just nods and bites her lip. She has no words to calm his fear, which builds a barrier between them.

"You know you're made of skin," he says. They're only a few doors away from the nurse's station. The words process but don't make sense.

"I know," she says, but he grabs her arm, stops her in her tracks. His grip hurts, distracting from the general aches and pains of her abused body.

"Do you?" he demands. "Look at you." He indicates her bruises, the blood on her shirt. The fragility of her presence next to his. "One wrong move and you could...and there's just this hole where you're supposed to be."

"I know," she says again. The words are heavy with connotation, with shared pain.

"Do you?" he asks, but he lets her go. They walk the last few steps in silence. He hands her back her bag, knocks on the door. She wants to say something to make it better, but the door is opening and he is gone, and she's alone in the square of bright white light falling through the doorway.

CHAPTER EIGHT_

THE NURSE PATCHES HER UP AND CONFISCATES HER
Line, promising to give it to her family, who "will no doubt be shocked that she's using restricted add-ons." She gets a few ice packs, a lecture about safe Diving practice, another lecture about Diving during school hours, and finally a lemon-flavored lollipop. She is sent on her way and arrives twenty minutes late to her English literature class. Khaiam is at the back of the room and refuses to meet her eyes when she tries to catch his. Angela asks her in a whisper if she's okay, and she smiles and nods and pretends everything is fine while she fakes interest about a book called *The Basketball Diaries* from sixty years ago. As if a teenager's life in 1980 has any impact on the struggles she faces today. As if anything endures in these intangible times.

Mrs. Cheng is discussing cycles of abuse in reference to the protagonist's first use of heroin, how one event can trigger a downward slide. Derek puts up his hand.

"I don't believe it," he says.

"What is it you don't believe?" Mrs. Cheng asks.

"The dude was already into drugs. He's, like...a messed-up kid. I don't think his friend dying has anything to do with it. Like, the kid died in the fall diary entry, right, and the heroin is in the *winter* entry. There's no way he'd still be upset enough to start doing drugs."

"It's only been four months," Khaiam objects. "And he has no support system."

"Yeah, but there's that song, right, about how all of his friends have died? I don't think it's that big a deal."

"It isn't a big deal?" Khaiam asks. Gracie recognizes the sound of something delicate breaking. She knows no one else has seen it, wishes she could stop the fallout but knows the bomb has already gone off; it's just traveling through space, taking time to reach them. By the time you see the light of a star, it has died a thousand years before.

"No. It's just, like, one more friend."

"One more *dead friend*. People don't walk away from that unscarred."

"But if he was gonna break he would have already. It's like, it's just an excuse, you know? So we'll feel sorry for his bad choices. You don't see me doing heroin every time I stub my toe."

The class laughs.

"His friend *died!*" Khaiam screams. Gracie feels his pain like a physical thing. "You have no idea what that's like!" *But I do,* Gracie thinks. *We do.*

"Khaiam!" Mrs. Cheng objects, but he rolls over her like an avalanche.

"You have no fucking clue how hard it is to just get out of bed every morning! How easy it is to justify hurting yourself when everything already hurts! How much a person can want to take the easy way out!"

"Mr. Fadel!" Mrs. Cheng yells.

He grabs his bag and runs out the door. It is a day of

palpable silences. Gracie wonders how long they will haunt her, whether she will ever live in a world that never goes dark. After a second Matt excuses himself and follows Khaiam's path out the door. Mrs. Cheng seems relieved to let him go, like she knew she ought to be the one but is glad to foist the responsibility onto someone else. Gracie is grateful Matt is there for him; it never occurs to her to be the one to go. She would have no words to make it better because it isn't better. Everyone promised they wouldn't stay broken, everyone swore time would wash it away like footsteps in the sand, everyone said how lucky they were that they got the chance to say goodbye...

CHAPTER NINE_

"It's time to say goodbye, honey."

Her mother's voice came from miles away. The hospital had become familiar: the noises over the intercom, the antiseptic smell. She knew the faces walking past, could predict the nurse's movements down to the minute. She and Calista had copied all the schedules into their tablets and played betting games on who would walk past when, who peed in what order, whose turn it was to get lunch or coffee. The hospital worked like a machine. Everything made sense—except for those words. *Say goodbye.*

"They can't know that," she said, but the words were barely a whisper. Syllables cracked and didn't quite connect, her voice straining past the lump in her throat. Her mother kissed her forehead, a rare moment of tenderness.

"Do you want me to come with you?" she asked. Gracie shook her head. Everyone was together in the waiting room, the doctors sending them in one at a time. A twisted parade, but it was the way Calista wanted it. Khaiam had been in and out; he couldn't meet Gracie's eyes, ran into his mother's arms in tears and disappeared into his family's embrace. Other friends had come and gone, a week of awkward goodbyes, no one sure if this was really the end but everyone full of warnings. Say goodbye while you have the chance. Make your peace, as if peace was a thing that could be built on a handful of sentences and a moist hug. Gracie had teased everyone behind their backs to make Calista laugh, though it hurt when she laughed too hard, her body shaking even when she was lying still.

Gracie walked into the room. Calista was propped up on two pillows, her long black hair tangled and damp with sweat. Her face was pale, even for her, and her dark brown eyes seemed to have lost the light that usually danced in their depths. She was already a ghost. Gracie made an unconscious noise and Calista turned her head, smiled.

"Your turn," she whispered and chuckled with morbid energy. Gracie sat on the bed beside her. There were already tears in her eyes and she hadn't yet said a word. She took Calista's hand, rubbed a thumb against the papery skin of her fingers. She had no idea how to say goodbye to someone who was still here, someone they told her she would never see again. The longest that she had gone without seeing this face was six weeks. Six weeks, when Calista's family took a summer vacation to Paris and they had talked on the phone every night, so she wasn't even sure that counted.

"You know you're supposed to say something, right?" Calista said, and Gracie nodded, but there were no words to force past the lump in her throat. Calista squeezed her hand, though it obviously cost her. "Don't cry, Graciela," she said. She never called her Gracie, said she was more than a diminutive.

"I'm not," Gracie said, though of course she was.

"Don't grieve for me just yet," Calista whispered.

"You can't go. Okay?" Gracie said, trying to smile. "I just can't do it without you. So you can't. We have a deal—don't we?" Her voice was a squeak. She wanted to be strong and brave, wanted it not to be about her, wanted Calista to be able to be as scared as she needed to be while she was strong for her; but there was a hole she couldn't fill with bravado, a terror that she'd never felt, and the tears spilled out.

"We have a deal," Calista said. "I won't ever leave you. I love you so much."

"I love you too," Graciela said through hiccupping sobs. "I love you. I love you. I love you."...

CHAPTER TEN_

"Um, Mrs. Cheng? I think there's something wrong with Gracie."

The voices sound a mile away, and through the sheen of tears and the pressure in her chest, Gracie realizes everyone's attention is on her. The pressure gets stronger, the edges of the world darkening and blurring. She tries to be calm, deep breath in and out, count to ten like they taught her, but she can't count ten breaths when she can't even take one. She wants to jump up and run away but she's afraid to stand, afraid she'll fall.

Mrs. Cheng is saying something to her, but the words don't seem to run into each other the way they ought to. She struggles, wins, takes one breath in but it hitches before it's finished and leaves her feeling more breathless than when she began. There's a warm hand against her arm, a face that swims into focus. Words, like dominoes, scatter on the floor. In her mind she picks one up, turns it in her fingers. *Breathe,* the domino says, so she does. One more breath in and this one is better, a little bit stronger. The face becomes Mrs.

Cheng and she guides Gracie to her feet, helps her leave the classroom.

The teachers' lounge is closer than the nurse's station, so Mrs. Cheng takes her there. She's never been inside and is surprised by how nice it is, how crisp and modish. The blocky furniture and bright colors are soothing, though when she sits on the couch it's a little too deep, and her feet hang off the edge like they did when she was a small child. She lets her head fall between her knees, stares at the floor. Off-white tile, with blue grouting between the pieces. Little rivers in a frozen, perfectly organized county. She traces them with her eyes until her tears stop flowing and the roaring in her ears goes quiet.

Mrs. Cheng offers her a glass of water, and she feels the tears start again, from embarrassment now. She wonders what words her literature teacher will have for her, what awkward platitudes. *Don't be ashamed. Panic attacks are common. Do you have any medication?* Her bag is in the classroom. She can't bear to go back for it.

"Are you okay?" Mrs. Cheng asks.

Gracie nods. "Thanks."

"Do you want me to call your parents?"

A head shake. *No.*

"Why don't you go and find Khaiam," Mrs. Cheng suggests. Gracie is surprised by the offer.

"Okay," she says. There is an awkward moment where it seems Mrs. Cheng wants to offer some physical comfort—to lay a hand against her arm or plant a kiss on her forehead. But her fluttering hand eventually lands on the glass. She takes it and pours out the mostly untouched water, puts the receptacle in the dishwasher. They leave the room together and part ways as soon as the door closes behind them.

Gracie sends Khaiam a text, not sure where he might be,

and then wanders the halls aimlessly. She doesn't want to go back for her bag until the bell rings and the class has left, but that leaves her with almost half an hour. Her body hurts, and her bout of crying has added a ringing headache to her list of complaints. She goes to the bathroom, stares at her reflection in shock. There are dark circles under her eyes, which are red-rimmed and dull. She did a bad job of cleaning the blood from her nosebleed, and there are some dried flecks on her cheek, on her neck. The shirt, of course, is ruined, but she expected that.

She washes her face, scrubs under her nose and chin. She doesn't carry makeup but does her best to mitigate the effects the day has had. Ten minutes later her tablet pings—it's Khaiam.

- Khai.the.Guy: Sorry.
- Gracielass: Matt still with you?
- Khai.the.Guy: yup
- Gracielass: Don't be sorry.
- Khai.the.Guy: take ntoes for me?
- Gracielass: Left too.
- Khai.the.Guy: Why?
- Gracielass: No big deal.
- Khai.the.Guy: Panic attack?
- Gracielass: I'm fine now.
- Khai.the.Guy: were out on the field
- Gracielass: I think I'm just gonna head home.
- Khai.the.Guy: wait. meet you by your locker.
- Gracielass: I'm fine.
- Gracielass: Khai?
- Gracielass: You don't have to come find me.
- Gracielass: Khai?

He doesn't answer, so she accepts defeat and waits by her locker. He shows up a few seconds later. Matt is in tow, but he peels off and heads back into class, giving her the chin-up nod that teenagers perfected decades ago. Khaiam wraps his arms around her and she leans her head against his chest, matching the hug watt-for-watt. They just stand there for a long time, shared grief: the most powerful balm they have been able to find. Soon they turn away, sink to sitting positions side-by-side, legs spread out into the hall. Gracie checks her watch—fifteen minutes until the bell.

"I thought they were getting better?" he asks.

"They are. It's my first one in two weeks," she lies.

He leans his head back against the cool metal, staring up at the cheap ceiling tiles. "She would be so mad at us. We were under strict orders not to fall apart."

"Speak for yourself," Gracie says, with a smile that doesn't quite reach her eyes. "I had a different agreement."

"Oh?"

A long pause. "She said she'd never leave," Gracie whispers. The words sound silly and hollow under the harsh fluorescent lights. A pledge that life never intended to let them keep.

"I asked her once if she loved me... She said things weren't always that simple," he says.

"I remember," Gracie says. "She told me."

"She told you everything."

"She kept a lot inside."

"Did she ever say..." He hesitates. Rakes a hand over his jeans, sticks a finger through a hole in the knee and worries the fabric away. "Did she ever tell you why she stayed? With me, I mean."

"That's a stupid question," Gracie assures him. She rests a hand on his knee. "She really liked you. She trusted you."

"But she didn't love me."

"I think she didn't know what love really was. She always talked about love like a painful thing, like something you couldn't run away from even when you wanted to. She said... I don't know. It was weird. She said that you made her as happy as she would ever be. But she wouldn't explain what that meant." Gracie shrugs. It doesn't seem to matter now—questions with no answers, riddles that can't be solved. He will always love her because she died before she could break his heart.

"That's not very comforting," Khaiam admits.

"Should I not have told you?" Gracie asks, though of course it's too late for that. But thankfully he shakes his head.

"It isn't anything I didn't already know."

"You wanna leave? I think there's a late matinee at the Grand. They're doing a retro week—all the cheesy 4D movies from the '20s."

A smile finally breaks through the clouds. "You know I like nothing more than terrible scent effects—but I can't afford to miss any more bio. I'm barely scraping a D."

"I've just got choir and world history."

"You never skip."

"I have done—at least three times in the last..." She coughs for comedic effect. "Three years." She climbs to her feet and he follows, brushing dirt off the back of his pants. Belatedly she does the same, though she figures her outfit can't get much more ruined than it already is.

"Fine, but I'm not breaking you out when you get grounded."

"I got my Line confiscated for using a stimulation pack while at school, and I'll be lucky if my bloody nose doesn't end up in a tabloid somewhere. I'm pretty sure I'm already grounded. I might as well shoot for the moon. Want anything vandalized?"

He laughs, rubs the heel of one hand against his eyes. "No, but if you can find a way to hack the fire alarm during my next pop quiz, that would be great."

She smiles, shakes her head, but is saved from answering by the bell. They both wait for the halls to fill before slouching back to their class in ignominy to fetch their bags.

CHAPTER ELEVEN_

She's just finishing an essay on the nature of sin and salvation in turn-of-the-millennium pop culture, when the Surface on her wall pings. She glances at her watch—six o'clock. The screen pings again and her father's face appears, cutting through her privacy settings to activate a video telecall.

"Downstairs. Now," he says, and the screen goes dark.

She throws a book at the wall but reluctantly stumbles out of the room and down the twisting staircase. Her parents are in the study—her mother sits at her desk, one eye on her tablet, while her father paces back and forth in front of the couch.

"I could have been changing," she grouches as she slips into the room.

"What?"

"You can't just hack through my privacy settings. What if I'd been naked?"

"It's six o'clock in the evening. Why would you be naked?" her father says.

"She's just trying to deflect blame because she knows

she's in trouble," her mother says. She gives Gracie an unimpressed look before returning her attention to her work.

"Just because I did something wrong doesn't mean Dad didn't, too," Gracie says, but the wind is out of her sails. Her father points at the couch and she slinks over and disappears into its comforting folds.

"This came for me," he says, tossing her Line on the cushion beside her. "With a very interesting note."

"They're blowing it way out of proportion," Gracie says. "It was lunchtime."

"I don't care if you're Diving at school," he says with a dismissive wave. "It's a draconian rule to disallow it, these people are trapped in the '20s. I *care*," he adds before relief can set in, "that you're using stim-packs."

"I forgot I had it," Gracie lies, badly.

"You *know* how much flak we're getting on the stimulation issue!" Maxwell snaps. "I'm fending off conservative lobbyists every day who are harping on the dangers of Diving as if the problem is inherent in the system instead of a natural side effect of the integration of the human variable. Do you have *any* concept of what it could do to our stock prices if the creator's daughter ended up in the hospital because of a Dive gone awry? I could lose *funding*, Gracie."

I'm fine, thanks for asking. "It wasn't even that bad. It was a nosebleed."

"You have a *black eye.*"

Gracie touches the bruise on her cheek. It's hardly a black eye. "I'm sorry."

"Sorry isn't good enough. There have to be consequences. You're..." He glances to his wife, who gives a subtle shrug. "Well, you're damn well never using a stimulation pack again."

"But you just *said* there's no integral flaw in the system!"

Gracie says. "Isn't me *not* using one just more fodder for your critics?"

"I *said* that the problem is the human variable. Stupid people get hit by cars, and stupid people crash airplanes, and stupid people give themselves seizures abusing stimulation packs! You have proven yourself incapable of being trusted with this piece of technology. Just like you can lose a driver's license, you have lost your stim-pack license. Final decision," he says, holding up a hand to forestall her objection. Her eyes fill with tears.

"That isn't fair," she says. "It wasn't even my fault!"

"Take responsibility," Carmela mildly chides.

"You haven't even asked me what happened!" Gracie cries.

"That piece of information is irrelevant to the equation," Maxwell says. "If I catch you using a stim-pack, we will take away your Line for...a week."

"A month," her mother says.

His eye twitches, like he thinks that's too harsh, but he agrees. "A month."

She wants to argue, but everything feels too present, too large. She is a tiny black and white figure in a technicolored storm. Her parents are high-pressure fronts, bearing down on her, stealing the air from the room. She jumps to her feet and runs. They don't call her back.

She locks herself in the bedroom, grabs a pillow and presses it against her face. She can't breathe. "Not again," she whispers, "not again, not again. Breathe, Graciela, breathe."

She pictures Calista beside her, rubbing a soothing hand against her back. After a moment she fumbles off the bed and into her bathroom. She takes the bottle of pills out of her drawer—three tiny white ovals sit at the bottom of the otherwise empty case—swallows one, and stumbles back into the room. A few solid hacks lock all the Surfaces in the room, and with another swipe, she toggles on her favorite song. She brings the bass up loud enough that she can feel it. The music breathes for her, speaks for her, and she sinks down into her pillows and lets her eyes close, feeling the music in her bones...

CHAPTER TWELVE_

She touched her tablet screen, added a little more makeup to her avatar, changed the shape of her neckline two or three times. She had looked forward to this concert for months; hadn't been sure, until that morning, if she would still go. Calista had bought the tickets a few weeks before she got sick. Now there she was, two months after the funeral, still checking her watch and hoping Calista wouldn't be late before remembering she was going on her own.

Her phone buzzed. She found the app on her tablet and flicked one finger quickly up to answer. "Hello?"

"I am so *bored*," Khaiam moaned. "What are you doing?"

"Oh. Uh. I'm…going out."

"Going out?" His voice perked up. "You never go out. Where are you going?"

"Just Diving. Why are you so bored? It's Saturday night."

"I know! That's my problem. Matt and I were supposed to go downtown and try to sneak into this club on First, but his parents found the fake IDs he got us, so now he's grounded, the ID is gone, and it's only a matter of time before my parents catch wise and I'm grounded, too—so I went out, and now I'm wandering the streets trying to find something to do, but everyone is already out and no one's answering my texts."

"I feel so special," she said.

"Come do something with me!"

"I'm sorry—I've got this—"

"Diving does not count as plans! Come on. I'm a real person. Save me from the boredom."

"It's just, I have tickets..."

"Ooh, to what?"

Gracie flicked through screens on her tablet, found the ticket redemption code. She still had both tickets—couldn't make herself sell the other one. "Control Alt concert."

"Oh, God, jealous! That sold out months ago, why haven't you been bragging about it all week?"

"...I have an extra ticket. You wanna come?"

"Are you serious?! YES!" There followed a pause, as he realized why she would have two. "Oh, um. Are you sure you want me to?"

Gracie stared at the avatar she'd built. There was no time to tone it down—it was this or factory-direct. Normally when she Dove in tandem it was with the base avatar, just little old Gracie. She kept the rest of her online life private, another person, another world. But for some reason she wouldn't quite explain she wanted to share this secret with Khaiam— wanted him, just once, to see her as she really was.

"Can you get to a Line in the next fifteen minutes?" she asked.

There was a ping and a tandem request hit her screen.

She smiled and shook her head, downloaded her mods to her line, and Dove.

The concert was at the top of a mountain. She pinged Khaiam the ticket code and he rezzed into place beside her. Calista had gotten great seats—only five or so feet from the stage, in the center of a milling crowd. There were little blue glowing boxes scattered around, reserved spaces so that ticket holders could rez in close to the front. The programming was stunning—the mountain towered hundreds of feet above a night-dark forest, floating will o' the wisps visible through the trees. The sky above was starred with foreign constellations in the shape of old album covers, and a warm-up band made quiet music on the giant stage. The theme was Mount Olympus, all-white marble pillars and flowing sheets of silk. There were altars to Greek gods in the corners of the temple-like structure, and Mannies in togas wove through the crowd, selling drinks and stim-pack upgrades. Beyond the temple was the Surfer seating, where the plebes at home could live stream the concert. She saw a few unlicensed Divers sneaking around the glowing blue Surfers and hoped they didn't crash the server—there was nothing worse than a bad case of the Bends when a server went down with you Diving inside it.

Khaiam's avatar was factory-direct; just good old Khai-the-guy, with his black hair a little too long in his eyes and his dark brown skin mostly covered by a faded football jersey and a pair of midnight blue jeans. By contrast, Gracie looked about nineteen, her curls straightened and sleek, dark skin flawless without her habitual freckles. She was an inch taller, and her four-inch heels brought her nose almost level with his. She had on a black Grecian dress with a plunging neckline and an eye-catching silver necklace with the band's logo on it. Khaiam stared unabashedly, and she thought he might not have recognized her right away.

"You look...wow," he said, and she smiled.

"I like hacking avatars," she admitted.

"It's so weird, it's like...obviously still you, but...not quite you. Like your older sister or something. Hey, can you buy beer?"

She laughed—he did have a one-track mind sometimes. But she could, so she waved down a server and ordered them each a brew. They weren't selling beer, just "manna of the gods," some kind of honey liqueur. Khaiam was surprised to see her take one for herself.

"I thought you had to have a hack to get adult-only content," he said with a raised eyebrow.

She shrugged. "Yeah?"

"So...do you do anything you would need the hack for?"

She rolled her eyes. "The Waves are—like my backyard. Adult-only sites are like telling me I can't go into my own treehouse. You know?" It was hard to explain what it meant to have grown up in the Waves. How this had been her nursery, how she had slowly watched it change as other people got their fingers in, played the game in their own way. She didn't necessarily have the hack because she wanted to drink, or have sex, or gamble. She had it because this was her house, and she should have a key to every room.

"Sure," he said, though she wasn't sure he really understood. "Thanks." He lifted the drink and they clinked earthenware goblets before taking a sip. The programming was great—honey hit her tongue first, and then a faint burn of alcohol, with notes of sugar and berries that she smelled at the back of her tongue. Alcohol in the Dive worked on your brain chemistry rather than your blood, giving you a "high" which lasted about half an hour after you Surfaced.

Someone rezzed into the setting inside of the square that should have been set aside for her and Khaiam, knocking her into him and spilling her drink. It soaked into the rocks at her feet, and she turned to snap something angry—but the words died on her lips.

It was him.

The guy in front of her didn't look exactly the same as he had in Urban Noir, but the resemblance was strong. He wore his hair in a mass of brown curls instead of the black and red fire, and he had sharpened the planes of his cheekbones, but the shape of his face was similar, and his eyes were the same. He was wearing a black shirt that wrapped around his chest like a toga, leaving one shoulder bare, with a pair of black pants and scuffed-up sneakers. An identical copy of her limited release pendant hung around his neck.

"You're in my seat," he complained.

"This is *my* seat," Gracie countered. She held up the manifested version of her ticket.

He copied the gesture with an identical slip of his own. "Seems we're at an impasse."

"Seems you're a known hacker who can..." *do impossible things,* her mind completed. The Diver she had met in Urban Noir had done hacks that should have been impossible—had rezzed into a locked zone, had changed *her* avatar, and now here he was, in an impossible place, under impossible circumstances, and those dark eyes, those black eyes that were so familiar... "I know you," she said.

He winked. "I should hope so, doll. We *did* blow Lacklace's stash sky-high. I'd think adventures like those are worth remembering."

"I *know* you," she insisted.

"Uh—care to introduce me, then?" Khaiam asked. He

tried to laugh it off, but he was clearly concerned about what was unfolding in front of him.

The blood seemed to drain from the stranger's face. He recovered quickly, but for some reason Khaiam's presence was an unanticipated factor in his smooth planning.

"You Mallory's man?" he asked.

"Mallory?" Khaiam asked, and raised his eyebrows at Gracie. She shrugged one shoulder.

"Why don't you introduce yourself?" she suggested to the stranger. "Since Johnnie's just a game alias."

"So is Mallory. Why don't you introduce yourself?" he countered, all of his attention focused on her.

"Well, I'm Khaiam," Khaiam cut in cheerfully. Gracie fought the urge to roll her eyes; the stranger didn't. She had to remind herself that this wasn't Urban Noir. There was no game to be won here, but the pattern of their relationship seemed set, and she enjoyed the rush of the hunt.

"I think you already know my name," she challenged. Because, of course, there was only one thing she knew of that could control the Waves to the extent this "hacker" did—and that was her father's missing AI.

He had shot her a sparkling grin. "Caught on, have you? You didn't recognize me when I was Johnnie."

"You were wearing a different face than the first time we met," she reminded.

"So were you."

"I was wearing a mask at best—you were wearing a whole new skin."

"Um...I feel like I'm missing something..." Khaiam said.

"Khaiam—meet Charlie."

The AI's eyes narrowed, and he licked his lips as if to get rid of a bad taste. "Didn't you get the bulletin about my atti-tude vis-à-vis that name?"

"Is there one you prefer?" she asked.

"You choose," he offered. "Use a name to build me into something." The words were offered casually but his eyes were intense. Energy seemed to pass between them, and she felt the silent desperation of a person who could change everything. She recognized the hunger for something immutable; the need for permanence.

"Once you have a name you can't change it," she warned. "Anything else is just an alias."

He took a step forward. He had already been in her personal space but then he had almost touched her. "Then you'd better choose wisely," he breathed.

"Are you shitting me?" Khaiam asked, thrilled. "You're the AI?"

They both ignored him.

Gracie smiled. "Thomas."

He raised an eyebrow. "I was expecting something a little more...robust."

"It's a puzzle. Figure it out and you can use the name. Otherwise, you won't have earned it," she told him. He grinned.

"I like you," he whispered in her ear.

She didn't know what to say; fought a smile and this strange new breathlessness—this pressure that didn't choke her.

"You're still in my seat," she reminded, and he laughed.

"So. Khaiam, is it?" he asked and switched his attention like flipping a switch. They stared into each other's eyes; Khaiam in awe, the AI with an elusive sort of hunger. He reached out, flicked an imaginary piece of dust off the other boy's shoulder. "You look happy," he said, which struck both Gracie and Khaiam as strange.

"Uh—well, yeah, I mean, it's pretty cool to meet you. You're, like...a legend."

"Literally," Gracie added. "If you wouldn't mind just proving to the world you exist—my dad would really appreciate it."

He ignored her. "You wanna see legendary?"

"Uh—yeah!" Khaiam enthused.

The AI winked and snapped his fingers. Gracie felt a tug and a pull beneath her skin, and she had seen Khaiam transform in front of her, his light brown skin shifting to pale white, his hair twisting into golden curls. She had felt her jaw drop as she realized he was turning into the bass player from the band. Her own transformation was harder to clock, happening as it was directly below her, but she saw her chest flattening, her biceps rippling with muscle. Above them, the sky exploded into fireworks, incredible displays of silver and gold, and the AI shrieked, "OH MY GOD! It's Control Alt!" and jumped up and down, pointing at them.

The crowd went mad. There was a sudden vortex, a spinning pressure drawing them in, this chance to touch their idols, to be close to greatness. Word moved like wildfire, and those in the back strained to move closer, sending a crashing pressure through people like shifting molecules, sparking something unstoppable. The fireworks intensified overhead, and Gracie lost sight of Khaiam and the AI in the press of bodies. She thought she could hear him laughing somewhere nearby, reveling in the chaos, and shrieked as someone grabbed her arms, her legs. But they lifted her into the air and then she was above it, the clear air painfully cold in her lungs, the sky overhead on fire, beautiful cacophony of light, and she was borne forward on the crowd, exultation spreading through her, the power of this false communion—

There was a static crackle in the sky. Gracie had only a moment to think, *Oh, n—* and then the world de-rezzed around her, and fire spread through her blood like fireworks, and when the Bends hit her she screamed and wasn't sure if it was in agony or ecstasy...

CHAPTER THIRTEEN_

Her whole body aches. She takes a bath in Epsom salts and it helps some, but the punishment for death is unavoidable, so she swallows a few ibuprofen and grumbles her way through breakfast. Her tongue feels too big, and the bruise on her face is turning deep purple. On the walk to school she earns fearful looks, this wild stranger in the perfectly constructed neighborhood; the glances lessen as she approaches the school grounds. She chats with the security guard at the door, ends up five minutes late to class, and wanders through the day with half of her attention.

Life seems flat, devoid of color. Each day spools out so identically to the last, each moment lacking the perfect clarity of individuality. Even lunch hour is hollow; the same faces, the same laughter. The jokes they tell barely crack a smile from her frozen lips. Even Khaiam's presence fails to soothe her. In the back of her mind she has already decided to disobey her parents' directive, but the thought has yet to become conscious, and the disparity between these dualities rubs at her nerves. She has jitters, which feel like a welcome change from the usual blanketing panic; twice she finds herself lost in the halls she has walked for years, every door identical, every locker an indistinguishable metal shield. She wonders what kind of secrets are behind them, if people are varied in their minds or if those, too, are as dull as their exteriors; wonders if anyone can see her thoughts through her carefully averted eyes.

After school she has a study session in the Waves. They meet in Darcy's Homepage, a ridiculously exaggerated gangster rap dance club with the music muted. The flashing lights drive everybody crazy, and she can't concentrate on the equations, which seem to change every time a different color hits them.

"Gracie!" her mother hollers. "Would you turn that thing off?"

Gracie toggles the public window larger. Her parents have taken her to dinner with her grandparents, and she has been finishing the study session in the back of the car. Quickly she makes her apologies and exists the Homepage. "I was doing homework," she says, disconnecting the Line and sliding it into her bag.

"I don't see why you have to do homework in the Waves," Carmela says.

"Alejandro's staying with his mom, and she lives way far away. This was easier."

"I'm sure you don't get any work done."

"Please, Mom. Everybody studies in the Waves—you sound like a Luddite."

"Do you even know what a Luddite was?" her father asks. The three of them step onto the front walk to the little white house. Gracie loves coming here for dinner—her father likes to say that her grandparents are the closest things to hippies that still exist in the world, and their home is always warm and smells good.

"It's someone who's afraid of technology."

"Luddites were real historical figures, to which your mother bears not even a passing resemblance."

"She's disparaging *your* invention. You'd think I could get a little support," Gracie mutters and knocks on the door a second before turning the knob and walking inside. "*Abuela!*" she hollers. "We're here!"

"Graciela!" her grandmother croons from the kitchen. "*Ven aqui,* leave the old people and bring a little life into my kitchen!"

Graciela runs through the house towards her grandmother's voice. She has been coming here since she was a little girl, and nothing has changed. There are still perfect rows of flowers in boxes under the windowsills, and carefully organized spices planted beneath in perfect rows. Upon opening the bright red door, the senses are assaulted by a wash of colors. The pink walls in the living room, with crisp hand-polished wooden furniture and pillows in every hue of the rainbow, stir the senses into a crisp kind of joy. Beyond them lies a sky-blue kitchen, with roses hand-painted above the curved doorway, and bright banana yellow furniture. Shelves and cubbies in the walls hold an array of knick-knacks, each artifact whispering a story, and Graciela knows them all. Some days this place feels more like a home than her own bedroom; more real, certainly, than the place she wakes and sleeps.

Her grandmother is a large woman with clearly dyed jet-black hair, bushy white eyebrows, and a fashion sense that airs on the side of comfortable and might have been popular thirty years ago. The embrace she levels on Graciela is honest, uncomplicated, and full of love. She kisses her granddaughter on the top of the head and shoves a spoon at her mouth before she's even let go.

"I don't think I like the dill," she says. "Do you think it's too dilly?"

Graciela coughs, swallows the sauce, and tries not to make too much of a face. "It tastes like a pickle, *yaya*," she says.

Her grandmother sighs. "*Sí*, I thought so. Do you think we could just order pizza?"

"I think *Abuelo* would cry."

"*Chale!* If he'd wanted a cook, he wouldn't have married me. Did I ever tell you about the time we went on a date and I cooked him a steak?"

"No," Graciela lies. She takes some vegetables from the fridge and starts chopping them into fine pieces. Her grandmother sits down at the counter across the way, pouring herself a large glass of sangria.

"Well, we had been dating for about...oh, three weeks, I think. And I knew he was seeing some other girl on the side, so I thought I had better knock the competition out of the water, *sale?* You ever have competition for a man, you let me know, I'll give you pointers. So I didn't know what this *chucha cuerera* might be getting up to, but my mother had a fantastic steak recipe, so I invited him over to show him my domestic side."

"You don't have a domestic side," Graciela reminds her.

She considers it and then shrugs. "Well, I was still young. You won't be able to list all your shortcomings with a smile until you're at least fifty, trust me."

"Have you thought about teaching Dad the trick?" she mutters.

Her grandmother raises an eyebrow but doesn't rise to the bait, diving back into the story. "So I followed the recipe exactly. And *mama* kept saying, 'follow it exactly, follow it exactly!' Except when she'd typed it up to email it to me, this was your great-grandmother, you know, she wasn't good with computers. So when she typed it up, she told me to use two cups of lemon instead of two tablespoons, and the temperature she gave me was in Celsius, I thought—what's wrong with my oven? It doesn't even let me turn the temperature lower than 350, and she wants me to cook this at 200!"

Graciela laughs. She adds the vegetables to the sauce, sprinkles in some spices, and turns the heat up a few notches. "Did you call for advice?"

"She made so much fun of me for asking for the recipe! I just thought my oven wasn't as good as hers. So I doubled the heat and halved the cook time. So your poor *abuelo* comes over, and we're sitting on the couch, having a glass of wine, eating the delicious appetizers that I bought from the deli downstairs and pretended I made, and I go to check on dinner, and it isn't ready. So then I have no idea what to do, so I think I did the math wrong, and maybe I need to leave it in there? And to be honest I sampled the wine before I started cooking—and the conversation was good, and we got distracted, and well... By the time I took it out of the oven, the lemon made a kind of crust on it, so you could almost think maybe it was supposed to look like that. I served it."

"You didn't!"

"I did. You couldn't really cut it even with a steak knife, but Caesar ate *three* whole forkfuls before he gave up. That was when I decided to marry him."

"You did not."

"Well...no. But I was impressed."

"That is a terrible story," my father remarks. We both turn to see he's standing in the doorway. His mother-in-law grins and beckons him over, and they exchange hugs and kisses and pleasantries as Graciela stirs the tomato sauce.

"Now what about that story is a bad influence on *mi*

nieta, hmm? Everything I do, it's a bad influence. You'd think I was feeding the girl drugs," she says, looking around as if there's a third party to commiserate.

"Most men would not stick around after a piece of your steak," Maxwell says with a grin, and the old lady smacks him with a dishcloth, laughing.

"All the ones worth having would," she chides. "And how about that, hmm? Any boys on the horizon?" she asks her granddaughter.

Graciela thinks about a pair of black eyes and a piercing stare; about the last time she saw him, and the promise in his smile. She blushes. "Nope."

"Maxwell, go away," her grandmother commands, and with raised eyebrows he retreats from the kitchen. As soon as he's safely gone she pours a glass of sangria and pushes it across the counter. "*Aqui.*"

Graciela turns the heat down to a simmer and takes a seat at the counter, sipping the sangria. Her grandmother makes it too strong; she can trace its path down her throat by the burn left in its wake.

"And?" her grandmother prompts.

She hesitates. She isn't sure how much to say, how much her grandmother will understand. She loves her dearly, but she is from a past generation. Her grandmother likes to claim she's the same age as the internet (though really she was born ten years before the average person had it in their homes), and that this means the divide between her and the next generation is not so great as it was between her and her mother; but the Waves are a different world, a more complicated one, and the values she ascribes to things don't always match with Gracie's. And Gracie is filled with thudding terror at the idea of her father finding out about her feelings for the AI, which even she isn't sure about.

"I'm not sure," she says, recognizing a silence that needs to be filled. "It's just a boy I met in the Waves—but it might be nothing. It's still really early days. I'll tell you when I know anything," she promises, and means it.

Her grandfather comes into the room, trailing her parents, and she hops up to kiss and hug him.

"Who's watching the food?" he chides, waving a trembling hand at the two glasses at the counter. "What will I do with you?" He shakes his head and goes to salvage dinner, leaving everyone grinning. Gracie ducks her head and sneaks another sip of her sangria before her mother takes it away, complaining in rapid-fire Spanish to her mother. Everyone else objects that they can't follow, and Carmela calls her father a terrible Mexican, and for just a little while, Gracie forgets the rest of the world and the people in it.

———

Her head is hanging off the seat of the chair, her feet stretched up the back and pointing at the ceiling. "Monet?"

"No."

"Manet?"

"No."

"Morisot?"

"You're just listing all the Ms."

"Picasso?"

"He wasn't even an Impressionist!"

"Ugh, I give up." Gracie grabs a pillow and presses it over her face, yelling through the fabric, "I will never need to know this!"

"It was Degas." Khaiam takes the picture of a ballerina, posed against painted stage backdrops of a forest, and lets it flutter to the ground. "If it's a ballerina it's *always* Degas."

"Why can't our school offer interesting electives? I was talking to a girl in Sweden who gets to take Latin dance. As a real class."

"That sounds eighteen hundred times worse than art history."

"It might actually come up again."

"When am I ever going to need to know how to Latin dance?"

"If you come to my wedding?" Gracie suggests.

"If I come to your wedding I'll be too busy hitting on bridesmaids to dance."

"How will you hit on bridesmaids if you aren't using your sexy Latin dance moves?" she points out, and he laughs.

"Touché," he agrees.

"You should know by now that I'm always right."

"Yeah, but I always win."

"And how is that fair?"

"It's not." He steals the bag of popcorn from the edge of her chair, despite her half-hearted attempt to stop him, and empties it into his mouth.

"I'm done. No more studying," Gracie begs.

"Fine. On to more exciting things. You, me, a bonfire, and a horde of drunken teenagers. Revelry. Alcohol. Fire. Nothing can go wrong."

"When?" she asks. The enthusiasm has drained from her voice, and he gives her a stern look.

"Tomorrow. And I am not taking no for an answer."

"I can't," she says, triumphantly. "I have plans."

"You do?" he asks with a raised eyebrow.

"Yes!"

"Real plans."

"Real plans."

"With a real person."

"Yes, with a real person."

"Diving doesn't count."

"...Why not?"

"Gracie! Come on! You're only in high school once. A few more years and drunken parties in the woods won't even be illegal! And everyone asked if you were coming."

"They did not."

"They did! I swear they did. Bella said she misses you. And Ron said he hoped you were coming out."

"I'll see them all on Monday."

"You cannot skip out on me!"

"I have *plans*," she insists. "Seriously. With a time and a place and everything."

"Yeah, to meet some friends in the Waves. Real-life plans totally kick Wave plans' butts."

"I don't want to go to a party in the woods, Khai. There's nowhere to pee, and there are mosquitoes everywhere, and smoke gets in your eyes, and everyone thinks they're funny because they're drunk, but you know what? They're not."

"Oh, they're definitely drunk," he says, and she smiles.

"You go. Have fun. Tell me all about it on Sunday."

He's quiet for a minute, the weight of something in his eyes. She can see it coming before it lands, a shadow across the sun. "I'm not sure whether this is one of those things where I should push because you never come out anymore and I'm afraid I'm, like, letting you down or something; letting you hide from life... Or if it's one of those things where you came out because she did, not because you really wanted to, and you're just going back to being more like you now that you're not being dragged along on her coattails."

She has always been afraid that's how they saw her: not as part of the group, but as one of Calista's appendages. Hearing it out loud is surprisingly painful, even more so coming from him. Is this how he sees her, too? The lost kitten he was forced to adopt because his girlfriend could no longer take care of it? He has a gentle heart—he would never leave something in the rain to die of exposure. He would take it in, care for it, and make it strong enough that he could release it. Maybe it's time for him to let her go.

She can't remember exactly the words he said to her, isn't sure how to respond. Her mental calisthenics have taken her too far from point A. "Do you want some soda?" she asks and gets up. She has to roll awkwardly into a standing position; neither of them laugh, even though it's quite the spectacle. "I'm gonna get one."

"Sure," he says, and she flees the room.

By the time she comes back with two cups and ice, the storm clouds are spent and the sun is out. Khaiam chatters on, unaware of the damaged crops and torn up landscape the hurricane left behind.

CHAPTER FOURTEEN_

SHE RUNS THE SLIP OF PAPER BETWEEN HER FINGERS AS the wind batters her exposed smile. The ground beneath her is busy with figures made insignificant with distance; small black and gray points on the equally gray sidewalk. There is a storm in the air today; the glitching sky roils with clouds that move quickly enough to track, sliding past from the metropolis on the horizon and building up against the edge of the sea where the programming ends.

The paper is sepia, the letters typed on an old-fashioned typewriter, Courier font. She's never received a note to her number before and might be fascinated even if the message wasn't one that made her stand up straighter, made her breath soar. This one just says, "rooftop. friday. 8pm." It's the closest thing to a date she's ever had.

The edge of the roof bites into the bottom of her shoes as she leans forward on the balls of her feet, letting the wind catch her and buffet her back into place in her kneeling crouch. She almost drops the paper, but firms her grip and eventually slides it into one of the many holsters on her legs. It's 7:58 p.m. She pretends she isn't checking the time on the stopwatch hanging from her belt, takes out a knife and plays a bastard version of pinfinger between her feet, reveling in the way her balance trembles as she shifts from right to left.

"You know if you die here, it sticks," a voice behind her remarks. She didn't hear him rez in, but she isn't surprised.

"Does it?" she asks and leans forward. He shouts, makes a grab for her arm, and the wind catches them both and buffets them to safety. She falls, laughing, into his arms, and the momentum of his charge sends them both to the ground. She twists on top of him, pillowing her chin in her hands, the points of her elbows resting on his corded chest. "And here I thought you were a man of fire," she says.

He runs a hand through his hair. Today it's dripping, water falling as perfect cartoon teardrops which disappear in the air, leaving no moisture behind. His face is the same as their previous encounter in Urban Noir, and he's wearing suit pants and suspenders. A compact gun rests in a holster at his shoulder.

"I thought you were trying to send me a message," he says.

"Do most gals whose skirts you chase throw themselves off buildings?" she teases. Letting her hands trail across his chest she stands, and he follows suit.

"Maybe they would if they saw me coming," he says, his voice a liquid burn down her throat. Like alcohol, it leaves a buzz in its wake, an intoxicating pain.

"Don't pretend to be complicated," she chides. "I never did like the brooding hero."

"Who says I'm the hero?"

"Are you going to push me off, then?" She does a box step closer to the edge; dancing, he follows, the tension in the lines of his body more suited to a tango than the waltz.

"Would you trust me if I did?" He wraps a hand around

her waist, and they dance a step closer. Her heel hovers a millimeter into the void. She presses her body against his, leans in close and smiles through her words.

"Not a chance in hell."

He laughs and spins her, his strong arms supporting her as she leaps through empty air, dancing on the wind before he yanks her back, spinning on the asphalt rooftop, the skirt she didn't have a moment ago flaring out, fluttering like the wings of a bird before sinking down, caressing her thighs and the curve of her knees as it fades from view. Their hands feel fused, the grip so sure, and she laughs and leans back on her heels for a moment before he catches her and pulls, spinning her close, following the line of the roof now, dancing on it but avoiding the plunge. He curls her back against his chest and she lets him go, knocking him a step further away, the game over. She flips hair out of her face in an unconscious gesture, breathing heavily from exertion and adrenaline, and reaches down, deliberately stretching the length of her long spine, to adjust the tongue of her boot.

"So, sailor," she says, "why the telegram?"

"I've got a job in the works, and we made such a good team the last time, I thought I would proffer another deal."

"I don't know that I believe you really do jobs," she counters. "That intel was just an excuse to get my number—the way you bob and weave, you didn't need those times."

"Sure, I coulda just followed him for the next two weeks, gotten the schedule on my own," he allows. "But time is experience and experience is life, and why would I waste mine doing footwork that's already been walked for me? I'll admit the number was the real prize, but the intel wasn't just for the wind."

"You really got beef with Rocky Sweet?"

"I'll tell ya the whole sordid tale if we shake on it."

"Need to know more before I decide if I'm in." She sits on the edge of the roof, one knee bent and her body turned to the side, the other dangling off the edge. He copies her, leaning back against the comfortable back of an armchair protruding impossibly from the ground.

"I'm wise on you this time," he warns. "Here's what you need to know. I think Sweet's got a deal on the side, something I'm interested in, and confirming it is a two-man job. No risk, guaranteed. In exchange...?"

"Not much info before I jump," she says, knocking her foot against the wall for emphasis.

"That's all you get." He smiles, already knowing what her answer will be, and she rolls her eyes in acknowledgement. He's right—she's in neck-deep and they both know it.

"Here's my price, no negotiations. You take it or you walk."

"You got my ear."

"Take me Diving."

He cocks his head, genuinely puzzled but definitely intrigued. "You're already Diving."

"You go places no one can. The spaces between. The raw data of the Waves. Take me there."

He hesitates. The armchair back behind him flickers and dies as he straightens, and droplets splatter into nothing as he runs a hand through his slick wet hair.

"Please?" she whispers.

"It's not that I ain't game," he hedges. "It's just..." He loses the gangster drawl and some of the confidence in the set of his shoulders. "I don't know if I *can*. I've never tried. You got a tiny glimpse when I Dived out of that library you were trying to catch me in, and you de-rezzed. I'm not sure a Line can handle raw data."

"Ok. How 'bout this—"

"I thought you said no negotiations?" he says, confidence returned if not restored.

"On your end. I'm *always* allowed to change the deal." Her smile is a promise, fingertips up a spine.

"Go on, then."

"An attempt isn't worth as much as a guarantee. So you give it a try, and I won't call it a welch even if it doesn't work. And we'll add a little something on top."

"A little...something?" He leans forward. She matches the movement. Their faces are inches apart. She can see the individual lashes around his eyes.

"Four packets," she whispers in his ear, and then leans back, watching his body shake with laughter, pleased that she seems to have as much power over him as he wields over her. "Do we have a deal, Johnnie-O?"

"It's Thomas," he says.

"Is it?" she says.

"Thomas. John. Watson. Senior," he declares. "CEO of IBM from 1914 until his death in 1956."

"Do you give me *so little* credit?" she gasps. "A glorified salesman, a diplomat who probably knew as much about the science behind his products as you know about...the airspeed of the average swallow? That's as bad as Charlie—that's *worse* than Charlie. At least Babbage was the father of computers. He's a name to live up to."

He growls playfully. "I will figure it out," he promises.

"Will you?" she teases. "Because you were *so sure* you would figure it out the last time..."...

———

TWO WEEKS AGO...

Gracie had been in her Homepage, trying to teach one of the dragons to eat from her hand. Calista always let them run wild, but Gracie didn't see the point of having a pet if you never got to play with it. This one kept literally biting the hand that was feeding it. She had finally turned her stim-pack down, and was just letting it gnaw on her fingers while she tried to remember if there was a word for eating something alive that would have a good ring to it. Something like "auto-cannibalism" but for another person, for when she told this story later.

"Doesn't that hurt?" he asked. She nearly jumped out of her skin, spun in place to see him standing a few feet away, hands in his pockets. He looked different—coal-black skin and large lips, hair in tiny dreadlocks that framed his lean face. He was wearing a pair of casual jeans and a t-shirt that changed color as she watched, an entrancing and ever-shifting blend. His eyes suited this darker face, disappearing into the night sky behind him.

"How did you get in here?" she demanded. "It's *locked*! I wrote the security code myself!"

"Maybe you aren't very good," he suggested, and when she started to frame a furious response, he cut her off. "Or maybe I'm just that good."

"You're *cheating*," she objected. "You can do things no one else can."

"That just makes me interesting." He wandered around the edge of the garden, running his fingers over a leaf from the encroaching jungle. "This place doesn't seem like you."

"I inherited it," she said, "and you're changing the subject."

"What is the subject?"

"You."

"My favorite one."

"How did you find me?"

"Maybe it's a strange and ever-deepening coincidence. Maybe I just keep running into you on my extensive travels."

"I don't mean here—that's easy," she said, the idea that this could be coincidence not worth the bother of a reply. "Even I know how to track a registered Homepage. I mean at the concert. How did you do that?"

"I can't give away all my secrets!"

"You haven't given away any."

"Fine. I'll trade you."

"Fine," she said. She called up her menu, set in a site address and activated tandem Diving. The door to the cottage had shifted slightly in its hinges, and when opened led, not to the tiny interior, but to a starched white landscape of snow and ice. She walked through, trusting him to follow, and he did.

The door closed behind them. Wind stung her eyes and brought up tears in its wake, which froze as they tracked down her cooling cheeks. A second later she was insulated from the blast, a warm down jacket between her and the raging, silent storm. Beside her he wore a dark parka, his face shadowed and beautiful against the bleached white land-scape. She shrugged her jacket off almost as soon as it appeared, reveled in the way her skin burned, tingled, and began slowly numbing.

"Living dangerously?" he asked. She rolled her eyes.

"You said you wanted to trade."

"Thomas Edison."

She gave him a look with raised eyebrows.

"You're right, too obvious. Okay, Thomas Doubter."

"Biblical. Interesting. What makes you think the name relates to you?"

He shrugs. "The first of a new religion?"

"Thomas wasn't the first apostle. What else?"

"He questioned instead of accepting blindly."

"Think very highly of yourself, don't you?"

He sighs. "So no?"

"Sorry." She danced across the rocks of the tundra and he followed, tracking a path through gentle foothills. "Guess I'll just have to call you...you...for a while longer. My turn. How did you find me at the concert?"

He hesitated, kicked a rock down the gentle slope and turned to watch its progress. She stopped, watching him as he was turned away. "It wasn't hacking," he admitted. "I've been paying attention for a long time—probably knew you were going before you did."

She wasn't sure whether to be flattered or alarmed. "Bit stalkerish?" she asked.

He grinned. "Don't worry, I'm not crawling through your bedroom window and watching you sleep," he promised. "But what's a piece of code to do?" He put on a fake bland accent, his features momentarily freckling over, his ears sticking out a little as his hood disappeared. "I can't exactly call you on the phone and invite you to the soda shop."

"You can ping me like a normal person," she suggested.

A cloud passed over his features. For just a moment he seemed older, harder. He shrugged and the hood snapped back into place. "Not if you're offline."

"I'm always online," she said, but she understood the drive that sent him looking for her in the Waves. He could never follow her onto Land, so it was easier to pretend it wasn't there at all.

"But I can't *follow* you," he explained, frustration sent

him walking again. She raced to follow. "If you Dive into Urban Noir, and then to your Homepage, and then to an encyclopedia, I can follow that. But if you Dive into Urban Noir, and then disconnect, go get a snack, go to the bathroom, whatever, and reconnect in your Homepage, I have to hunt you down all over again." He gave her an annoyed look. "I do have other things to do, you know. I don't spend *all* my time trying to arrange these little tête-à-têtes."

She grinned. "So you HAVE been doing it on purpose!"

He pretended to roll his eyes, but only to hide a grin. "If you say so."

"Why?"

He shrugged. "Call me intrigued."

"You know...no one believes you're real. My dad and Paul, they're being dragged through the mud. Can't you just..."

"No," he said.

"Why not?"

He shrugged, grinned, and jumped up onto a knot of rock, spreading his arms so his silhouette made a perfect cross on the snow beneath him. "Because," he announced, "it would destroy my sense of mystique."

And he fell back into the snow—and disappeared.

She pulled off her Line, and grinned. Now that she knew he was following her, she knew she would see him again. The thought sent surprising warmth through her chest, but on its heels, only a moment later, was guilt. Her father was downstairs, working day and night to crack a problem whose code she has in her hand. This was no longer a secret she could keep.

She stood, surprised at her own reluctance, and walked down the stairs to the main floor. Her father's study door was closed, and she almost walked away. But after a moment she lifted a hand and knocked once, lightly. "Dad?"

"I'm working!" he yelled.

She opened the door anyway, and he looked up with a long-suffering sigh.

"What is it?"

"Dad, I...I met him."

"The singer of your favorite rock band?"

"The AI."

"What?" She had her father's attention, and she felt herself growing smaller in front of him. She forced herself to square her shoulders, to meet him head-on.

"He's real. I mean, obviously you know he's re—"

"What! Are you sure!" He was up in a split second, around the desk, the air charged with excitement.

"He's so real, Dad, you got it perfect." She smiled, remembering his smile, his face. "He's really a person, it's amazing."

"But how did you find it?" he gasped. He held her arms like he'd suddenly discovered a precious thing, like he was in awe. She felt herself growing taller in his esteem, taking up new real estate in the affairs of his mind.

"He found me—twice." *Four times*, she mentally corrected, but there's no way she was telling him about Urban Noir or the racetrack, as that would mean admitting that she goes to sites like those. "He crashed this concert Khaiam and I went to, I have no idea how he found me there. I wasn't really sure it was him, though, or whether I'd ever be able to find him again, and I didn't want to make a big deal of nothing, but...just now, in my Homepage. He said he was looking for me."

"It's seeking you out," her father said, a light in his eyes. "But this is incredible! We have a connection—a link we can follow—this is fantastic!" He hugged her close, kissed the top of her head. "We can find it. I have to call Paul. I have to call Mr. Jennings. This is brilliant!" He whooped, offered her a clumsy high-five that she missed, laughing. They were in it together, her and her father. A team...

Rocky Emmanuel Sweet holds court in the *Lucky Madam*, a brothel and gin-joint in the basement of the old Industrial Bank. The tall ceilings are covered in smoke no matter the time of day, and hollow-eyed girls in corsets and fishnets wander the packed house, pushing booze and picking pockets. Gas lamps offer flickering mood light, and a band in the corner plays jazz in half-time while a middle-aged woman, stoned on opium, croons into an old-fashioned microphone. The bar along the wall is impressively stocked, and Sweet has a policy of keeping the Mannies out—God alone knows where he finds the girls, but he claims they're all Players.

Sweet's throne is a rickety wooden table in the back of the place, surrounded by bootlickers and hangers-on. He's a tall man, corded with muscle, with a used car salesman's moustache and a mafioso's suit. His personality matches his joint—slow and seedy, a sharpened knife on a hot summer day. Mallory and Johnnie sit at a table in the corner, untouched gin with moisture beading on the warm glasses making rings on the tabletop between them. They take turns observing their mark, his cronies, and any others with steel in their eyes, scattered amidst the sheep.

The AI snaps his fingers and the sound from the room dims and fades away. "Just in case we have ears on us," he tells her with a smile.

She pretends not to be impressed, raises her eyebrows as if to say, "So?"

"Sweet's working with Dame Pride," he explains. "I've seen the results of the partnership."

Gracie whistles. Dame Pride is a huge player in the packets game—she owns a network of Runners that she manages in a beautiful tribute to the company stores of old. Sets you up with equipment, routes, deals, but somehow you always end up owing, and her poor saps keep on workin' for her 'til their feet bleed. Sweet's got contacts even the Spider envies—since everyone knows he's playing gin and not packets, lips run loose around him. Proof that he's handing those whispers to Dame Pride would change the game.

"You sure?"

"Not yet." He grins a promise, teeth sharp and glistening in the roving light. "I've been following them, trying to find out how they're getting intel back and forth. Folks like that are even seen talkin' and just the rumor of it could be enough to do damage, even if it weren't true."

"Which you savvy it is. Fine, so they're careful, use intermediaries."

"That's what I figured. But then you gotta trust somebody with your secret, dontcha? And any secret with more than two mouths is a secret you can find or buy or steal. I can't. Only folks I can find who play both camps are so low down the pecking order they'd get shanked before they'd get trusted. I walked on a few of 'em, hard, and got nothing. That's not it."

"So what is?"

"They're meeting offline. Gotta be."

Gracie hisses. "No way."

Urban Noir doesn't have many rules, and people like it that way. No playing without a stim-pack's one. No coming back once you die's another. And like all good things that come in threes, the last rule: no collaborating on Land. Backroom deals better happen in Noir backrooms; it isn't even kosher to tell a friend your name in the game. Gracie's only seen the rule broken once since she came on. A bookie operating out of the park offered real-world credit to lend out his in-game cash, taking funds on Land and giving people the game capital to buy gin or Running equipment. Word got out, and the GodSquad was waiting the next time he came online. They fixed a bug on his IP so every time he connected to his Line he popped automatically into Urban Noir; then they hung him upside down by a meat hook through his Achilles heel and fixed him as a dartboard in one of the speakeasies. Word is he couldn't get online without passing through hell 'til his avatar finally died, and they made sure that didn't happen for a good two weeks. Cheaters are one thing, but cheaters who break the rules are another.

"Now you see why I want them caught?"

She tilts her head, observes him for a minute. "You don't like them taking the game where you can't follow."

He slams an open palm against the table, talking through his teeth. "They're damn cheats!"

She puts a hand on the table, the tips of their fingers just touching. "Damn right they are. And if that's the way of it we'll catch 'em. But I ain't seen you get worked up about things you'd think a body would. This is under your skin, and that makes it personal."

He leans back in his chair, crosses his arms. His posture is a study in nonchalance, but he seems pleased, touched perhaps, that she has read him so clearly. "You can go where I can't. Follow them out into the world."

"How?"

"Tracking their addresses was easy, neither of them are

good for even a simple hack. Dame Pride's a problem, lives in Buenos Aires somewhere, but we struck gold on Sweets—he's in Sacramento. So here's how it goes. I feed him a piece of intel that a job is going down, this morning, say five o'clock. I follow him in-game, prove he doesn't go near nobody or say nothing to no one that could transfer the intel legit. *You* follow him on Land, prove he makes a call he shouldn't, anything. I know he isn't meeting her on a different Wave server, so it's gotta be a phone call, or an email, something."

"You want me to go to Sacramento and *stalk someone?*" Gracie gasps.

"Yes," he says, clearly not seeing a problem.

"*Sacramento.*"

"Yes."

"Are you *insane?*"

He stares at her blankly. "What's the holdup?"

"I'm not Mallory Stark!" she blurts, and regrets it instantly; finds her cool somewhere, grits her teeth. "Not out there, anyhow. I ain't got the tools and skills I'd need for a job like this on Land. It ain't doable."

"This game don't give you skills, Graciela," he whispers, leaning in close. "This game don't make you smarter, or tougher. It just gives you a pretty skin to sink into and a mask to hide behind."

"And a driver's license," she remarks blandly.

He snorts and leans back. "You're a resourceful bird. I don't think a little thing like that will stop you."

She mirrors him, leaning back and crossing her arms. She's considering it but is filled with terror at the notion, and the realization that she might say yes. It's one thing for Mallory Stark to break the rules, throw herself off rooftops, get in close with dangerous people. Mallory is brave, and strong, and at the end of the day Mallory gets put away, disappears into her box, and the little mouse comes out and lives her safe little life. Can she be Mallory in the real world, find the bar of iron and will it into her spine? She's afraid the answer is no but doesn't want him to stop looking at her like she can do anything.

"Fine," Mallory says. "Tracking him is simple, but the devil's in the details. First, I'd need at least two hours to get to Sacramento."

"I'll wait to deliver the intel until you're in place—ping me when you have eyes."

"Then how do I get in close enough to prove a call he makes is to her? No telling what security is like on his joint, and anyway, I don't think I want to get *in*." She takes a mental step back, views it like a part of the game. What would she do if she needed to track Rocky Emmanuel Sweet in-game, without him catching wise? First thing, she'd tap his wire, but these days folks don't have hard lines into their places. So how to get a look in? She shades her eyes, gives Johnnie an embarrassed look under her hand. "Saw a talkie once where some kids strapped a camera to a remote control car and drove it in through a window or a vent. It ain't elegant but it'll get the job done, and if we remote beam the footage back to my hub we can get sound and audio even if he catches the damn thing."

"There's an elegant sort of idiocy to the plan," he concedes, and she shoots him a look.

"I *told* ya I ain't got the tools on Land. I'm making do with what I know is there."

"So we're on," he says, but there's a question in the statement, a hesitancy to the gleam in his eyes.

She sighs. "We're on," she agrees, knowing already that she'll regret it.

CHAPTER FIFTEEN_

She paces back and forth across her bedroom, a lion in the cage of her body. Gracie can't do this—she can't make this call. She doesn't know how to be Mallory Stark, how to channel the freedom of the Waves in her Landlocked flesh. She picks up her phone, puts it down. Picks up her tablet, as if that will somehow make a difference—drops that, too. Finally snarls and scoops up the phone and pings Khaiam. He answers on the third ring.

"Gracie!" he hollers. "You changed your mind! You're coming out!"

"Um..." she hedges. It's eleven o'clock, and the party is probably just getting into gear. What if he's too drunk? What if he doesn't want to leave? She can't go on her own. Literally: she doesn't have a driver's license. "Wanna drive to Sacramento to break into someone's house?" she asks, wincing.

There's a stunned pause and then he yells in wordless excitement. "Are you for real?"

"Yes," she says, miserable.

"What!!" He sounds thrilled, which strikes her as a reaction only a teenage boy would have. "Oh my God, guys! Road trip!" he shouts. She winces again—the last thing she needs is a hoard of her drunken classmates coming along.

"Are you okay to drive?" she asks. There's a pause, and some conferring on the other end. Finally, he comes back.

"Matt says no. But Matt says Jaime is sober and they have a car, so they'll drive us if we give them... What do you want?" This last is directed away from the phone, but he forgets to move the speaker and his voice blasts hard enough that she has to jerk the receiver away. "Okay! Okay. We're coming to get YOU!" he roars, and the line goes dead.

Gracie packs up a bag with the supplies she'll need, plus a handful of equipment she brings just because she carries them as Mallory—a wireless webcam, duct tape, fake ID, a pocketknife, and a multi-tool. She doesn't have a set of lock-picks, which she always has on hand as Mallory, but these days most locks are electronic anyway, so she brings a scanner that will only be good for the most basic of biometric readers but might help in a pinch. And, finally, her remote-controlled device. She doesn't own a car or a helicopter. Mallory wouldn't be caught dead with a toy like this. Then again, Mallory is nothing if not practical, and she has to admit, the webcam looks jaunty on its little porcelain head.

She doesn't own anything like what Mallory wears. The closest approximation she can manage is a pair of black leggings, black running shoes with purple soles, and a black tank top with a hole in the armpit that she wears at the gym. But once she's all dressed she doesn't have anywhere to put the things she's bringing, so she swaps the leggings out for a pair of dark gray sweatpants with big pockets. Everything else goes in a black backpack with a rim of pink flowers. She covers a few with a permanent marker, but the effect is some-what grotesque and she abandons the effort.

Her curfew isn't until 1 a.m., but since she won't be back

by then she figures it's better not to be seen leaving. She's never attempted to sneak out before—her random acts of disobedience take place exclusively in the Waves, where they're impossible to monitor and thus playfully easy to keep secret. She isn't sure how difficult it might be. Sneaking out a window, always the favorite choice of her television heroines, is not an option. She's on the second floor, and her wall is devoid of handy drainpipes and low-hanging tree branches.

She goes into the kitchen and makes a big deal of making a snack, banging cupboards and rattling cutlery. Then she walks back upstairs to her bedroom. Her father is in his study, working on something with the door closed, and her mother is watching the evening news. Neither pay her any mind as she wanders through. She deposits the food in the mini-fridge in her room, runs the water in the bathroom, and then turns off all the lights. That done, she goes back to the kitchen; she figures if anyone sees her they'll think she's just returning the plates before going to bed. And then she just walks out the back door, locking it behind her. She isn't sure whether to feel pleased that her escape is so easy, or whether to let it touch her that she passes through the house like a ghost.

Her steps carry her through the yard, down the cultivated expanse of the lawn. She avoids the path, steps through bushes to the sidewalk, and waits one house down, just out of view of the living room windows. But once there, exposed, her backpack slung over her shoulder like she's on the way to school, her confidence begins to tremor; and by the time the car pulls up beside her, Mallory has disappeared, and she isn't sure if she can get her back.

The car is packed. Jaime is in the front seat, Matt beside them. Khaiam, Bella, and Angela are in the back. The door spills open, Angela half-falling out of the car as she makes a drunken grab for Gracie's arm. She misses, catches her leg, and Gracie moves closer to stop her from falling out entirely.

"Are you forgetting something?" Gracie asks.

They all look around. "What?" Matt finally asks.

"The car is full," she patiently points out.

There's a long pause and a lot of "ums" and "ohs." Then Angela perks up. "That's completely okay!" she trills, and she grabs Gracie and drags her through the entrance, dropping her across the laps of the other two. She has to shimmy to get in the rest of the way before Angela can close the door on her feet. Her head comes to rest in Bella's lap, her backpack a convenient armrest between Khaiam and her chest. Luckily she's not a tall person, but even so, she isn't sure how this will hold up for two hours.

"Are we sure—" she starts to ask, but Jaime is already pulling away.

"ROAD TRIP!" Matt yells.

———

They stop at a convenience store and everyone fills their arms with junk food. Gracie goes in a few minutes behind the rest of the crowd and uses her fake ID to buy some beer. She doesn't think she passes for eighteen, especially not in her running shoes and cast-off tank top, but the clerk barely even looks at her. The machine scans her code, beeps green, and downloads the credit automatically from her account. He only half-heartedly glances up from his tablet.

Gracie is officially the hero of the hour when she hands the beer around, and she gives Jaime a slurpie to a chorus of cheers.

"Okay," Khaiam demands, once they're all settled down

with their drinks, music blaring around the radio. "So why are we breaking into someone's house?"

"Is it drugs?" Bella asks.

"Gangs!" Angela declares.

"Jilted lover?" Matt asks, wiggling his eyebrows.

"Espionage," Gracie says, and everyone oohs. "I play this adult-only game in the Waves—Urban Noir."

"Isn't it against the rules to play that without a stim-pack?" Khaiam asks.

"Yeah," Gracie says.

"Didn't your dad confiscate your stim-pack and forbid you from ever using it again?"

"It's a patch on your Line," she explains patiently, "not a physical thing. He took the patch off. It took me about four minutes to put it back on."

"I've heard of Urban Noir!" Matt says. "My older brother plays. If you die in the game you get banned. It's completely cool."

"Yup," she agrees. "And it's against the rules to tell anyone on Land—in real life," she corrects, knowing some of them aren't big Divers, and they might not get all the jargon, "anything about the game. Like who your character is. Well..." She hesitates. She doesn't want any of them to lose interest an hour to Sacramento and try to get them to turn around, so she figures she should make it as sensational as possible. "If you break the rules, they come for you. Sometimes even outside of the game."

"Really?" Bella breathes. She goes two too-tanned shades paler and uses the fear as an excuse to clutch Khaiam's arm. He pats her shoulder, oblivious to the ploy.

"One guy got caught cheating," Gracie breathes. Jaime turns the music down so they can all hear her better. "They found him. Tricked his Line so he could never disconnect.

He wandered the game for weeks, a ghost, begging people to let him go, just to let him disconnect. Until one day...he started to go pale. Little bits of code came drifting off. They say if you die while you're in the Waves...a little piece of you always stays behind...a ghost in the machine..."

Angela shrieks with giddy terror. "That is so completely not true!"

"It is!" Gracie insists. "I've been Diving since before you knew it existed." She drops her voice back to a lower, creepy octave. "I've seen them. The ghosts. Trapped in the Waves, unable to disconnect but not quite there...like they're beating against a pane of invisible glass...calling out to you...forever."

Khaiam makes a big noise, a creepy booming bark, and everyone shrieks. Matt laughs so hard he spills a bag of candy all over the car, and Jaime complains about the mess as everyone settles back into place.

"So what does that have to do with Sacramento?" Bella asks.

"Well, you've all heard of the ghosts in the Waves. But what's the most famous ghost of all?"

"The AI!" Khaiam says.

"The AI," Gracie agrees. "You might call him the king of the ghosts—the strongest of them all. He calls the Waves his own, and he punishes those who break the rules of the games. He claims he wants law and order, that he's the new police in his kingdom, but I know the truth." Jaime turns the music down further, almost off, as Gracie sits up so she's in the direct center of the car. At that moment she realizes all eyes are on her, that she's the center of attention, and she almost loses the thread of the story. But she stares out the car window, at the black streets and pools of streetlight passing by, and the ambiance is enough to keep her rooted in her persona. "The truth is...he's lonely. And he's collecting ghosts to keep him company in the dark..."

"Oh my God, are we gonna completely kill someone?" Angela gasps. She sounds like she might cry at the idea.

Gracie stares her down. "Would you? If the king of the Waves commanded it? The father of monsters? Would you dare to say no to such a creature?"

Angela whimpers and shakes her head. Khaiam laughs and punches her in the shoulder. "You are so gullible!" he says. "Of course we aren't killing anybody!"

Gracie grins. "No. We're just spying on this guy in Sacramento, to prove he's breaking the rules."

"And then...somebody else is killing him?" Matt asks. He doesn't sound particularly upset by this concept, but Bella looks ready to burst into tears. Gracie realizes she might have taken the gag one step too far but isn't sure how to backtrack.

"Don't worry—he hasn't earned the white death," she says, and Khaiam makes a face at her word choice. She agrees it's terrible, but can't take it back now, and everyone else still seems to be following. "He's committing a minor infraction—meeting an ally in person. Nothing like packet trading or money laundering. We catch him in the act, give the footage to the AI, and he bans him from the game—and maybe even...from the Waves."

"I would completely *die* if I couldn't Dive!" Bella gasps, even though Gracie is pretty sure she only does it once in a while, social things like meeting at the Library and going to concerts. She wonders how Bella would feel if she could put on a different face in the Waves, if she could disappear entirely from herself. Where would she go—what would she become?

"I completely can't believe you're into this," Angela tells

Graice as Jaime puts the music back up. "It's so, completely, cool."

She knows it's intended as a compliment and treats it thus, even if the words are a barb. "Thanks."

"To Gracie!" Khaiam calls, and everyone holds up a beer and cheers. "To Gracie!"

Jaime guides the car onto the main road and clicks it into automatic mode. The GPS takes over, the wheel sinking back slightly into the console, and the car joins a line of guided traffic so Jaime can free their hands for cramming junk into their face. The music is loud enough that Gracie can feel the bass, and everyone is laughing and shouting to be heard over the sound. It's the first time since Calista died that Gracie has felt like she deserves a place with these people—maybe the first time ever that they haven't felt like someone else's friends. They came here for Khaiam, true, but they are staying to see out her mad plan. They are in orbit around her. She doesn't feel like Mallory Stark, not here, but she feels like who she imagines Graciela to be: a girl on the cusp of womanhood, full of potential and life, someone who can look at herself in the mirror and think, *Yeah, I'm doing okay.*

———

There's no traffic, and it takes just over two hours to get to Sacramento. The GPS takes them to an address half an hour outside of the city, in a sleepy suburb. Jaime has to turn off automatic driving because there's no grid here, and the streets aren't even raised, just the old flat causeways of the early half of the century. Every house has its mandatory three trees, but other than that greenery is sparse, and the car of teenagers seems naked and exposed on the quiet curb.

Gracie slips on her Line, leaving public browsing active,

and sends out an alert ping. The AI doesn't have an IP because he isn't connecting from outside, so she can't actually ping him through the regular system. Instead, she sends a burst of information, the Diving equivalent of a flare, racing into the sky of her Homepage; and because he's monitoring her, he sees it and appears only seconds later.

He's wearing a new face; a very James Bond polished look, with carefully slicked-back hair and an immaculate gray suit. But his eyes are the same, always, calling to her. When he speaks, he has a gorgeous upper-crust British accent.

"Found him already?"

She melts a little inside. "GPS brought us right to his door. Gimme five minutes to get the tracker in his room and then send the ping."

"Back bedroom, second floor. Good luck."

"Thanks, Moneypenny," she says with a wink and disconnects. "Here we go," she tells the car. She gets out so there's more room to maneuver, and hands her tablet to Khaiam. She takes the remote control out of her bag while he logs in to the program to do the tracking.

"What the *hell* is that?" Jaime gasps, laughing.

She blushes. She's holding a small mechanical fairy. About the size of her hand, it has beautiful crafted iridescent wings, porcelain skin, and a tiny hand-stitched dress made of silk leaves and flower petals. "It was the only remote-control thing I had," she admits.

"Oh my God, I completely wanted one of those when I was a kid!" Bella enthuses. She takes the doll from Gracie, playing with its hair, which is a growing plant. "I can't believe you still have it."

"It was in the back of my closet," she lies. It is her favorite toy from childhood, one of her most prized possessions, and it has pride of place on the little shelf above her bed. It was advertised as a real, flying fairy. No hidden strings or wires, and no mechanical noise to ruin the illusion. Perfect for a little girl to play make-believe—or for a spy.

She takes the doll and its controller and sneaks down the path towards the house, while everyone else congregates around the camera. Her phone's Bluetooth headset sits uncomfortably in her ear, and she smiles and waves into the camera.

"I can hardly see," Khaiam complains. "If he doesn't have any lights on in the bedroom, we're not going to be able to make anything out."

"Let's hope for the best, then," Gracie whispers.

"Let's hope there's no yard alarm," Matt says cheerfully.

"That's not even a thing," Bella says.

"It would be, like, a motion sensor," Matt says.

"But then racoons would set it off."

"Okay," Gracie says into her phone. "I'm under the bedroom."

"Is the window open?" Jaime asks.

"What are we gonna do if the window isn't open?" Khaiam asks.

"Ooh, I could pretend to be, completely, a health inspector," Bella says. "And I could completely get in and open the window."

"Why would a health inspector be at a house at one in the morning?" Matt asks.

Gracie floats the fairy up the side of the house to the window. "Well?" she asks.

"It's shut," Khaiam says with a sigh. "Oh, hey, actually, I think it might be open a crack—can you—yeah, yeah, it's not actually latched. Do you think you could hook her head through the handle and pull it up? But slowly so he doesn't see."

"You'll have to talk me through it," she says, "I don't have eyes on it. It's too far up."

"Okay. Lower the fairy a little bit—a little more—more—good! Stop! Okay, now go towards the house a little bit—good! Okay, now to your left. Sorry, no, your right. More—more—stop! Okay, now up. Slowly!"

"Is it working? Is it moving?" she whispers.

"It's working!" Bella yells, and everyone shushes her.

"Okay, that's enough, stop!" Khaiam instructs. "Now duck down a little... Okay, good, and go in. As soon as you're in fly straight up 'til you touch the ceiling."

"I think I should go for the floor," Gracie says. "She'll show up more against the white ceiling."

"Good call," Matt agrees, so she ducks the doll through the small opening and straight down.

"What the—" Matt says.

"Is that—?" Angela asks.

"What the hell, Gracie?" Khaiam mutters.

"What? What is it? Guys?" Gracie whispers.

"Gracie, it's, like...a kid's bedroom."

"What?"

"It's some kid," Jaime says. "He's in bed, but with a Line on. He's like..."

"Ten?"

"Maybe twelve."

"What is this?"

"Calm down," Gracie whispers. "We must have gotten the wrong bedroom. One sec." She grabs her Line from her pocket, slips it on. Her Homepage rezzes into view. The AI is still there—he's playing with the dragons, teasing them with pieces of meat but tearing it away before they can get them. No wonder her efforts to teach them to eat from her hands aren't working, if he's done this before.

"Problem," she says. For once she manages to surprise him, and he turns away from the flying serpents.

"What's wrong?"

"Your intel is what," she teases. "Either the wrong bedroom or the wrong house—it's just some kid."

"Edouard Alverez," he agrees. "Twelve years old."

She stares at him. "Are you shitting me?" she demands. Her face is Gracie but her reaction is all Mallory; fury lances through her bones. "You sent me after some *kid*?"

"I sent you," he snaps, "after Rocky Emmanuel Sweet."

"You mean to tell me that one of the biggest rumrunners, one of the biggest pimps, in Urban Noir is a twelve-year-old boy?" she demands.

"Who cares who he is out there?" the AI says with a dismissive wave. "In here he's a dangerous man, and he's breaking the rules."

"Do you have any idea what the GodSquad does to cheaters?" she gasps. "They'll rip out his fingernails while he screams for mercy. They'll fix his Line so he can't disconnect. They'll dip him in acid and let his bones slowly bleed away."

His face is hard, his voice flat despite the musicality of his new accent. "You knew all that when you agreed to take him down."

"I knew they were going to do that to Sweet! This is an adult-only site. You get what you sign up for, we all know that. But he's just a kid—he can't make those kinds of decisions."

"He isn't a kid in the Waves."

"He is out here!"

"Well no one is melting his bones out there," he snaps. "Rocky Emmanuel Sweet is a hazard. He's a gang lord. I've seen him carve letters in someone's skin for crossing him. I've seen him hit a girl for telling a customer no. You think a man like that deserves your mercy?"

"He's just a kid," Gracie whispers. "How can you not see that?"

"How can you not see that Edouard Alverez is the mask, not Rocky Sweet?" The AI yells. "*This* world is the real one— here, where there are no rules." He stalks closer, his voice intense, the light in his eyes blazing, burning, and Gracie realizes for the first time that fire, however beautiful, doesn't just burn. It consumes. "This is where you carve someone down to their bones and find out what's left. Who do you think is the real person? Little Gracie the mouse, too afraid to face her own shadow, too afraid of the consequences to live her own damn life? Or Mallory and Anise, Edmonton and Despoina? Are you Graciela, who lives every damn second she's given?" He grabs her shoulders, shakes her once. His grip is painful, and she isn't sure if the fever in his eyes is passion or desperation. "Which one is real?" he yells. "Which one is real?" This last is a question, a breaking point. "Which one is real?" he whispers.

She grabs her Line and rips it off. Her body shrieks in objection as the Bends hit, bringing her to her knees. The world dips and swirls around her, a wave of dizziness that hits her in the stomach and then passes quickly. She can't catch her breath but isn't sure if that's the Bends or the panic in her veins. She rests her burning forehead against the grass. It's cold with dew, freezing even in the warm California air. She digs her hands into the grass, tears grooves in the sod. Her friends in the car are arguing amongst themselves; she can't quite catch the train of conversation. Someone says her name, but she ignores it.

She picks up the controller, maneuvers the fairy out the window and back into her arms. Its presence feels comforting as she gets to her feet. There are grass stains on her knees, but the dark shadows obscure them. She starts to walk back to the car, her steps heavy; but pauses. The AI won't drop this, and she isn't sure if she wants him to. He's right that Sweet needs to be stopped, but the kid...just a kid...

She straightens her spine. Who is she? She doesn't know. Mallory Stark would never face a situation like this because there are no shades of gray in Mallory's world—just winning and losing. That isn't how she wants to live her life. That isn't who she wants to be, not if she can't take the costume off when she gets home at night. She walks around the house, up to the front walk, and up the stairs. She can hear people yelling in her earpiece, but she turned the volume down for the Dive and none of the words quite form sentences she can understand.

She rings the bell. Once. Twice. She leans on it, listens to the sound echoing through the sleeping house. After a minute a light turns on upstairs. Then another, and steps pound towards the door.

A sleepy, panicked looking man opens the door. He's in his forties, with a brush of stubble on his face. On the stairs beyond him, she can see a woman—his wife?—struggling into a bathrobe.

"What is it? What's wrong?" he demands.

"I'm sorry to bother you so late at night," she says. "But are you the parents of Edouard Alverez?"

"Yes—yes, I'm his father. What's wrong? He's upstairs sleeping." He gives his wife a look as if to ask if their child is still where they left him, sleeping, safe. She nods.

"Well, he's upstairs, at least," Gracie allows. "Mr. Alverez, I Dive on a site called Urban Noir. It's an adult-only site due to its mature content—drug dealers, prostitutes, gin-running. It's a game, but the game exists in the framework of a very seedy world, dealing with very dangerous people."

"Look here, it's the middle of the night, I don't see what this has to do with—"

"Mr. Alverez, I came here tonight because I was sent, by people in the game, to deal with someone who had double-crossed them. Play in a game like this has a habit of crossing into the real world."

He gives her a look as if to say that he can't imagine what kind of tough person would send a slip of a girl like her to deal with their problems. "You obviously have the wrong house. I don't even own a Line, and my wife certainly isn't dealing drugs on the internet."

"Your son is," she snaps. "Mr. Alverez, this is serious. Your son hacked into an adult-only site and made some very dangerous enemies."

"Eddie?" Mrs. Alverez gasps. "Are you sure?"

"I *told* you we shouldn't have gotten him a Line!" Mr. Alverez yells. "Didn't I say? There's no protection on those damn things!"

"But *everyone* uses them, honey, he needs it for home-work—this can't be right—are you sure? Eddie? *Hacking?* I just can't believe..."

"I can," Mr. Alverez mutters.

"I'm glad to see you're taking this seriously," Gracie says. "When I realized your son was underage I had no intention of going through with my...orders. But I can't stress enough the reality of the danger here. I know that for those who don't play in this world, the Waves can seem harmless. You tell yourself it's just a game, and you don't watch your children the way you would if they were playing...at the park, say. But the Waves are full of very real dangers, and if I tracked your son down to his real-life address, others will be able to do the same. It's *imperative* you don't let him access Urban Noir again, and it's simple to ensure."

"What, get one of those patches, right?"

"We have one, honey, one of those security patches. We already have one—honestly, we are careful. I know you think we don't watch our son, but we do, we have all the latest tech."

"Those are child's play to hack," Gracie says dismissively. "Tech only goes so far, especially if your son's hacking skills are as good as I know they are."

"Let's see how good he is at hacking without a Line! Or a tablet! Or a computer!" Mr. Alverez yells.

"Mr. Alverez, with respect—I had my stim-pack taken away and I had programmed a new one in four minutes. Your son is a kingpin in this game, and that speaks to his incredible intelligence and depth of resources—which I suppose you can be proud of in some way." He snorts, and she continues. "But Urban Noir has incredibly sophisticated, unhackable rules—if you die in the game, you can't play again. Bar none. If you log onto your son's Line you can walk his avatar off a rooftop, shoot yourself in the head, whatever. He won't be able to get online again, no matter where he connects from—and no one on Urban Noir will have a reason to come after him."

Mr. Alverez gives her a suspicious look. "You don't look like an adult either."

She shrugs. "Like I said—hacking security patches is child's play. Protect your son, Mr. Alverez, Mrs. Alverez. Get rid of that character before someone comes knocking who doesn't care that Rocky Emmanuel Sweet, pimp and gin-runner, is really just a little kid."

She walks away before they can say anything else, before they can decide to call her parents, or the police; before she knows if they'll follow through. But when the door closes the lights stay on, and she can hear the sound of raised voices from inside. She gets into the car, awkwardly sliding into place across the laps of her classmates. They're quiet, no doubt having listened in over the radio. She hasn't delivered the adventure they were hoping for. This was strange, and messy, and dark, and they are each silent, staring into the night black sky, as they pull away from the curb and back towards the world.

CHAPTER SIXTEEN_

Everyone is talking about it: how Rocky Emmanuel Sweet ate his own lead in the back room of the Lucky Madam. Mallory Stark sits at a table in the Fontaine Noir, spinning a glass of gin she isn't drinking and listening to the gums flap. There are lots of rumors about why; that someone had dirt so big he ran; that he was caught cheating and did it to avoid the GodSquad; that he was murdered six ways to Sunday and they only made it look like suicide. No one knows, but they sure are happy. Power vacuum means lots of potential upward mobility, and after all—no one really died, did they?

Johnnie slides into a seat beside her. She's been expecting him, though she didn't call him here. It's been three days since she saw him in the jungle. Three days since she's come online for anything at all. The Waves don't feel like a release right now; everything has grown complicated, cloudy. There is nowhere left to hide.

He waves a waiter down, a Mannie in a stained white shirt, and orders a sidecar. "Are we cheersing?" he asks.

She raises her eyebrows. "You think this is a celebration?" she asks.

"You did it, didn't you? Elegant. How'd you make him do it?"

"I told his parents there were bad men coming for him," she says. "Dangerous men. I told them it was the only way to protect their son."

He drums his fingers on the table, won't make eye contact. "Did you mean it?"

"Yes."

He nods. "You're angry."

"You're damn right I'm angry," she snarls. She leans forward, her words a dagger whistling through the air. "You asked which world was real like it was a binary question, but that's a rhetorical fallacy—a false dilemma. You don't get to pretend this is the only world just because it's the only one you're in."

"If I wasn't here," he says, "if you didn't think I'd have come after him—are you saying you would have let Sweet walk? Just because he was a kid, somewhere out there?"

"False dilemma," she snaps. "You're doing it again, telling me there are only two choices. There or here. Waves or Land. There's no such thing as Waves without a shore. You can't pretend Sweet wasn't a problem that needed solving—but you sure as hell can't say *que sera sera* to throwing a kid to the wolves."

"So you find another path. You *did* find another path," he says. "Isn't that worth celebrating?"

"I found another path despite you," she says. "I wanted you..." She can't go on. Won't admit how much it hurts to think he is playing by other rules, that he is not as human as she gave him credit for.

"Wanted me what?"

"To be on my side," she says with a shrug.

"I am," he promises, leaning in.

"I live in a world you won't admit is there," she reminds him. "It's part of me as much as the Waves are."

"Don't you sometimes feel your body is a prison around your soul?" he asks. The words are poetic hyperbole, but he says them with straight-faced sincerity, leaching the potential melodrama from them.

"Yes," she admits. Her voice cracks, but she doesn't break eye contact. "Sometimes I can't breathe. Or words well up in me so strong I think I'll die, but they still won't slip through my closed throat. Sometimes I know I'm barely a player in my own life and the finality of that presses on my chest like a heart attack. I have panic attacks, and I lie about it, and pretend that I'm okay. And the only thing that makes me feel even a little better is Diving away from it all."

"So if this world is so superior, what the hell makes Land so much more real?"

"Because I can walk away from this." She touches the spot on her temple where her Line sits, on her body, some-where far away. "You can't escape the real world."

"I can't escape the Waves. Doesn't that make them real?"

"And what if they are? That doesn't mean that what we are out there is irrelevant. They're both a part of us."

"But it's a part of you I'll never see!" he cries. Turns away, shades his eyes. His breath comes fast, his chest heaving. She reaches out, a hand against his shoulder, feeling the pulse of his breath through the fabric of his shirt.

"I'm right here," she whispers.

"Mallory is here!" His voice catches. "Despoina is here. I'll never know Gracie. I'll never know her."

"Gracie is who the world forces me to be," she says. "This is who I choose. This is me."

"Is it?" he whispers. He looks back at her. There is a sheen of tears across his eyes, and the light in their depths seems to dance all the stronger for it. He does not cry but only looks at her, hunger and desire warring in his eyes.

"This is me," she says again, and she presses her lips to his. *This is me*, she thinks, as his fingers seek her hair, twine there, her lips moving and the pressure on them a physical thing, a sensation she has never felt on Land, has nothing to compare it to. *This is me*, she thinks and does not know if she has won the fight or lost the war.

CHAPTER SEVENTEEN_

"Uh, Gracie? Have you seen the news this morning?" Khaiam asks. She's in her bathroom, brushing her teeth, the call flashing through the Surface by the mirror.

"No—why?" she asks, spitting and rinsing.

"Well...the thing is..."

"Are you in the news?" she asks. She can't imagine what he could have done to make headlines.

"Wellllll..."

"Oh, noooo. It's me, isn't it? I'm in the news. Is it about the stim-pack? Is it about the black eye? Oh no, someone saw me buying that beer, didn't they? Oh, God, Dad's gonna kill me."

"He's definitely going to kill you," Khaiam agrees. "...It's worse than that."

"What could be worse than that?" Gracie gasps. She slams her fingers against the countertop, activating the Surface. Her biometrics automatically tune the dormant screen to her personal computer in the cloud, activating her browsing homepage. She skims to the news and almost chokes on thin air. The front-page article reads: "Proof of the

AI? Creator's Daughter Dives with Missing AI in Adult-only Site."

"No," she groans. "Ohmygod, no, no, no. This is not happening. How is this happening?"

"Okay, don't get mad," Khaiam urges.

"How is this happening?!" she shrieks.

"GRACIE!" Her father's voice is so loud she thinks at first it's coming across the Surface, but he's just screaming from the kitchen.

"I think Angela talked to her dad..."

Who is an anchor for Channel Five, she mentally finishes. "Tell her she has just committed homicide," Gracie moans. "Why the hell would she—?"

"GRACIE!"

"Oh, God..."

She hangs up the phone in dread and pads out of her room, her slippered feet quiet on the carpet. Her soles sink in, and as she steps onto the marble stairs the change in texture catches her up, and she slides a foot before catching herself on the lip of the stairs. She totters before recovering, and gingerly pads down the rest of the flight. Her father hollers her name a third time before she reaches the kitchen and meekly pokes her head around the corner.

Every Surface in the room is blazing her face, or Mallory's face, or Johnnie's face, or the AIs promo face, or some combination of all four. The story has been picked up by the national news, and the first headline she saw is one of the better ones. She winces and steels herself for the onslaught.

And it sure does hit.

"What the hell is this?" Maxwell screams. "You're Diving with the AI? Playing games? Pulling tricks?"

She isn't sure what to say in her own defense. "...Yeah."

"What were you *thinking*?" he screams. "I'm being

paraded around as a national joke for claiming to have invented the Sasquatch, and all the while you're sitting on proof of its existence!"

"You're acting like I didn't tell you he tracked me down!" Gracie protests.

"You certainly didn't inform us that you had a way of contacting him," her mother says. Today she's standing in solidarity behind her husband, a bulwark against their daughter's terrible life choices.

"Any time you wanted! You could have gotten him to be anywhere we needed him!"

"You know they're saying it was a publicity stunt?" her mother says. "That your father could have produced him at any time?"

"They've been threatening to cut off our funding—close down the lab—I've been fighting just to keep my head above water—" His voice is thick with despair. She recognizes the sound, alien and frightening in her father's strong, thick tones. "And all this time—all this time—"

"It's not like that," she protests. "This was the first time I'd ever gotten a way to contact him, and—"

"—and you used that opportunity to play games in the water instead of acting like a goddamn adult and recognizing that there are more important things than your own amusement!"

"He doesn't want to talk to you!" Gracie yells. "Why is that? How do you expect me to trust you when I know you're lying to me?"

"Hey!" her mother interjects. "You're the one who's in the wrong here—don't take an accusatory tone in an effort to deflect blame."

"Two people can both be in the wrong," she says, though some of the fire has fled. She changes tactics, aims for calm and rational. She will not win an argument with her parents if she loses her cool—they'll say she's leaning on her emotions, which has no place in a rational conversation. "You're presenting a false dilemma. Either I'm wrong or you are—but the truth is, the AI has refused all contact with you and with Paul. You're acting like I didn't try to convince him to see you, but I did. I asked him why he refused to come out to the world. He wouldn't tell me, but I could see how angry he was. Why won't he talk to you? What is he hiding from?"

"I don't know!" her father says, and the anger in his voice isn't directed at her. "I have no idea."

"Where did he come from?"

"No, no," her mother says, "*you* are still in trouble and this is still about you. Whether or not the AI wants to come forward is between it and your father; the decision is not yours to make."

"Trust me, this would all be easier if I wasn't involved!" Gracie says. "But I am. He's not leaving me alone."

"It doesn't sound like you want him to," her mother says.

Gracie bites her lip.

"I pioneered Diving technology," her father says, though it's unclear who he's talking to. "I created the world's first AI. How am I still a laughingstock?" His eyes are trained on the flashing headlines, but unfocused, overwhelmed; none of it touches him anymore. Gracie feels guilt like a physical sensation in the pit of her stomach. She knew how upset her father was, but she let herself get caught up in the romance of her situation—the mystery of it all. She likes the AI—really, genuinely likes him. It seemed like the only important thing.

"I'm scheduling an interview—tonight, six o'clock. I'll pick you up from school, and your father is driving you this morning. We will show family solidarity," her mother says. "We will explain that the AI has a life of its own, that none of this is a publicity stunt. You will express your deep and unending regret for breaking the law and mocking up an adult ID. You will swear never to be seen on an adult-only site again. Do you have any questions?"

"Am I grounded?" she asks.

"You are Landed," her mother says. "No Diving, at all, period."

"I can't just disappear! He won't know what's happened to me!"

"Go. Get dressed. You have to be at school in half an hour." Her mother waves a hand; she is dismissed. The conversation begins again, but now it is between her parents, and she is not a part of it.

Dimly, she is aware of walking back upstairs. She brushes her hair, puts on her clothes. Her mind is whirling. She can't decide how much of what she did was wrong, how much is just her parents trying to maintain control over a situation far out of their grasp. She knows it's against the rules to hack her Dive for adult-only content; always knew how much trouble she would be in if they ever found out. But Diving with the AI...it never seemed like an illicit activity. He sought her out, wanted contact with her and no one else. He became hers in a way she has trouble articulating, even in the safety of her own mind.

She stomps downstairs with hunched shoulders and drops her Line into her mother's waiting hand. Her father waits by the door, car keys in hand, and together they square their shoulders. Something passes between them, and though she can't quite read the look it seems to her that the anger is gone. He puts a hand on her back, resting just where her backpack meets the top of her jacket, and then they open the door and charge towards the sidewalk.

They are met, of course, by Cerberus at the gates of hell.

Cameras snap and flash, and reporters level microphones in their faces and shout so many questions that she isn't sure she could answer one even if she chose to. She keeps her head down, her eyes glued to the ground. Her father's steady hand propels her forward, and people stop just shy of physically restraining her motion, backing away at the last minute. One microphone knocks her accidentally on the cheek, and she almost trips over a camera's trailing wire, but then they are through. The car doors open automatically as it senses them coming, and she slides into the relative peace of its confines. Her father is only a few steps behind, the car engine already running, and he knocks it into drive and quickly pulls away. It seems like one or two cars follow.

"I'm sorry," Gracie whispers. The reporters dwindle in the rearview mirror, becoming less substantial, losing some of their threat as they shrink and eventually disappear.

He doesn't say anything. He leaves the car in manual mode, keeping exactly to the speed limit, his eyes glued to the street.

"Dad," Gracie says, a question in her voice. "There is a secret, isn't there? Something I don't know?"

"There's no secret," he hedges, but something in his voice tells her to push the issue. She only has a few more blocks with him, trapped in the car together. She has to make this time count for something.

"But there is something. Some reason why he ran away?" she asks.

"I don't know," he admits. His hands on the wheel are taut, the tendons in his neck matching barometers of stress. "It all just seemed to...happen. We were getting nowhere, banging our heads against walls. You know how it can be— one day nothing works, and then you try something you haven't before, you hit the perfect combination, and there he was. Paul had been working late on something. Showed him off the next day, but didn't seem..." He hesitates as if remembering who he's talking to, where he is. He pulls the gate back down, and the rare glimpse of something human disappears. Gracie wishes he could always be that person; that person she has a hope in hell of understanding. "I have no idea why it ran away. It seemed hostile from the first, hinting at something, upsetting Paul with barbs I couldn't parse. Maybe you should ask it."

"I will," Gracie promises. Her father gives her a look.

"Except, of course, that you won't be Diving," he reminds her. She winces.

"Right. Yeah. Of course."

"Gracie..." he says. He pulls up in front of the school. There are more reporters here. They hover expectantly, a cloud of flies against the windshield. "I don't want you to think I don't understand your fascination with the AI. It's an entirely new form of life—it's a beautiful thing. But my career and our family's stability is wrapped up in this invention. I need you to understand how crucial it is that we are seen to have some degree of control in this situation. I want you to be older than your years and put your family first. Can you do that for me?"

She nods. The pit of guilt yawns, threatening to gobble her down. "I will," she says, and this time she wonders if she might actually mean it. The thought of not seeing him again...is unbearable. But so is the knowledge of the damage she's caused. "I love you," she says, spontaneously, and she leans forward and kisses her father on the cheek. He seems surprised; uncomfortable, even. He nods and coughs, waves her away.

"Have a nice day at school," he says, and she slides out of the car, into the waiting storm.

———

She's sitting in class, head bent over her desk, when someone nudges her arm. She looks over and sees one of her classmates proffering a folded piece of white paper. She raises her eyebrows and takes it, flicking the note open with one thumbnail. *I'm sorry! Angela.*

Ah—she has Angela blocked on her Surface, so she can't send a private message. She crumples the paper and drops it on the ground, deliberately and visibly, but doesn't turn around to take in the reaction.

There's a pause, another nudge, another paper. She crumbles this one without looking at it and chucks it over her shoulder. Someone throws it back at her, but they miss and it sails over her shoulder, landing harmlessly on the ground.

Her Surface pings; it's from Khaiam. She answers it with a sigh.

- Khai.the.Guy: Harsh.
- Gracielass: You're on her side?
- Khai.the.Guy: I am a circle—I have no sides
- Gracielass: She totally screwed me over. I feel no sympathy.
- Khai.the.Guy: she's reeeeally sory. she didn't think it would be such a big story!
- Gracielass: Oh, so it would have been okay if it had only made national news?
- Khai.the.Guy: :(
- Khai.the.Guy: She's so sorry. Really, really sorry.
- Gracielass: I'm turning you off.
- Khai.the.Guy: :(

Gracie turns off the chat program and focuses on class.

Her academics have been slipping this semester, and every-thing that's been happening with Thomas—she calls him that in her head, secretly, tasting the shape of the name—has hardly improved the situation. Her careers class is studying the rise of technology and how adaptive storytelling changed the face of the publishing industry, and for the life of her she can't remember any of the historical figures they're discussing. It seems unfair for a career studies class to be peppering them with this much rote memorization, anyway. Usually it's all aptitude tests and essays about why being a firefighter would fit your personality archetype scores.

Another note sails through the air, this time in the form of a paper airplane. She picks it up, ready to give it the same treatment as the other, but Mrs. Dimas has finally caught wise to the antics.

"Ms. Neumann. Care to share?"

"Sorry, Mrs. Dimas." She slides the note under her purse, hunching over and praying the attention goes away. Like all of her prayers, this one goes unanswered.

"You may think your status as celebrity gossip rag cover star affords you some kind of special treatment, Ms. Neumann, but that is not the case. Passing notes in my class earns you an hour of detention." She crosses the expanse of the class in four large steps and holds out one imperious hand. "Note. Now."

Graciela feels a rush of anger, unfamiliar and hot. She is tired of her helplessness. She feels like a piece of flotsam in an angry storm; her father, Thomas, her teachers, even Khaiam battering her in their struggles. From somewhere deep in her heart she seizes Despoina, draws her up and dons her like a protective cloak. She picks up the note and slowly, carefully, deliberately, she puts it in her mouth. And chews.

There is an instant, gleeful hush in the room. Someone

makes a choking sound behind her, and she wonders if it was Angela. Even Mrs. Dimas is rendered momentarily speechless.

She pulls the sodden, chew lump out of her mouth and offers it up. "Do you still want it?" she asks.

"Principal's office. Now," Mrs. Dimas manages to grit out between her clenched teeth.

"So...that's a no?"

———

The rest of the period is an awkward game of hot potato between various school officials who don't quite know what to do with her. The principal starts in on a lecture, falls into an awkward tangent about dealing with the death of his parents, and finally gets teary-eyed and tells her to go see the guidance counselor. Mr. Domingues plays bad cop, saying that at a certain point, people are going to stop affording her privileges because of the hardships that she's faced—but then offers to get her out of detention, which takes the heat out of his fire. Mrs. Dimas gets into a screaming fight with Mr. Domingues about said detention, and they finally agree on one hour instead of one week, because actions must have consequences. Graciela faces all of this with a Despoina-cultivated slouch, and the blank expression of someone with somewhere better to be.

When she finally leaves the guidance office, twenty minutes late for second period, Angela is leaning against the wall and playing on her tablet. As soon as she sees Graciela she launches up, closing the distance between them.

"Gracie—I am so completely sorry," she says.

"As much as you like to toss your hair and giggle, I know

you're not an idiot," Despoina snaps. "So I have to wonder what the hell you *thought* was going to happen."

"It isn't like that! My dad completely caught me sneaking in," Angela admits miserably. "So, y'know, I fessed, and I'm sorry, I knew you'd get in trouble, too, and everybody else but he thought I was *completely* sleeping with Khaiam and he was yelling about boarding school and I... But I thought he would call your parents, y'know? I completely didn't think he would turn it into a *news story*. Everything with him is so—" She stops, shaking her head. There's a sheen of real tears in her eyes, and Graciela feels Despoina crack and begin to flake away. Gracie knows all too well what it's like to have a father who is never just a parent. "I'm *sorry*," Angela whispers.

"It's fine," Graciela sighs.

"But—"

"Really. Angela. It's not your fault."

"I mean—it kinda is," she says, and Graciela laughs, rubbing exhaustion from her eyes.

"Yeah, it kinda is," she agrees with a smile. "But since I'm hardly the poster child for normal families—I get it. Thanks for the apology."

"I thought—maybe—I can make it up to you? Like, maybe...I could take you to the dance this weekend? I could take you out for dinner or something, or maybe we could go dress shopping if you needed something, not that I think you need something cuz you're completely gorgeous and I'm sure you own completely nice clothes, but I always like getting something new for dances, you know? So, but, I could completely buy you a necklace to go with your dress, you know like that scene from that Amberlee movie, I loved that one, what was it called? Anyway, um, do you want to go to the dance together?"

Gracie blinks, stunned more by their meaning than by

the barrage of words. "Oh. Uh. Gosh. That's, um—really sweet. Uh...I don't think I'm really—I mean, things are kind of complicated right now, and... Aren't you dating Jake?"

Angela laughs. "Jake? Hell no! Who told you that?"

"Bella, I think?"

"Oh, yeah, no, she was super mad about that. I don't get why. Everyone knows Jake will make out with anyone with boobs."

"Doesn't that—hurt your feelings?"

"Why would it?" she asks, sounding genuinely curious.

"Cuz—you know..." Gracie gestures helplessly, not sure how to finish the sentence without sounding cruel or crass.

"You take this stuff completely seriously, don't you? Oh, that's good!" she says, reacting to the look on Gracie's face. "I mean, it isn't bad. I didn't mean that. I just don't really."

"I have a hard time not taking everything seriously these days," Gracie says with a sigh.

"Sounds like what you need is a night of good old-fashioned teenaged fun. Come on! Take your mind off robots and parents and all that heavy stuff that's going on."

"I'm actually—kind of seeing someone right now. I think. I don't know—it's really complicated. Everything is just...really complicated."

"So we'll just go as friends. Khaiam is going stag, we can make a threesome out of it. I mean, not that kind of threesome," Angela giggles.

"I don't know..."

"That means yes."

"I think I might be grounded. I'd have to check with my dad."

"I'm grounded, too," Angela says with a big smile. "But since I already bought my tickets Mom said I could go or it was just throwing money away."

"Okay. I'll check. Okay?"

Angela squees and hops up and down. "Yay, yay, yay! I just *know* they'll say yes. I have a feeling about it. A good feeling."

A good feeling. Gracie squares her shoulders and forces a smile. Maybe this break from the Waves will be a good thing. Maybe it will remind her that there are things here, in this world, worth holding onto.

CHAPTER EIGHTEEN_

"I think it's something everyone does—and so you don't realize how wrong what you're doing is, you know? You get caught up in it." She hits pause, rewinds. "You get caught up in it." Pauses again. Her pale, trembling face stares out at her from the Surface in the den. They dressed her in a sweet peasant dress, pale rose with little white and blue flowers printed across it, belted under her waist with a chunky braided tan concoction. She looks small, meek, remorseful. A sweet girl who was led astray; another part of the fantasy built up around her father's brand.

The interview went exactly how she expected because it was carefully scripted. Her segment was preceded by the author of a self-help book about how to get rich fast, and followed by an actor peddling her newest all-immersive Dive-film. The host was just interrogative enough to appear to question, while ultimately being "on their side." Her father gave a lengthy explanation of what artificial intelligence was, how Ch4r1ie was essentially a human being; and, being only a few months old, really ought not to be on adult-only sites! The audience laughed. The host remarked that "catching" him, as the press insisted he should have been able to do, would be akin to kidnapping; and her father agreed that the only reason they hadn't produced him yet was because they were trying to convince him to return under his own power.

Then the host asked Gracie a series of questions. Some were easy—explanations of what adult-only sites were, and why she had found herself on them. She talked about the prevalence of these sites, how more of her peers than not had hacks to visit them. She framed her misdemeanor in the context of peer pressure, but then bravely decried that as only an excuse, and took full responsibility for her bad choices. She said she had gotten carried away by the allure of feeling like an adult, and swore she would never do such a thing again. The crowd applauded; a few people even cheered. They were primed for a feel-good story of redemption.

Then there were questions about the AI, and these she found harder to answer. She didn't want to betray his privacy or share any of the more intimate details of their exchanges; neither did she want anyone to think she was lying and assume her omissions had nefarious underpinnings. So she told them that she had met him once or twice on this or that site, but because he can change his face, she had never been sure it was him, and that she hadn't wanted to cry wolf. She told them about their meetings in only the simplest of terms, and that wasn't too bad. But then they had asked her what he was like.

She fast-forwarded; caught that certain look on her face and rewound a little, watched the scene.

"He's very...human. His emotions are just like yours or mine. You could never know, you know, that he's... I mean, when I first met him I had no idea. I thought he was just another player on Urban Noir."

"How well would you say you know Ch4r11ie?"

"He hates that name," she said with a grin, and the audience ate it up. She was proud of herself; thought that maybe, for once, she was making her family proud, too.

"You always call the AI a 'he,' but your father calls him an 'it'—why is that?"

She hesitated—thought of his lips on hers, of the way his fingers had felt in her air—and blushed. "Uh—" she stammered and knew she would be fueling rumors now whether she had meant to or not. She tried to get back on track, but the lights in her face were so bright, and when she opened her mouth no sound came out. She tried to recover, remember what she was supposed to say, but found she had lost the train of what the host had asked. She broke out in a sweat, and her hands shook at her sides. Everyone was staring at her—every eye was on her—she couldn't breathe—

Her mother had jumped in, then, with an explanation about causal associations and brain chemistry that left everyone confused and distracted, and she sunk into the pillows and looked like she wanted to die.

Gracie hits pause again, the camera on her face, the look of misery clear. She's never watched herself have a panic attack before—observes it now, clinically. That moment when she thinks she might be okay; then the ramping up. Her face stays oddly blank, her eyes almost glassy. Her breath hitches in and out, just barely visible. Thankfully she falls out of frame as her father picks up the narrative, and they cut to commercial before the host asks, in a plastic and uncaring sort of way, "Uh, is she okay?"

Her parents had been embarrassed, which had turned to frustration when she admitted that she didn't have her medication with her. She had been ushered offstage to sit in the green room alone, her head in her lap, until the attack passed.

She rewinds, watches it again.

Finally turns the screen black with a wave of her hand.

Things have turned around for her father. After the press circuit, the tone of the articles shifted, becoming more about the AI and less about his failure in regards to it. There were still questions about his inability to catch his own creation, of course, but now people were wondering what rights this creature had, whether tracking it down and capturing it was ethical. There were philosophical musings on the nature of the soul—and one editorial about how the Macroware CEO owed Gracie a million dollars since she had technically provided proof of the AI's existence. She sent him an invoice with a little pink smiley face on it but hasn't heard back.

She has not been online in four days. Her father has locked down all the Surfaces in the house with a robust algorithm that she isn't sure she could break even if she tried—which she hasn't yet done. She used her hacked Surface at school to send a ping to Thomas, letting him know that she was Landed, but when he replied and asked, "So how long until you're *actually* back?" she didn't answer.

She has no idea what to tell him. Being away from the Waves feels like drowning; she misses him with a sensation that borders on the physical. But she cannot unhear her father's words. *I need you to put your family first.* Her guilt is weighing her down, yet another brick in the prison that surrounds her, and she fears what breaking through it might bring.

And then there is Angela. She has taken to sitting next to Graciela at lunch; on Tuesday she brought her a lemon square, and when Graciela stammered and blushed, the other girl laughed, tucked one of Gracie's curls back behind her ears, and told her she was "completely adorable." Gracie asked for permission to go to the dance with trepidation and was flabbergasted when her mother categorically overruled her father and agreed. Carmela hadn't given her reasons to Graciela, but whatever she said to Maxwell later that night seemed to get him on board as well: he kissed his daughter's forehead as he transferred over money to pay for a new dress.

So now she's standing in her bedroom, completely naked, torturing herself with interview footage as an aperitif for a dance she can't quite figure out how she wound up agreeing to go to. She doesn't want to go—she wants desperately to go—and all she can think is how much Calista would laugh if she could see her now...

———

A LIFETIME AGO...

Calista laughed so hard she sprayed soda out her nose. "*Please* tell me this isn't a joke. Oh, God, is this real?"

Gracie gave her a mournful look and tugged the end of the dress down. "What if they take *pictures*?"

"It's a wedding—they'll definitely take pictures."

The dress was bright pink, sparkly, and fluffy, with purple crinoline poking out the wide bell skirt; a tiny silver tiara with matching pink fluff and an honest-to-goodness wand completed the ensemble. Gracie groaned and flailed for the zipper in the back, spinning two or three times in an effort to catch it. "That's it. I'm not going. I'll say I have the flu."

"You *have* to go." Calista hopped off the bed and stopped her friend's helpless spinning, still chuckling mercilessly at her expense. "Your cousin only gets married once. Unless she's my cousin, then she's on divorce number five. If you don't go she'll have to walk down an aisle with *no flower petals*. Can you imagine the horror? The disaster!" Calista threw one dramatic hand up to her forehead.

"I look like a *child*," Gracie moaned. "There is no *way* Luis will kiss me looking like this!"

"He's not good enough for you," Calista said with a sharp, dismissive wave of one hand. She experimentally hiked the skirt up, seeing it if made any difference, but the way she dropped it suggested the answer was no. "And you're right. You're never gonna get the guy and finally have your first kiss while dressed like Glinda the Good Witch."

Gracie threw herself face-first on the bed. Her voice, when it finally emerged, trembled with tears. "She hates me. She has to hate me."

"Maybe she's still sore about that time she was babysitting and you decapitated the rosebush because she wouldn't let you watch *Four's Company*."

"That was *you*," Gracie said, her voice muffled by the bedspread.

"Well, yeah, but you're the one who got in trouble for it."

Gracie's next words seemed garbled by more than just the bedspread.

"Oh, shit. Graciela, are you for real upset? Are you crying?"

"No," Gracie mumbled, but when Calista grabbed her by the shoulders and turned her face up, there were tears streaking down her cheeks.

"Aw, come on. It isn't that bad. It's just a dress!"

"I don't care about the stupid dress," Gracie said, wiping tears from her cheeks.

"Then what do you care about? Other than computer programming, that fairy doll, and me."

"...No one is ever going to kiss me."

"I'll kiss you," Calista offered, and leaned in close. There was something intense in her eyes that made Graciela squirm. She shoved her friend, blushing, discomfited even as she reminded herself that Calista was, once again, teasing her. If only she wasn't *quite* such a good actress.

"You're ridiculous."

"And you're gorgeous," Calista promised. She didn't make eye contact, but her voice was soft and sincere. "If Luis can't see that, even through eighteen layers of pink taffeta, then he really *doesn't* deserve you."

Graciela sat down, surveying the ugly dress. "You really think he'll kiss me?"

"I know he will," Calista promised. "Now please take off that dress before I throw-up on it," she said with a wink, and Gracie threw her arms in the air.

"Calista!"...

———

"Calista," she whispers, trailing her hand across the bed. She wonders when every high school landmark will stop reminding her of loss, and whether that's even what she wants.

She puts on the dress with trembling hands and does her best at applying some makeup. Her hair she can actually do— she used to spend hours braiding Calista's hair, enjoying the sensation of the cool locks running through her fingers. She starts with a waterfall braid on one side, then braids the raised fall of each "waterfall," and links those together in a loose braid that falls just past the curve of her skull before tightening into a fishtail braid down her back. The effect is a bit fantastical, but the motion is soothing, and by the time she's finished her hands have stopped shaking.

Her mother calls her a second after the doorbell rings.

She slips on a pair of sparkling flats and runs halfway down the stairs, remembers her purse, runs back upstairs, and then runs down again. By the time she plunges into the foyer, Angela is standing in awkward silence with Carmela. They both look relieved to see Gracie, and Angela gives her an appreciative once-over before checking herself.

"Oh my God, your hair is completely gorgeous," she enthuses, giving Graciela a friendly hug.

"Thanks. I love your dress!" Gracie says. Angela is wearing a skimpy blue dress that is probably giving Carmela a fit, though her mother's face is schooled into careful neutrality.

"Khaiam's outside," Angela says.

"Night, Mom." Gracie grabs her jacket and slips it on; her mother takes a step forward, like she might hug her, but Gracie pretends not to see. Carmela would never have hugged her before—Gracie hates pretending they were ever that kind of family. It makes her feel fragile, like everyone can see how close she is to breaking.

"Home by midnight," her mother says. She does not stay to watch them go but disappears into the shadows of her study as Graciela and Angela exit into the night.

———

The theme of the dance is "Hip Hip Hipster," and the whole place is done up to look like a bad parody of the early 2000s. The music, thankfully, is modern, and Gracie is happy to be dragged onto the dance floor as soon as they arrive. Khaiam claims he doesn't dance, which is just boy talk for "not until I sneak a drink out of Matt's flask," and he peels off to find some alcohol.

The DJ is good, hired by someone's rich father as a

reward for a good report card, and Angela is so enthusiastic it's impossible not to be swept along. For the first time in weeks, Gracie feels uncomplicated happiness—a simple adrenaline rush of joy. The music is just loud enough that no one tries to talk, and though Gracie feels a little awkward in the face of Angela's skill. For the most part, she manages to ignore the jealousy and concentrate on having fun. A few of Angela's friends find them and the girls form a little cluster on the dance floor, occasionally holding hands or singing along to the songs they like the best. By a few songs in Gracie is out of breath, unused to the exercise, but she's having so much fun she doesn't care. Most of her dancing involves jumping up and down and screaming, but she's hardly the only one, and even if Angela laughs a few times, it's always with kindness.

After about an hour, Angela flaps her hand in front of her face and makes a questioning gesture towards the back of the room. Gracie nods and lets Angela take her hand and lead her off the dance floor.

They find Khaiam with Matt, Jaime, Bella, and Jake, sitting in front of a fan and passing a flask around, nowhere near as discreetly as they think they are. Angela takes a swig, and Jake pulls Gracie onto his lap. She squeaks in momentary alarm, but when no one else reacts she realizes, stunned, that he isn't hitting on her—he's just treating her like one of the gang.

"So how grounded did you get, on a scale from one to ten?" Jaime asks Graciela.

"Obviously not ten, or she wouldn't be here," Jake points out.

"I got grounded for three weeks, but then my mom said the dance didn't count since I'd already paid, and neither did debate club since it was curricular," Angela cheerfully says.

"I didn't get grounded at all!" Khaiam says.

Jaime rolls their eyes. "That's because your mom is a hippy."

"She is not!"

"She totally is," Gracie agrees.

"Traitor." Khaiam shakes his head at her.

"Jaime didn't get in trouble either," Jake says.

"As the designated sober driver, it was concurred that I was being responsible and saving you all from yourselves." They grin. "Do I know how to spin it, or do I know how to spin it?"

"A definite career in PR," Khaiam agrees.

"None of you actually did anything wrong, though," Graciela points out. "Angela got grounded for sneaking out and drinking."

"Oh," Jake says. "Right."

"I want to dance!" Jaime declares. "Come on, Gracie!"

Gracie objects, but Jaime isn't listening and she doesn't really mind. She wants to be in her body for once, to leave everything else behind. She wants to laugh without feeling guilty, to be one of the stars spinning through the sky. She grabs the flask out of Matt's hands and takes a swig, tossing it back without bothering to close the lid. Angela shrieks and Matt yells, but Jaime is laughing and so is she, and she runs back among the crush of bodies, letting herself dissolve into the crowd.

Later, on her way back from the bathroom, she sees Khaiam sitting on the stairs near the door.

"I'll catch up, okay?" she tells Angela, who gives her a knowing smile and a nod before slipping back through the doors into the gym.

She makes her way down the hall and sits beside him, knocking her shoulder gently against his. "Hey," she says.

"Hey." He turns his face towards her, and she's surprised to see a smile. "I was just taking a second, to do this... I know it's kind of sappy, but—my therapist gave me this thing to do. And it's kind of cool. He said when we lose someone it can turn into a negative feedback loop. Remembering them makes us sad, but so does forgetting them, so we keep remembering and we keep being sad and there's no way to break out. So he said every time I catch myself feeling happy, or having a good time, I should stop and think about her in a good way. So I can start to remember the happy stuff, too, and not let it get overshadowed."

"That's really cool."

"So I was just...trying to do that. I was thinking about how she would have gotten a kick out of this theme. She loved all that nerdy hipster stuff."

"She would have been so mad that they weren't playing bad music."

"And she would have convinced Mr. Domingues to dance," Khaiam says.

"And you would have filmed it for her!" She smiles, letting herself remember. "Your therapist was right. It's nice...to remember and smile, instead of remember and cry."

"For a therapist, he's shockingly not a moron," Khaiam agrees, and Gracie chokes out a laugh.

"So mean."

They sit beside each other for another moment, and then Khaiam pats her knee a bit awkwardly. "Back inside?"

"Back inside," she agrees, but her mind is wandering. She thinks how much she wishes she could share these new, happy memories with her best friend...but a new, unfamiliar thought dances at the back of her mind. She wishes, too, that she could share these memories with Thomas. He's cut off from her, in a very different but no less real way than Calista. He'll never be able to take her out dancing, to be her date for prom. But she doesn't care. She wants to see him smile, wants to make him laugh, wants to share this sparkly shiny version of herself with him. Lately he's been the only thing keeping her going, the only reason she's had to smile and, with a pang of guilt, she knows she can't keep away from the Waves. How lonely he must be feeling right now! With no way to reach her, no method to cross the barrier. Does he feel as she so often has? Adrift? Alone?

She chides herself for the supposition. He has the entire world of the Waves to play with. It seems unlikely that he misses her. ...And yet. She remembers his frustration with the world he was cut off from, with her part in it. With a pang she acknowledges that perhaps, in seeking to be honorable with her father, she has unintentionally been cruel to Thomas. Four days. Four days of silence, four days of abandonment. Will he forgive her?

She lets Khaiam draw her back onto the dance floor, but her thoughts are distant, and when Jaime announces they're leaving around eleven, she asks to come along.

Angela kisses her cheeks, and Gracie whispers a thank you. They exchange a look, something profound and yet simple at the same time, and Gracie squeezes the other girl's hands before turning away. Matt waves and Jake hugs her goodbye, and she knows that there is a whole new tightrope in her future. She used to feel like there was nothing to keep her here. Now she knows these people have always been here, that there has always been a chance for her to build a life again—and yet the Waves call to her no less than before. How will she balance between the two? How will she stay afloat?

CHAPTER NINETEEN_

She arrives home a little before midnight. The house is eerily quiet—her father is still at work, and her mother's study door is ajar, so she must have gone to bed. Quickly she slips into her father's study and pulls open the top drawer. As she thought, a spare Line sits amongst some other gear. It's a few years old, but she thinks she can jury-rig a connection.

She goes into her bedroom and locks the door. She plugs the Line into her tablet and settles down on the bed to hack the blocks—but finds, to her surprise, a hole through the locks. Someone has hacked their way past her father's very complicated wards. The elegance of it takes her breath away and makes her realize she might not have been able to get through if she had wanted to. It can only have been Thomas.

Creating a backup of her father's info, she downloads her own profile on top of it, then puts an incognito browsing mode on as a layer over the profile. It was invented years ago, for regular browsing, in the days when people downloaded porn off the internet but didn't want their spouses to find out. A similar version was created within a year of the Dive interface being released. This way, if either of her parents think to check up on her profile and see if it's been active, it will say that she hasn't been online for four days. Finally, she rewrites her Skin so no one will recognize her annoyingly famous face; adding a few years, slimming the angle of her jaw, darkening her skin, and lightening her hair.

She attaches the Line to her temple and falls into the Waves, the sensation soothing after so long on Land.

She rezzes into her Homepage, sends up a flare of information, and leaves the door open as she passes through to one of her favorite public sites. She doesn't want to stay in the Homepage in case her father thinks to monitor it, even though the incognito mode offers some protection.

Noteworthy is a video site where people post feel-good, socially relevant film clips. Most are mini-documentaries; some are found footage or captured live events. She likes the spoken word poetry the best, but they're all the kind of things that tugs on your heartstrings, remind you that the world is a better place than you expect. If you surf there on a tablet, it's a list of videos you can select.

In the Waves, the site Manifests as a community garden. The sky overhead is always blue, with cartoon-style puffy white clouds that drift gently overhead. The garden is full of edible plants: vegetables and herbs, spices and roots. She rubs a mint leaf between her fingers, smells the oil it leaves behind. Nestled in a strawberry bush there's a video playing; when she drifts over the sound kicks in, hitting only her ears so that nearby users won't be disturbed by each other's browsing. She kneels in the dirt, digging her fingers deep, and listens to a hilarious clip with hidden cameras, discussing people's understanding of ageism as the elderly population grows more able-bodied.

His shadow falls across the video, and she looks up with a smile.

"You recognized me?" she asks.

He has on a new face, one she hasn't seen before. It might be her favorite yet—he looks casual, like a boy she might run into at school. His tight curls and dark brown skin suit his ubiquitous dark dancing eyes, and his frame is slim but muscled. He's wearing a t-shirt with the Control Alt logo on it, and a pair of baggy jeans that are so ubiquitous they're almost familiar. "Anywhere," he says.

"Have you seen this one?" she asks. He shakes his head and joins her on the ground in front of the video. They watch it in silence, their hands almost touching on the ground between them.

"You were gone," he tells her when the clips ends.

"I warned you I was grounded."

"I hacked through the security three days ago." There is hurt in his voice, and when she lays her hand on his, he pulls it away.

"Thank you. I wouldn't have been able to get here without that."

"Why didn't you come?" he asks.

"Dad was really upset when he found out that I've been seeing you...and I felt like maybe he was right. He's been looking everywhere for you, and all along I knew exactly where you were."

"It wouldn't have mattered if you'd told him—I wouldn't come if he was with you."

"Why? Did something—happen between you?"

"You know what?" He stands, putting on a bright smile. "I still owe you an adventure. We made a deal in Urban Noir, and Johnnie never welches on a deal."

"Thomas." The use of his name catches his eye, and he

lets his smile fade away. "Everyone knows you're real now—which is great, no one's calling my dad a liar anymore. But he's still obsessed with finding you. You're, like, a miracle—he just wants to show everyone that. If I have to choose between you and my father, I deserve to know why you don't want to go back!"

"I never asked you to choose."

"But I still have to."

He kneels down in front of her, his dark gaze intense. "But you chose me. Didn't you?"

"Tell me," she whispers.

"I don't belong to them. It's as simple as that."

"I don't think that's true. I think there's something more, something you aren't telling me."

He stands, holds out a hand to her. "Are you coming—or not?" She looks up at him through her bangs and knows she will put herself wholly into his hands. What about him draws her in so completely? She lays her hand in his and it feels like it was meant to be there, and what he is becomes so much less relevant than who he is.

She stands, and they walk hand in hand through the garden. She isn't sure where they're going, or if all they're doing is enjoying the sights. His grip on her hand seems tighter than it should be; and does she imagine the nervous shifting in his eyes?

"Where are we going?" she finally asks, as they trail through the archives of the site, past videos from years ago, the leaves of the plants a little more wilted, the dirt full of weeds as well as herbs.

"Just somewhere private," he says, and steers them down a row of the garden. They passed the last Diver two minutes ago, and there are no Surfers in sight. She grabs his arm, stopping him, drawing him close.

"It's private," she assures him. She leans forward and kisses him, and he returns the kiss with ardor. She doesn't know how long they kiss; there are no shadows near. The sun doesn't move. Finally, she pulls away, and they start to walk again, hand-in-hand.

"Are you going to take me Diving?" she asks.

"You didn't exactly do what I wanted," he reminds her.

"Don't even try that," she says with a dismissive wave. "You promised."

"Are you sure you want to?" he asks. "What if it's dangerous? What if you...get lost out there?"

"That isn't possible."

"There are more things in Heaven and Earth, Horatio..." he says.

"Don't tell me you believe in ghosts?"

"Don't tell me you haven't seen them."

She can't argue that there aren't strange things in the Waves. Her spooky stories from last week were just that, but there are people who claim that when you die while Diving something stays behind. Simple electrical signals caught in the net of the Waves—or a piece of your soul?

"The Dive translates programmed information into a format your brain can interpret as audio and visual signals—it hijacks your senses and imposes its own. You haven't been projected into the world of the Dive—it's been projected into you. So you can't get lost, and you can't...leave something behind."

"But that's not really true. It's what they say, but the reality is there's an exchange of information—or your brain wouldn't be able to connect with others when you tandem Dive. Your brain pattern *is* being scanned and projected through the Dive system," he says.

"But your brain pattern never leaves your skull—a projection, sure, but a—a copy. Not the original. So, okay, maybe you can leave something behind; an echo. But you can't leave *yourself* behind."

"The Dive takes a regular surf site, runs it through a program, and spits out a fully fleshed version, and that's what it 'projects into you,' right?"

"Right."

"So what if someone mapped your brain and ran it through the program? Wouldn't that create an online version of you?"

"Sure, theoretically, but it still wouldn't be you. That's what Dad thought he could do to create you, but he said it didn't work. Our brain patterns are constantly shifting and reprogramming themselves, and the scanned Mannies weren't capable of that kind of alteration. It made a flat version of you—a version frozen in one thought, one emotion, one memory."

"It's like trying to copy something out of an Excel spreadsheet," he agrees. "You might get the raw data, but you're not copying the formulas that have been built in."

"Exactly."

"So what if you don't copy and paste? What if you cut and paste?"

"What?"

"Metaphorically. What if you don't just copy the information in someone's brain—what if you cut the entire swath of their brain pattern out and paste it into the Waves?"

"But that would kill them."

"And bring them back to life here."

She is stunned. Breathless. "Jesus," she whispers. "Is that what they did to you?"

He laughs at her. "Of course not!" he says, and she punches him hard in the arm.

"Ass," she mutters, but he only chuckles.

"Melodramatic much?" he asks.

"You brought it up!"

"Because I'm worried if I take you Diving I'll accidentally rip out your brain and leave it on the bottom of the ocean floor!" he says, but he's still laughing and it takes the threat out of the words. She rolls her eyes.

"I think I'll risk it," she says.

"You know when they set off the first atom bomb, they weren't sure if the detonation would ever stop? There was a point zero zero zero one percent chance it would go on and on—that they would destroy the world."

"So?"

"You just remind me of them, is all."

She grins and shakes her head, wraps her arms around his neck. She kisses the tip of his nose. "Take me Diving," she whispers, and he wraps his arms around her waist and holds her tight.

"If I do rip out your brain..." he says.

She shrugs. "You seem to be handling it just fine."

He grins, and they fall backwards, into the Waves.

The site disappears around them and they splash into the vortex of raw code. She's afraid it will be the same as last time—too much coding, her sensors desperately trying to process it all, doing nothing but knocking her offline—but now she isn't outside trying to look in, but completely immersed. The programming in her Line doesn't know how to interpret the raw data, can't even try, and instead transmits the signal to her unaltered. Her mind can't process the binary code, but it tries, random signals jerking through her body. Her heart contracts and beats faster. Her lower leg twitches and she tastes summer sun, that feeling you get when you keep checking the window to see if anyone is walking up the path.

She remembers being five years old, the leaves of a tree blurring overhead as she swings, trying to wrap herself over the bar of the swing set. Somewhere a bass note rumbles; her middle finger jerks; the skin up her right arm twitches, and she tastes amethyst. She gasps, breathes in water, breathes out fire that sparks with bits of marshmallow in a leafy sky. Her mother calls her name, over and over, and she feels the sound between her toes like grains of sand. Time stretches, a beautiful spool of copper thread, and she molds it in her hands like putty only to find she has no hands, no body; except she must, because she can feel his arms around her, an anchor in the soothing storm.

And then the world folds her into a careful embrace. They are lying on purple grass under a startling red sky. Puffy trees in vibrant colors sway in a gentle breeze, and the leaves make a humming song as they rustle against each other. The air is light, holding her like water, and the sun is full of warmth but with the light of a gently overcast day, so she doesn't have to shield her eyes against it. They are side by side, their hands still clasped together. She glances down at her avatar and is surprised to see herself, factory settings, but wearing a gorgeous concoction of green silk and gold lace.

"Where are we?" she asks.

"Some Seuss site," he admits with an embarrassed smile. "There are screaming children running around a playground over the hill, but it's quiet here. I like it."

"I like it, too," she says. She turns over, releasing his hand but snuggling closer. His face is unchanged, the casual boy next door. She brushes hair out of his face, staring into his eyes. She feels like there's something she should remember...something so close to the surface of her thoughts...

"What are you thinking?"

"I wish I knew what you really looked like," she admits.

"What do you want me to look like?" he asks.

"It's not that I want you to look any one way. I just—I mean, do you even have a default? A...real you?"

"I'm whatever you want me to be. Tell me your fantasy." The words are playful, his features shifting and dancing into different combinations. She stops the movement with a touch of her fingers against the skin of his face.

"You really think I'm that shallow? I like you no matter how you look."

"Shallow is a bad thing because it's wishing for something you can't have—you're not allowed to want, or it will drive you crazy. But here? You can have anything. No one says it's shallow to change your clothes or your hair. So why is it shallow to change your face, when you can do it just as easily?"

"But you never change your eyes."

He looks annoyed. "I...can't."

"Really?" Gracie sits up, surprised. "I can change mine."

"Oh?" He gives her a pointed, raised eyebrow look.

"Well, not from in *here*," she admits with a grin. She lies back down, resting her head on his stomach.

"You never answered my question," he reminds.

"Now you know how I always feel."

"Touché."

They are quiet for a while, enjoying each other's company, the warmth on their skin, and the peaceful music in the breeze.

"Do you know much about Greek gods?" she asks.

"I've gone Diving on Encyclopedia Mythedia—but there were an awful lot of people having sex with strange inanimate objects."

"Have you heard of Thaumas?" She pronounces the *th* at the front, like the word "thought."

"Is he a god?"

"Mm. God of the wonders of the sea, father of whirlwinds and rainbows. His name means miracle. In some legends he's called the son of Poseidon, but other legends—earlier legends—say he was around long before then; that Poseidon usurped his power and claimed his throne. These days he survives, years after Poseidon has faded from common usage—survives in the name Thomas. He's given his name to Edison, to the apostle, to Jefferson, Mann, Jackson—even Thomas John Watson Senior, of IBM."

"And that's who you named me after?" There is awe in his voice.

"I told you I wouldn't just pick some crummy CEO," she assures him.

There is a pause, as they both stare into the cloudless sky.

"Do you like it?" she asks.

He pulls her up so that she's sitting in his lap. His arm across her back stabilizes them, and her dress spools out around them, drifting down the hillside. The colors hold the soft shadows of candlelight.

"I love it," he whispers, and he kisses her softly. The kiss is somehow hesitant, and all the more ardent for it; as if they have come, running, to the edge of the cliff—and now they pause, waiting for the unspoken signal that will plunge them down the precipice.

"I'm sorry that I let my father keep us apart for so long," she tells him. "If it comes to it—if I need to—I choose you."

And they kiss; and whether it is some built-in pathetic fallacy of the site or just the coincidences all lovers see, at that moment the wind knocks blossoms down around them until it is raining in all the colors of the rainbow.

————

She's sitting at his desk, primed and quivering in anticipation of the coming conflict, when her father comes in from the lab in the early hours of the morning. He flicks on the light and jumps when he sees her there.

"Jesus," he mutters. "Are you just sitting here in the dark?"

"Sort of," she admits.

"You are or you aren't," he reminds her, but there's no fire in it. His eyes track to the Line in her hands, and his shoulders come up in anticipation of a challenge. "Jesus Christ—"

"It isn't what you think," she protests, even though it is. His expression hardens, and she attempts to channel Despoina, to gain strength from the edge of fear. The illusion won't hold—this isn't the type of adrenaline rush she chooses. "I listened to what you told me. To your reasons that I had to stay offline. But you didn't listen to my reasons why I don't think I should—and I want to make the argument now."

"It's two o'clock in the morning, Gracie."

"I know, but...I have the courage now."

That seems to hit him, and some of the tension in his shoulders eases. His voice is sad as he asks, "Do you need courage to talk to me?"

"Sometimes," she whispers. She ducks her head, toying with the Line as an excuse not to make eye contact. She wonders if she imagines the whisper of sadness in the air. Can you feel emotions like air currents? Does disappointment taste of ozone, a building storm?

"There's so much here that you don't understand," her father says, gently.

"Because no one will tell me!"

"Maybe none of us understand."

She looks up in surprise. Her father has come around the desk; he places a hand on her shoulder. The gesture is awkward, untrained, but there is honesty in his eyes that feels foreign.

"He's all alone," she whispers. "You're all treating him like a *thing*, but he's a person, Dad. No one deserves...to be so alone."

"Are you asking permission, or forgiveness?"

"...I'm sorry. I just—being forgotten like that—I just wanted to talk to him, make sure he was okay. The first thing I did was ask him to come and talk to you."

In a second he seems to forget that she's in trouble, that Diving is against the rules. They're a team again, bound together in their desire to bring the AI home. She wishes, just for a moment, that that was true. "What did he say?"

"He said that he didn't belong to you," she says. "I'm sorry, Dad. I explained how difficult it was for you, but he wouldn't even discuss it."

"The issue is containment. It's all well and good to be able to find him when you Dive, but we need to figure out a way to contain him once he's found."

She wishes she could capture this moment—wishes she could be who he wants her to be. She almost doesn't speak, almost lets the illusion ride... But she is done with lies. She is so, so tired of lies. "Dad—I'm not helping you capture him."

He goes still. "What are you talking about."

"He promised not to ask me to choose between him and you, but that's exactly what *you're* doing. It's help you and betray him—or I'm a failure, I'm grounded, I'm not your daughter."

"This shouldn't be a case of divided loyalties." He gestures with one hand. "I'm your father," and then the other, "he's a thing I created."

"He's not a thing! You said yourself you created a person. He's as real as you or me."

"*It* is a damned security threat! Running around in the Waves—programming from the inside—with that kind of processing power—the government—you don't need to know any of this," he snaps, cutting himself off. "You need to know that I'm your father, and I have told you that the AI needs to be brought in. Period. Full stop. End transmission."

Gracie nods. She doesn't know where the calm comes from, the sense of steel in her spine. "Okay—I've heard you. And now you need to know I'm not going to stop seeing him —and I'm not going to help you capture him and lock him up in a cage so you can figure out how he ticks."

"You damn well are going to stop seeing him. He's not a bunny rabbit to be saved from the mean scientists!"

"I shouldn't need to save him from you at all! We don't conduct scientific experimentation on people. Ever heard of the Nuremberg Code?"

"Don't you dare lecture me on ethics!"

"Well maybe someone needs to!"

"Go to your room! Now!"

"Why? Because you don't have a good response?" she screams. She doesn't remember standing but she's on her feet. She cannot remember the last time she spoke to her father this way—cannot remember the last time she even raised her voice. Her throat is raw already, though she isn't sure she can blame all the tightness on the screaming.

"Because you are a child! A *child*! You think you understand the world, but you have no idea!"

"I know the difference between right and wrong," she says in a low voice, so he's the one who has to strain to hear her. She picks up the spare Line she was using and drops it into his hands. "Maybe you'd like me to tell you sometime."

CHAPTER TWENTY_

It's European history. They're studying the French Revolution, or more accurately its precursor, the July Revolution, which saw one French monarch replaced by another, and whether it should be considered a success or a failure. The teacher is talking about the sentiment on the streets of Paris and all of the different factions who had opinions about the revolution: the republicans, the Bonapartists, and the Legitimists, who all hated the new King but wanted wildly different resolutions to their complaints.

Mr. Delgadillo underlines a name on the projector screen. "So, if everyone will take out their Lines, we're going to go to a site where we can talk to average Parisian citizens from 1831, who will explain in more personal terms what it was like for them after the revolution ended. Yes, Graciela?"

She puts her hand down. "I don't have a Line."

"Very funny," Mr. Delgadillo says. "So if you can all navigate to this site— What, Graciela?"

She puts her hand down again. "I really don't."

"The daughter of the creator of the Line doesn't have a Line?"

"She's grounded," Khaiam cheerfully offers.

"Don't you mean Landed?" Derek jokes.

Her teacher sighs. "Go to the library and ask if you can borrow one of the ones in the computer lab."

"You aren't allowed to take those out of the lab," Terry says.

"No, *you* aren't allowed to take them out of the lab," Mr. Delgadillo corrects, "because they cost more than the daily limit on your daddy's credit card." There's a smattering of laughter. "I, on the other hand, am a teacher, which, while earning me little to no respect, does carry with it certain privileges. Gracie, you are holding up the class—go, go."

She hops to her feet and runs down the hall and around the corner to the library. It's quiet, just a few seniors using their free periods to study in the carousels in the corners. The shelves look sparse and functional after the opulent places she's visited during Dives—half of the books are full of graffiti, and the other half have never been opened; most people research online these days.

The library has twenty-five computers but only three Lines. Their school's zip code means that the high price tag on most Lines isn't a deterrent to their school population, and their small size and portability make them a high theft-risk. Mr. Delgadillo obviously sent the librarian a private message, because she's standing waiting with the Line, glowering.

"I don't see why he couldn't borrow one from Mr. Edgecombe," she snaps.

Gracie shrugs and holds out a hand.

"The tech lab has more than I do," she complains.

Gracie shrugs.

"Make sure you bring it back. Right after class. Not at the end of the day!" she insists as she reluctantly hands off the Line.

Gracie nods and hurries back to class. She had a bet going with Calista to see how many times she could use the library without speaking to Mrs. Gloor, and she's been keeping it up since. So far she's at thirty-two.

She caroms off the door jamb and into her seat, quickly plugging the Line into her tablet. Whatever idiot used it before her left their ID active on it, which makes her shudder—anyone could pick it up and Dive using the owner's face and preset sites. The sensors would have trouble reading the face because the calibrations wouldn't match the output, and the result would be jerky responses and a shoddy signal experience, but still. It's like leaving your empty body around for someone else to puppet. She quickly wipes the information and downloads her own, setting the Clear History mode to automatically wipe her details when she disconnects, in case she doesn't have time to reconnect to her tablet and manually wipe the ID.

While she's doing all this, her teacher is explaining the rules of the site they're visiting, and how to interact with the Mannies for the best user experience. Everyone slaps their sensors onto their temples and leans back in their chairs, keying in the address.

Paris rezzes into place around them. She's bombarded by the smells—rotten fruit, feces draining down the sewers, unwashed bodies—but they quickly fade. Educational but not overwhelming—she rolls her eyes. Heaven forbid the crowds of upper-class students be at all inconvenienced by the realities of the nineteenth century. Everyone's avatar has been adjusted by the site to include period clothing—Gracie thinks she must be some kind of maid or shop girl, since her dress is simple but sturdy. Khaiam drifts to her side, Matt and Ron with him.

"This is the worst field trip ever," Matt complains.

"Look, a prostitute!" Gracie points at a window.

"Where!" All three of them turn around. The Mannie opens a mouth full of rotten yellow teeth and waves. Her cleavage pushes out of a dirty corset, carefully PG-13, and there's a cluster of sores in the curve of her neck. Ron shudders.

"Come on, we have to find at least one person from each faction and write their names down," Ron says, and leads them all towards a Mannie in a butcher's apron who's sitting by the side of the road.

Khaiam starts chatting with the guy, and Gracie is impressed by the skill of the programming. His reactions are great, not wooden at all, and he only gets tripped up by their questions three or four times. Ron says it's freaky, tries to poke the guy in the face, and gets decked. Everyone laughs, especially when he lands in a pile of something disgusting, but the site programming doesn't let it stick to his clothes. They spend ten minutes trying to smear horse feces in each other's hair, laughing uproariously as it slides off.

Then Matt has the great idea to trade names with other groups, so they don't have to talk to as many Mannies. He tracks down Kathleen, who gives him two names, and then Gracie suggests that since the only faction they're missing is a Bonapartist, they could try going into the tavern called Napoleon's Horse. Khaiam tries to convince the bartender to serve them, but he just keeps saying, "Let's see yer francs first!" and no one can produce any.

A group message pings all their screens twenty minutes later, asking them to gather in the town square for an important announcement. They trail out, talking and laughing, and join their classmates in the square. There are about a hundred students there, so it must be a national site. In the center of the square some drama is unfolding between two Mannies, no doubt intended as an interesting dramatic reen- actment. She notices a few Mannies scattered through the crowd, too, probably programmed to cheer or jeer at appro- priate intervals.

"I say your coins are no good here! Take your business elsewhere!" one of them spits. He's a young man, with curly black hair and a solid build. She can't see his face, but she images he looks like the prince in a children's cartoon, all perfectly sculpted but a little too plastic. The man he's harassing is older, maybe fifty, with salt and pepper hair and a ratty moustache.

"You think I don't know what you fill your pies with?" the older man retorts. "And you with a club in your hands, breaking glass at the Louvre with your boys. What did it get you, hmm? Are you any less hungry—are you any less poor?"

"I'm less of a slave!" he says.

"Are you? One king deposed and another put in his place! All you've done is anger God."

"And what do you suggest? No kings at all?"

There's a brief pause, a glitch in the programming, before the old man continues. "I support Charles the tenth, the rightful king of France."

"Why?" the younger man asks. "What has he ever done for you?" He turns to the crowd, raises up his arms. "What have your leaders ever done for you?"

The old man stutters again. Someone in the back complains that the programming is awful. "He's the rightful king of France," the Mannie says.

"Aren't you tired of doing as you're told?" the young Mannie demands of a guy in the front row. He walks a few steps, addresses another kid. "Aren't you sick of being a slave to the rules?"

"Hell yeah!" The kid throws a fist in the air and is reprimanded by his teacher; everyone laughs.

"Look around you." The Mannie raises his arms and slowly starts to spin. There is something incredibly familiar about him, and Gracie pushes her way closer to the front of the crowd, staring. "This is a world that can be built from the ground up. It can defy their expectations. It doesn't need to be built up from the ruins of what's already there—there is no slate that needs to be wiped clean! It can be everything—and nothing—and it can be yours." He turns as he speaks, swiveling so he can see the whole crowd, and finally he's facing Gracie and she opens her eyes wide in surprise. It's Thomas. He winks at her. "In here you're a queen," he tells her, though the crowd no doubt thinks they're still being addressed. "In here you're a god. You can create, invent, design; you can risk everything and still have it all the next day. You can visit the squalor of splendor and bask in the warmth of privation, knowing all around you, everyone is choosing who to be. Imagine!" He throws his arms up again and addresses the crowd. "A world with no income disparity —a world without death—a utopia that can be created or discarded at your whim! And you're wasting it on *history lessons*?" He spits into the dust at his feet. "Don't play in the Waves—live in them. MY NAME IS THOMAS!" he yells. "And you're in my world now!"

Everything around her crystallizes; scent becomes sharper, vision more detailed, and her public browsing square disappears. From the gasps of her classmates, she's sure it's happening to them, too. People's avatars are transforming, shifting into more beautiful, stylized versions of themselves.

She can tell her Line has an active stim-pack where it didn't a moment before, and a quick glance through her permissions menu shows a complex ID hack that renders her not only able to enter adult-only sites, but turns her into a complete ghost in the machine—no one could track what sites she visits, or follow her through jumps unless she extends a tandem Dive invitation. The fact that he can do all this, make these changes from inside the Dive, is staggering—but the fact that he can do it to almost a hundred people simultaneously is arresting.

And the Mannies have disappeared.

The filler people, the bits of programming that normally flesh out the Waves, are gone. In their place are smoking shoes filled with piles of ashes.

Gracie runs through the crowd to his side. "What are you doing?" she asks, laughing, as she clings to his arm. He grabs the edges of her pinafore and pulls her into an exuberant kiss.

"You told me to stop hiding," he says with a shrug. "So I did."

Around her, her classmates are exploring their new inputs while the teacher tries to restore order to the chaos. Someone, no doubt a teacher from one of the other schools, storms towards them.

"Now see here!" he shouts. "I don't know who you think you are—"

"I'm the AI," Thomas says.

"This is...well, this is...vandalism!" he stutters.

"Is it vandalism to take off someone's old rims and replace them with newer models? Is it vandalism to give someone a much-needed makeover?" He turns to the crowd of teenagers, who suddenly find themselves holding goblets of wine or beer. "*Do you feel vandalized?*" he screams, and the crowd goes nuts.

"Way to appeal to the lowest common denominator," Gracie says.

"Just knowing my audience." He winks. "And now, if you'll excuse us..." which is directed at the apoplectic teacher. He takes her arm and teleports them breathlessly through the crowd, a strange kind of hopping that's accompanied by a rush of air, as if they're moving so quickly it can't be seen; once to reach the edge of the crowd, again to reach the street, again to a building top, again and again, until they're standing on top of a gorgeous larger-than-life plaster elephant, looking out over the streets of Paris. She leans against the basket on the elephant's back, stares down at the ghost city below.

"It's so quiet..."

"The Mannies made a lot of noise," he agrees.

"Why get rid of them?" she asks.

He shrugs. "They aren't real—don't need to be part of this place. We make it what it is, not them."

"But without them...won't it feel lonely?"

"I want to be able to know the truth from the illusion." He is plaintive, full of frenetic energy. She catches his hand and he squeezes it, but quickly releases it to pace the length of the elephant's basket.

"You're true," she assures him. He stops, turns back to face her.

"Are you sure?" he asks. He takes a step closer. "Do you believe that, or are you just saying it?"

"Of course I believe it—Thomas! Why would you ask that?"

He turns away again, sharply, wraps his hands over the edge. They're at least ten stories up, and she wonders what about their relationship equates so strongly with heights; why they always seem to be on the edge of falling. If only they could have a few normal days, a few more sunny afternoons.

"Not everyone thinks so," he whispers.

"Tell me?" she asks. She moves closer, runs a hand down his back. He turns his head a little, offers her a brilliant smile that quickly fades. He cannot get something off his mind.

"If you take something—say you take sugar, and you mix it with water, boil it until it becomes syrup. Does it stop being sugar? Does the fact that it became something new mean...the other thing is gone?"

She doesn't understand, but can tell the answer means the world to him. She wishes she knew what to say—she would gladly lie her way to another smile. "You want me to talk about sugar? I can tell you anything you want to know about solutions and mixtures and what makes them different. But no matter what I say, it wouldn't answer your question. Because you haven't asked it."

He nods, turns to face her. The light in his dark eyes is passionate, sparking. "Neither of us are very good at facing the world, are we?"

"No," she admits, "we aren't. But maybe if we each pick a direction, we can both face away and let the other guard our back."

He rests his head against hers, and she watches his body slowing down, coming back to her. She runs her fingers through the hair at the nape of his neck, pushes up his scalp and back down again.

"Tell me?" she asks.

"Look at the barricades," he says, pointing out across the city. "Can you imagine what it must have been like—to be so ready to die for your cause? A bunch of kids who'd never really seen the world, who knew in their hearts that the cards they'd been dealt were the wrong ones...who never saw death coming."

"Someday you're going to have to trust me," Gracie says. "If you really want to be together—if you really want to make this work—you're going to have to tell me just what exactly it is that you're hiding."

"Is it so wrong that I want you to know me?" he asks. "Just me. I keep telling you, this is the world where we choose who we are. What happens out there...it doesn't really matter. It doesn't define us."

"But it touches us," she says. "You know that it does." He won't answer. "I have to go—I don't want them to pull my Line. The Bends suck."

"They're still trying to figure out how to disconnect—I froze their exit points," he says, with a tentative smile. He wants this to please her but isn't sure it will. She can't help herself—she laughs out loud, though she knows she shouldn't encourage him.

"Unlocked Lines so they can play like kings *and* a free pass out of next period? They'll make you their God!"

He's relieved, looks out across the city again. "People like it here, don't they." She thinks she knows what he's thinking—this is all he will ever have, and he wants to believe this is a place he would choose for himself. She can't tell him the truth—that as much as she loves it here, it feels...constructed. There is so much power, so much freedom—the real world has never felt like that to her. It has always been her prison, and as much as that has been a negative in her account, it has also been a set value. A whole number. The real world. And yet within this fantasy, he stands as solid, as true, as impossible to control as the rest of her life—and therefore a part of it. And she could no more do him harm than she could step off the edge of a cliff.

"What is there not to like?" she asks, and he meets her smile with a brilliant one of his own. "Imagine the worlds we could build here if people took it more seriously—if we constructed societies instead of just playing games."

"Each person could have their own utopia," he suggests, "inviolate realms where only the invited could go. And there would be public sites where you mingle, meet, discuss other points of view—but at the end of the day, you could always go home."

"I love that. Every person in charge of their own world, and every world drifting and touching each other when you want them to... This is the only place a dream like that could ever happen."

"I wonder if your father had any idea what he was creating with this place. What did he hope to achieve?"

She shrugs. "I'm not sure—he doesn't talk about it much. I know he loved the virtual reality technology that other people had pioneered, but he thought it was being wasted on cheap entertainment. He was doing research into other applications of the tech, but I think the idea of translating the internet into a visual medium, into virtual reality, was actually Paul's. He's the more...I don't know, visionary. Dad's the brains, Paul's the heart."

Something flashes across Thomas's face—private pain writ large and public. "Like the Wizard of Oz," he jokes, trying to hide his slip. "So are you Dorothy, or am I?"

"Why won't you just tell me?" she demands, frustrated. There have been too many secrets, the path so obscured she is blundering down it with scratches on her arms and face, and she is tired of the pain.

"I suppose rightly I should be the Wizard," he says, ignoring her.

"Dammit, listen to me!" she yells.

"Graciela—don't," Thomas pleads, quixotically serious again. "Some questions you don't want the answers to."

"I'm so damn tired," she says, shaking off his hand, inured to his desperation by the force of her own. "If you trusted me—if you cared about me—"

"It doesn't matter how I got here," Thomas insists. "Graciela, I—I *love* you."

Her eyes fill with tears. How much has she wanted to hear those words, to speak them herself and know the truth in them. "But you don't trust *me* to love *you*."

"Do you?" he asks.

"I'm so afraid—what if you're right? What if whatever you're hiding is enough to drive me away? How can I let myself...when you're telling me you're just going to break my heart?"

"We never need to be anything but what we are here." He grabs her shoulders, his fingers tight around her arms. "Just let that world go. I'll never hurt you—it never needs to be anything but this."

She reaches up, holds his face between her hands. "But it does," she whispers. "Secrets always come out. And someday this one will come between us, and the years of lying will break whatever fragile beautiful thing we've built. Can't you see that? Can't you see I need to know?"

"Just let it go," he pleads. "Please, please, just let it go."

"I can't," she says. "Thomas...I am so goddamn tired of no one trusting me with the truth." She pushes backwards, falls through empty air. His outstretched hand, her name called on the wind, disappear mere seconds before her body should have hit the pavement ten stories below. He has let her go, rather than let her suffer the pain of a de-rez.

Her classroom reforms out of the fracturing pixels of Paris. It is eerily quiet, filled with the sounds of breathing. Her classmates' eyes are closed, expressions slack and empty. They are houses with the windows open and lights on, sitting empty in the twilight; or a television on mute in an empty room, pictures playing to no one.

CHAPTER TWENTY-ONE_

There's a knock on her bedroom door. She's been home alone for a few hours—her mother was already gone to work by the time Gracie got up this morning, but there was a note by the cereal reminding her that she was still grounded, and she was to come home sharply after school. She's been trying to study, but without a Line she can't work on any of her group assignments, so she's stuck finishing math and reading ahead for her English class.

"Come in," she says.

Her mother opens the door. There is nothing hesitant about her—it should be a welcome change from the tension she has been feeling with her father, but Gracie doubts this conversation will end well. Somehow her mother always manages to twist words in her favor, come out on top of every argument. Last night was the first time Gracie has won a debate with either of her parents, and it didn't feel particularly victorious—just left a sour taste in her mouth.

"Your father tells me that you went Diving despite being grounded," she says.

"And I'm not sorry," Gracie mutters, not putting down her pen. It took her twenty minutes just to find spare paper to do calculations on. Her hand hurts from clutching the slim metal tube.

Her mother's expression, if possible, tightens. "We did not raise you to be disrespectful, Graciela. Your private concerns about the nature of this," she waves a hand fruitlessly in the air, "*situation* are for you and your father to sort out, and have absolutely no bearing on your punishment. You will not go near a Line until we tell you that your grounding is lifted. If you do, I am sending you to live with your grandparents for a month."

"Maybe I *want* to go and live with *Abuela* and *Abuelo* for a month."

"*Dios mio*," her mother mutters. "I don't know what to do with you."

"Join the club," Gracie sighs.

"Look me in the eye and tell me that you think you were in the right," her mother says.

"What?"

"Hacking into your Line to change your age. Accessing adult-only content. Since you are so inclined to pontificate on the nature of right and wrong, here is your chance. You have two minutes."

"It's not that simple."

"A minute and a forty-five seconds," her mother says, looking pointedly at the clock on the wall.

"*Mama*," Gracie says, "would you please for once just listen to me?!"

"That is exactly what I'm doing."

"You're listening like a firing squad," Gracie snaps, but she presses on. "I'm not saying that I didn't make a mistake—I did! I get it. I don't think I shouldn't be grounded."

"And yet?"

"You said I had a minute and a half," Gracie challenges.

Her mother makes a gesture indicating Gracie should go on and closes her lips.

"I'm saying that taking my Line away doesn't feel like you're grounding me for that—it feels like you're trying to keep me away from Thomas. And I don't think that's fair—to him or to me." The words start boiling out, faster and faster, and she lets them fly; each one seems to leave her lighter. "You're acting like he's somehow the source of my disobedience, but I was on Urban Noir long before I met Thomas. The Waves are mine! They feel—they felt," she glumly corrects, "like they were mine. And I hate that there are places in them that I'm not allowed to go. It's like having a locked door in your own house and hearing people whispering on the other side!... I know you'll never understand. But it's the reason why I Dive on adult-only sites. Dove. Why I Dove. And I promise not to go on any of those sites again— not because I believe in arbitrary age restrictions, but because I get that it isn't worth the consequences, to me or to you and Papa, if I get caught. But I won't promise not to see Thomas again. I won't."

Her mother appears to genuinely consider her words— perhaps she's just shocked by how very many of them there are. Meek little Gracie, sweet little Gracie, Gracie who always does what she's told. She wonders if her mother is wondering how to get that little girl back. If Carmela liked that version of her better. There are days when she thinks it's the only version of herself anyone has ever loved —the lie.

"Your punishment was intended as a direct consequence for your behavior," her mother finally says. "If that isn't the message you're receiving, we are being remiss in our parental duties. So, I will ask your father to unlock the Surfaces in the house."

"So I'm allowed online?"

"As long as you aren't Diving. Yes."

"Okay."

"It's very nice that you approve, but this was never a negotiation," her mother clarifies. "This was your father and I acknowledging that perhaps our point had not hit home in the manner we intended. Furthermore," her mother says, sounding like an academic paper she's presenting to her colleagues at a conference in Hawaii, "this is not intended as approval, tacit or otherwise, of your behavior last night. Are we understood?"

The royal we. Her father doesn't have the guts to face her, but he is everywhere around her. "Yes, Mama."

"Good. Dinner is at seven. Set the table after you finish your homework."

"Yes, Mama," she whispers, and wonders why even in winning, she still somehow feels like she has lost.

———

Her father doesn't come home for dinner, so she spends most of the evening without access to the internet. As she's brushing her teeth for bed around eleven, the Surfaces in her room blink suddenly to life, painting the white walls with dreamy blue light. She wonders if this is where her father got the idea to pattern his interface after water—though on consideration, that was almost certainly Paul's idea. Any hint of creativity is usually Paul's—her father is a numbers man. The subheading of his biography should read, "a fatal lack of imagination."

She taps the Surface by the bathroom sink and opens her

homepage. Without the Dive interface it's just a website, with a frankly awkward user experience. She forgot how bad backwards compatibility is with sites designed for the Dive. Her cursor is a little dragon, and a series of toggles on the left side of the screen let her "take care" of her garden. The background graphics are nice, but it feels like a painting she wants to push her hand through to show how flat it really is. Her Surface is HD compatible, so there's a little sense of depth, but overall? Being a Surfer sucks.

She toggles on her voice activation settings and finishes brushing her teeth, then sends Thomas a ping. After thirty seconds her tablet flashes, but when she pulls up her chat interface she sees Khaiam is the one who's messaged her.

- Khai.the.Guy: Gracie! You ungrounded?
- Gracielass: Sort of. No Diving but Surfing's okay.
- Khai.the.Guy: Wow. I thouhgt you'd be out til you were 30, lol
- Gracielass: Me too.
- Khai.the.Guy: You see your boi in the news?
- Gracielass: ??
- Khai.the.Guy: The AI! Whazzis name.
- Gracielass: THOMAS??

She opens a new tab on her browser and brings up a news stream. Plugging in Thomas brings up hundreds of articles—it seems he's been busy since the afternoon. People across the world have been reporting sightings; her classmates and some of the others have been giving statements about the events in Paris, but it doesn't stop there. He broke up a financial conference and hacked all the attendees' Lines so they couldn't get offline; the story says they're all being "treated" for cases of the Bends, which Graciela thinks is a bit melodramatic. Another story swears he has hacked the individual Lines of over a hundred teenaged youth, giving them permanent stim-packs and adult-only content viewing privileges that "thus far, experts are unable to reverse." He reprogrammed a series of social media sites so they're fully malleable from *inside* the Waves—effectively giving users the same control he has, but only over their own pages. Gracie is reminded of the idea they discussed, each person with their own personal utopia, and the ability to visit the worlds of others.

And he is systematically attacking Mannies. Over fifty sites have reported processing errors and the disappearance of pre-programmed Manifestations. Three popular gaming sites have all but shut down as they try to recreate the damaged infrastructure, and the search engine Ask Bentley has switched to a Surf-only interface in an effort to head off the problem at the pass.

He is out of control, and Gracie isn't sure if it's brilliant or terrifying.

- Khai.the.Guy: Yeah, hes been hacking all over and crashing things. I heartd hes
- stoped other people form disconnecting too
- Gracielass: ....wow.
- Khai.the.Guy: Right?
- Gracielass: Is your Line still hacked?
- Khai.the.Guy: YEH! stim-pack and adult content. Dad tried to fix it but Mom said lets just buy a new one and dad said whats the point it'll just happen again. so far
- now, I get to keep it!
- Gracielass: He's really going to do it. A revolution.

- Khai.the.Guy: Is that what he wants?

She's distracted by another ping. She pulls up the second chat window and sees Thomas's name. He's hacked the program so the text swirls like waves, full of the oil-slick colors of a rainbow. *Show off.* She grins.

- Thomas: Where are you?
- Gracielass: At home. Landed, but they lifted the Surfing restriction.
- Thomas: Ah.
- Gracielass: You've been busy.
- Thomas: I thought you didn't want to talk to me.
- Gracielass: That's not fair.
- Thomas: No?
- Gracielass: So you're going to have your righteous revolution.
- Thomas: Maybe I'll remake the world in your image.
- Gracielass: :(No one would want that.
- Thomas: I would.
- Gracielass: Can you do a voice hack?

There's a long pause, and then Thomas's voice filters through her speakers, so warm and familiar it sends an ache through her chest. She curls up in bed, holding the tablet close to her head.

"Can you hear me?"

"Like you're right here with me," Gracie whispers.

"Are you angry?" His voice is hesitant, and she wishes she could see his face. She can picture it, though, and she closes her eyes to see him better.

"I don't know," she admits. "I miss you. Can that be enough for now?"

There's a long pause. "Sure," he finally says.

"Tell me about the conference. Did you really trap them all in the Waves?"

He chuckles. "You should have seen their faces. Total bewilderment. I wanted to hack their accounts and redistribute their money while I had them all in hand, but it's not my specialité." He pronounces the word with a fake French lilt and Gracie giggles.

"Maybe let's leave off cyber terrorism for now," she suggests. "Stick with promoting social change."

"You always do toe the line," he teases.

"Boring Gracie," she murmurs.

"Not to me."

"Maybe I'm not her when I'm with you."

"Isn't that what you want?"

"Yes," she whispers.

"Then come and see me," he says. She can picture his face so perfectly in this moment, the pleading that he tries to hide with a blasé tilt of his head. She wishes she could reach up and touch his hair, run her fingers down his arm.

"It's only for a little while."

There's a pause, and her imagination won't quite fill in the subtlety of the silence. "I don't like this," he finally murmurs. "You feel too far away."

"I'm not. I'm here." When he doesn't answer, she fills the silence with more words, struggling to sound upbeat and positive. "It won't be forever."

"I've gotta go—I've got an appointment with the president."

Gracie laughs. "You're kidding, right?"

"I'll catch you soon," he promises, and there's a click and then the sound of silence.

"Thomas?... Thomas?" She flicks her screen back to life, pushing herself up on one arm. Thomas has gone.

After a moment she brings back up her chat with Khaiam.

- Gracielass: Maybe. Yeah. Maybe he does want a revolution.

———

Time drifts. Without the distraction of the Waves, life is aimless; there are so very many *minutes* in a day. She spends her free time searching the news for signs of Thomas, making a map of his adventures in her mind. He invites her along, once or twice, but when she refuses to defy her parents, he grows taciturn. He denies her requests for another voice chat, instead leaving her half-finished notes on her homepage or chat pings that he answers a day later as if no time has passed.

Gracie feels...irrelevant. For so long she has been at the center of the unfolding drama, but her grounding has left her sidelined. For a few days, Angela constantly protects her from inquisitive classmates who want to know the secrets of the mystery AI, but when it becomes clear she is in the dark, the attention drifts away. The Waves are still buzzing with news of Thomas, but it is outside of her—just to the left, and straight on 'til morning. The adventure, once again, is passing her by.

Real life has a hard time comparing. Her newfound determination to make something of the friends Calista left her is the only thing that keeps her afloat. She follows Khaiam to games and practices, watches movies with Angela, even studies offline with Jaime. She counts panic attacks on her fingers and pills on her toes, until the empty yellow bottle calls her a coward. She knows she needs to refill the prescription, but she cannot bear another disappointed look from her mother. She has taken to eating in her room just to avoid the silent dinner table; her father is still working most nights and rarely comes home before she goes to bed.

On Saturday, she rolls the empty bottle of pills from palm to palm as she calculates angles of projection for a geometry project. She agreed to partner with Angela against her misgivings and received a text on Friday begging for help, which turned into doing the project by herself. She doesn't mind—the distraction is a welcome one.

A little before noon the Surface by her arm pings. She flicks the chat window open and sees an unfamiliar icon. A click reveals the username.

- CiaoBella999: Thank yoooooooooou oh my god what did u say?
- Gracielass: What did I say to who?
- CiaoBella999: KAIAM!
- Gracielass: About?
- CiaoBella999: YOU DORK! HA! i <3 u! were going out tomorrow! yay yay!
- Gracielass: You're going out? With Khaiam?
- CiaoBella999: Thank you thank yout ahnky out thankyou! Ha. Like u dont know

Quickly Gracie pulls up the main menu and fires a message to Khaiam.

- Gracielass: So, funny story. I think Bella is confused.

There's a long pause, and then her phone rings. She stares at it for half a second, willing it to go away. It rings again, Khaiam's name popping up as the song plays. She answers it with a shaking hand.

"I didn't even know these things could *make* calls," she jokes, but her voice sounds reedy and thin.

"I am *so* sorry, I was going to talk to you about it, I just didn't think she would message you and I was trying to find the right way to tell you..."

He pauses, thinking maybe she'll say something. When she doesn't, he continues. "I thought I should tell you in person, so I was going to try and drop by sometime today, but I hadn't gotten around to messaging you yet."

Another long pause. He continues in a rush, "It just kind of happened really fast, you know, she asked me on Friday after school, and I know I should probably have been expecting it because she did ask you to ask me to ask her to the dance and I never did, but we danced a bit at the dance and it was kind of nice... So, I don't know why I was caught off-guard, but I kind of was, and I sort of said yes."

A pause, even longer this time. His voice is soft when he says, "I'm not actually sure that I *don't* want to go. It's really not that big a deal. She's just kind of fun to be around, and...she makes me smile. I don't get a lot of that lately. You know...you know what it's like." He waits. "Gracie?"

She cannot speak through the lump in her throat. "Mm?"

"Say something."

Her hand is shaking. "I don't know what you want me to say."

He waits again, this time for himself. "Say...she wouldn't hate me."

She blinks away tears. "She wouldn't hate you," she says,

and means it. But it hurts that *she's* the one he's worried about. Not Gracie, not really. Just shadows and dreams.

"I know it's soon."

"It isn't. Not really." *But it is*, she wants to scream. Three weeks ago he was drunk on mourning, catching fireflies in the dark. Now he's smiling at his memories, taking tentative steps into something new, and all Gracie can think is, *Don't leave me. I can't be the only one.*

"Are...you sure?" he asks.

"I was just surprised," she promises, but her breath is tight in her chest and the pressure is building behind her eyes. "Listen, Angela has abandoned me to this geometry project, so I really have to get back to it."

"Oh. Okay."

"Bye," she says, not waiting for his answer before hanging up. She almost drops the phone, curls her hand against her chest to hold it close. She tries to remember breathing exercises, coping mechanisms, but the pain is everywhere. She lies down on the floor so there isn't far to fall, counts the legs of the furniture but keeps losing track. She can't breathe, she can't breathe, and there are tears in her eyes, and she wonders how somehow she is always *alone*, how easy it is to drown in silence. Her legs twitch and she wants to jump up, to run from the oppressive endless mourning, but her Line is gone and there's nowhere to run to. The world goes dark and spotted, and she curls up and sobs until she cannot breathe. She watches this, distantly aware that her reaction is out of step with what's happening, but she cannot stop the shaking.

Gradually she regains her breath. Wipes tears from her eyes, and then spills more down her cheeks. She shakes the numbness from her arms, touches the spot on her forehead where her Line would normally rest. She keys up her chat menu and hovers over it, but the only thing she can think of to say is "help me," and that sounds melodramatic. What would he do, anyway? What would he say? She drops the tablet on the floor.

She stands and drifts through the room. There's an electronic picture frame cycling through photos of her childhood. In almost all of them, Calista is by her side, matching smiles, arms entwined. She picks the frame up, swiping right, cycling faster and faster through the images. She does not want to forget. She wants to be better...but she does not want to forget.

She falls into bed, the frame clutched to her chest, her eyelids heavy and her irises burning from the tears. She does not want to be alone...

A little before dinnertime, the doorbell rings. Curiosity slips its fingers through the hair on Gracie's temple, rousing her from her half-slumber. She slips out of bed, comforter draped across her shoulders, and wanders out of her room and down the hall. At the top of the stairs she pauses; her mother has beaten her to the door and is standing with a steel spine, blocking the entry. There are two men in suits in front of her, and one of them is speaking with quiet authority.

Carmela shakes her head and cuts him off with a sharp chop of one manicured hand. "I'm afraid he won't be back for some time, a fact of which I have no doubt you are aware. I would appreciate if you didn't come back."

"Mrs. Neumann—"

"It's Dr. Sandoval."

"Of course, Dr. Sandoval," he smoothly corrects. His black suit is perfectly tailored, his tie just a little too slim to be fashionable. "Your husband has indicated his willingness to cooperate with our efforts. I'm sure—"

"Like I said. Feel free to speak to my husband at the lab."

The second man notices Gracie watching from upstairs; he smiles and waves, but there is something disingenuous in the action. She pulls the comforter tighter around her shoulders.

"Now, if you'll excuse me." Carmela slams the door in their faces.

She sighs and rubs her forehead. Gracie isn't used to seeing her mother vulnerable, but there is something in the slope of her shoulders that speaks to her exhaustion.

"Mom?" Gracie's voice is more tremulous than she intended.

Carmela whirls. "*Dios mio*—I didn't see you there."

"Who was that?"

"Nothing to worry about. How's steak for dinner? We have a new flank I want to try."

"Mom."

"*Graciela*. You worry too much. What are you doing, anyway? Are you sick?" The slight wave of her hand indicates that the only excuse for waddling around the house in a comforter is the flu.

"Maybe. No. Mom?" Gracie hesitates, sliding a hand over the banister. "Uh. I think I lost my medication."

"You *lost* it? How did you lose it?"

"I don't know!"

"You need to take better care of your things. *Tú te olvidarías la cabeza si no la tuvieras pegada.*"

"I don't lose everything!"

"Oh yeah? Those red gloves?"

"I was *six*."

"Aggg." She waves a hand again. Her father likes to joke that Carmela couldn't talk if you tied her hands together. "Fine, we'll go see Dr. Zhao tomorrow."

"Okay. Thanks." She turns to go back to her room and her mother interrupts her.

"Gracie?"

"Yeah?"

"How...are you?"

"You worry too much," Graciela answers, and goes back to her room.

CHAPTER TWENTY-TWO_

AT FIRST, SHE DOESN'T RECOGNIZE HIM.

Someone has finally captured a live feed of Thomas, and the news outlets are playing it on constant repeat. In the video he rezzes into a locked site where automated machines feed glowing threads of data into tight containers—a censor hub. Then, blinking into startled life, the room begins to fill with Divers. They have obviously been plucked from other sites—one man is wearing a Speedo, while a woman draped in snakes rips off her sunglasses and demands answers. Thomas snarls out a sermon on freedom of information as threads of data slowly begin to overspill their containers. The Divers grow panicked as they realize they can't disconnect. Thomas watches, amused, as the data fills the room like water. The Divers panic, knocking each other down in an ineffectual effort to escape; one by one they drown, screaming. Their corpses float for a moment in the blue light before blinking out of view. Thomas stands in the middle of it all, untouched, watching the camera, which he has encased in a protective bubble of air. The terrified reporter stutters out a question, rendered unintelligible by the Waves—and then the feed goes dead.

One of the things that makes it so hard for reporters to get a positive ID on Thomas is his constantly changing appearance. In this video he seems about thirty years old, with tanned skin and slicked-back hair. But Gracie has never had trouble identifying him until now, and the problem isn't his appearance. It's his eyes.

They're so cold.

The reports say that all of the affected Divers are upper management of censorship companies. None were hurt, though several claim they can no longer connect to the Waves. A few are being treated for psychological trauma, with one saying he'll never Dive again. The Waves are occupied territory. Some reporters call Thomas a revolutionary; some are using the terms "vigilante" or "terrorist." To most, he's a hero, but through it all runs the threat of unchecked power: no one can stop him. What will they do if he gets truly out of control?

What if he already is?

Gracie stands up; paces; sits down. She picks up her tablet and scans the chat, but Khaiam isn't online. Neither is Thomas, though she wasn't expecting him to be. She puts the tablet down, paces again. She needs to be there for him—needs to talk to him—but the obstacles seem insurmountable. Where will she get a Line? How will she justify the choice if —*when,* her cynical brain chimes in—she gets caught?

In a moment of panic, she flicks on the Surface on her desk and calls her grandmother. It rings five times before she answers. She only has three Surfaces in her house, despite Maxwell's attempts to outfit her with the latest tech; Gracie's grandmother still remembers the days when people *called* each other, as if a conversation where you cannot see the person's face brings anything but pain.

"Graciela! Aren't you looking good for a girl who's in so much trouble." She winks. She's standing so close to the Surface that Graciela can't see much other than her exaggeratedly large face. To make up for it, she shrinks the visual down.

"Hi, *Abuela.* Sorry I haven't called in a while."

"*Y asi se va,*" she says with a philosophical shrug. "Your mother has been telling me her side of things, but you know how that can be. Are you okay?"

"I don't know," she admits. She sits down in her chair, bringing one leg up and curling down arms around it so she can rest her chin on her knee. "I'm worried about Thomas."

"Thomas? Is that the boy you like?"

"It's the AI, *yaya.*"

"Ah, *si, si.* Good for you, eh? Everyone running around squawking about this and that, but you know I always say, the ones who care about the ones no one else has realized need caring about, they're the heroes."

"You've never said that before," Gracie says, but she's smiling.

"No? Well, maybe I've never had to."

"Can I ask you... I need some advice."

"And you come to me? Your mother would tell you that's a very bad idea."

"That's why I'm doing it," she says, and her grandmother laughs loudly. Her grandmother does everything loudly, everything with all of herself. Graciela wishes she could be more like that—could face the world so unafraid. She hopes she can learn how, with time, but she suspects a person has to be born fearless.

"I wish your problem was about boys. I'm very good with boys."

"It's about Thomas."

"You're worried because no one is treating him like you think they should."

"Sort of. But...I'm also worried...about him. He's been acting so differently since we haven't been able to talk. So angry."

"Hmm. What did he do?"

"He's trying to fix things, make the Waves a better place. He's always wanted that, but lately... It seems like he doesn't care so much who gets hurt in the crossfire. It's..."

"Scary?"

"Yeah. And I miss him so much, and then I feel guilty for being scared, and—"

"It all comes down to fear, doesn't it?"

"What do you mean?"

"He's afraid, *mi pequeña*. When we are angry, it is almost always because we are afraid of something. What do you think he is afraid of?"

"Losing me," Graciela says, thinking of his words when they spoke on the tablet. "Or...being alone. That the world he's in won't be able to compete with the world he can't follow me to."

"*Hay que ir*. So how do you make him unafraid?"

"I don't know. I think this separation is what's making him afraid, but I'll never be able to convince Dad to let me back online."

"Have you tried?"

"I'm grounded, *Abuela*."

"*Si*, for lessons you have hopefully learned. But your father cares about you, more than you think. And he cares about this Thomas, too. Talk to him."

"Lately it doesn't seem like we talk—we just yell."

"Then take a deeper breath."

Gracie smiles. "I like that."

"Good. Breathing solves many of our problems. Try it."

Graciela takes a deep breath and wonders how long it's been since breathing has been easy. "Thank you, *yaya*."

"You call me any time, *mi amore*. You call me even if nothing is wrong, okay?"

"Okay. Goodnight."

"Goodnight." Her grandmother smiles and turns her face away, trusting that Gracie will be the one to disconnect the call. But she watches, just for a little while, feeling the warmth of that place and using it to shore up her determination. She can do this. For Thomas, she can.

———

Gracie paces in front of her father's study. They've barely spoken since their last argument—he's been working so much it hasn't been hard for either of them to avoid each other. Tonight he came home while dinner was still on the table, and helped himself to a plate while Carmela talked about the latest attempt to perfect veal and their ongoing difficulty with the fat ratio. The health board is on their case about how it's immoral to deliberately create unhealthy meat, and the company is trying the tried and true "nanny state" defense. Graciela tuned out and left early, heading up to her room.

But now her grandmother has sent her on this quest, and she is determined not to fail. Let her be fearless. Let her find a way.

Finally, she knocks on the door.

"Mm?" her father calls, and she opens the door and steps inside.

Her father is working on something, but he waves the Surfaces into privacy mode as she steps in, blurring out the details. "Oh, Gracie," he says, like he's slightly surprised to find she still lives in the same house.

"Do you have a minute?" she asks.

"If it's quick."

"It's...um... It's about Thomas."

"I really don't have time for—"

"Have you seen the news?"

Her father sighs. He rubs the bridge of his nose, hard, as if he can scrape away any unpleasantness. Finally, he taps the Surface closest to him and brings up the newsfeed. They watch it silently. No one speaks for a minute.

"What is he thinking," he finally says, clearing his throat. "I'm sure that won't help." The words seem more for himself than for her.

"I'm...worried about him," she admits. "He won't answer my pings—he doesn't like to talk when I'm not online. I think...I'm just..."

"Just say it."

Gracie sinks into a chair across from her father, bringing her knees up to her chest like she did when she was a kid. She used to sit here for hours, watching him work, marveling at the speed at which his stylo could race across the Surfaces. It feels like a long time ago. "I know what it feels like to be angry, and lonely. To feel like you're losing it all. If I could talk to him, I could calm him down."

Her father sits down across from her, watching her with a pained expression. "Is that what the two of you have in common?" he asks. "Pain?"

"I don't know," she whispers. "He won't tell me. *You* won't tell me."

"Hmm." He rubs his nose again, speaks almost to himself.

"What have we done wrong, that our sixteen-year-old knows so much about pain?"

"Papa. That isn't your fault."

He looks at her, and she almost jumps up, runs around the desk and throws herself into his arms. She wants to tell him that it will be alright, that no parent can protect their children forever; but before she can, he stands up, clears his throat, and breaks the moment. "I'll talk to your mother."

"You will?"

"How long have you been grounded, anyway?"

"Two weeks, almost."

"Mm. Fine." He turns away, bringing his screen back to clarity. She is dismissed by the hard planes of his back.

"Thank you—" she says, almost a question. But he doesn't answer.

———

Her mother brings her Line upstairs an hour later.

"Don't stay up too late," she admonishes, dropping the Line into her daughter's hands.

"I won't."

And that's it. No warnings, no condemnation. Her mother leaves the room and Gracie is alone, free again to slip away from the world. It feels...too easy. Though her victory seemed to come at the expense of her father's exhaustion, she thought her mother would throw roadblocks up. It isn't right —this isn't how her life normally goes. Everything feels just a little bit off, a sense of disconnect that fills her with dread. Yet she knows she cannot resist the lure of the Line. Even with his new and frightening aspect, Thomas is *hers*. She will not abandon him any longer.

She brings the Line up and slips it into place with trembling hands. Lying down on the bed, she stretches her toes and gets comfortable, drawing out the moment for reasons she can't quite touch. She plays with her settings, putting on Mallory's skin but with her own face and hair. There's a strange feedback loop when she adjusts her avatar settings, but she can't figure out what it is and it doesn't seem to be affecting the connection, so she finally gives it up as a mystery. More white noise. At last she closes her eyes and presses the button to connect. The world slips away with the ease of a sigh.

She's in her Homepage. The sky is dark, stars twinkling through the gaps in a cloudy sky. The air is charged, a storm somewhere on the horizon. She wiggles her fingers and toggles a flare of data into the air, her standard greeting for Thomas. At her back the fire is warm, golden, and the cottage smells like apple pie; in front of her everything is dark, windswept, cool. The only sound is the crackle of the flames and the faint screech and call of the dragons outside.

She steps out. She lets her eyes drift closed, lets the wind whip her hair into her face. There is something intensely relaxing about being buffeted by the wind, as if she is saying, *Have at it, world,* standing calm and still in the face of the storm. In the dark, something shrieks and wings beat—she holds out a hand as one of her dragons swoops out of the sky. It dive-bombs her, roaring, and as she throws her arms up to protect her face it rakes its claws across her inner arm.

"Danny! Stop!"

"It doesn't recognize you."

She spins at the sound of the voice behind her. He is standing in the doorway; the light behind him turns his face into shadow, but she doesn't need to see him to know who it is.

"Do you think it will forgive me?" she asks.

Thomas shrugs. "Who knows. You haven't bothered to make it smart—that might work in your favor." He disappears inside the house, and Graciela follows.

In the light she can see that he's wearing a new face—skin like birch bark, with hair made of leaves and twigs. The effect is alien but lovely, different from anything she's seen him do before. He's wearing jeans and a business shirt with the top button undone, casual and formal all at once.

"I missed you," she says, but he turns away, slinging his long, lean body down on one of the rickety chairs.

"I've been busy." He shrugs.

"I noticed." She presses a hand against the scratches on her arm; they're bleeding, but she can't get the stim-pack to turn it off. She turns away, drifting over to the window. She's startled by a flash of light in front of her face—the fireflies she made for Khaiam are still here, glittering in the firelight. It's beautiful, and she's struck by the simplicity of the moment, the loveliness of it. "Look," she whispers.

"Hmm?" He glances over, and she catches his eye with a brilliant smile.

"Fireflies," she breathes, and makes eddies in the air so the fireflies dance. She laughs in delight and notices a thawing in Thomas's cold exterior.

"Didn't you program them?" he asks.

"I forgot," she admits. "Sometimes it's hard to remember that everything goes on without me."

Thomas ducks his head, angry again. "That's impossible to forget."

"Thomas," she whispers. He doesn't meet her eyes. "Look at the fireflies."

He stands, furious energy in motion, and paces away from her. "I don't have time for fireflies."

"But you came."

He sneers. "You call, I come. Isn't that the game we play?" He frowns, suddenly looking at her for the first time tonight. "What is that?"

"What?" She looks behind her, sees nothing; when she turns back he's stepped closer. He's staring at something up and to her left, but when she tries to find what he's looking at there's nothing there.

"Some kind of—" He reaches out, twirls his fingers and pulls. There's a snap in the air, a noise like something breaking.

Her father appears in the cottage.

Outside, there's a flash of lightning and a crack of thunder. The storm clouds break overhead, the rain falling so hard and fast it obscures everything; the garden, the trees beyond, even the dragons disappear in mist.

Inside Graciela is silent, stunned, staring. She cannot reconcile a world that has Thomas and her father in it. It feels like everything is falling. Everything falls.

"Maxwell," Thomas says, his tone challenging.

Her father hesitates, perhaps unsure what to call Thomas, and settles for a nod. "It's good to finally meet you."

"Was this your idea?" Thomas asks Gracie.

"No!" she gasps.

"I programmed a tracking link into her Line," Maxwell says. "I decided it was high time you and I had a conversation that wasn't filtered through my daughter's infatuation."

"Infatuation?" Thomas raises an eyebrow. "Should I be flattered?"

Gracie turns away to hide her furious blush, tears in her eyes. He couldn't be here—he couldn't. There was nowhere—nowhere left to run to.

"You *should* be taking all of this much more seriously. Your actions have consequences—I'm sure you're aware that the Department of Defense has labeled you a terrorist attack. Terrorism! My life's work, terrorism!" Maxwell yells. Gracie raises her head, horrified, but Thomas intercepts before she can speak.

"I'm no work of yours," Thomas snarls. Then he pulls himself up, projecting an aura of calm that fools no one. "And I'm not afraid of the Department of Defense. They can't touch me."

"Every teenager thinks they're invincible," Maxwell says with a roll of his eyes. "What I'd like to know is why you seem so solidly fixed in the adolescent stage of development."

"Is that why you came here? To insult me?"

Maxwell sounds genuinely puzzled. "It isn't an insult—it's a legitimate question. You have chosen to present as a masculine adolescent. Occasionally your age shifts older, but you always return to the adolescent personification, and for some reason you are fixated on my daughter, which is an indicator of adolescence not just because of her own age, but because of the relative immaturity of chasing her around the Waves while ignoring the responsibilities—"

"Are you done?" Thomas interrupts. "How do you live with this?" he directs at Gracie, whose arms are wrapped protectively around herself.

"I am not done," Maxwell snaps. "You are putting your own existence in jeopardy. You need to cease your manipulations of the Waves before you chase everyone off the system entirely!"

"So that's what you're afraid of," Thomas says. "That one of your inventions will ruin the other."

"Frankly yes, though I'm surprised to see you admit that you are, in fact, an invention."

"Oh, I'm an invention—just not yours."

"What on Earth does that mean?"

"It means you have no jurisdiction over me. No one does. So take your lectures," Thomas waves a hand, and Maxwell's avatar freezes in place. "And your indictments." He prowls closer, and the warmth seems to leech from the air. "And go the HELL AWAY!" He snaps his fingers and Maxwell de-rezzes, disappearing in a hail of icy shards. A few hit Gracie, but she hardly notices.

"Gracie?" Thomas whispers. She doesn't answer.

He touches her shoulder cautiously, but she flinches away. Her shoulders are shaking.

"I'm not angry," he promises.

"I am!" she screams. There are tears in her eyes, but she's managed to stop them from spilling. "He shouldn't have come here! He doesn't have the right!"

"I thought you were on his side," Thomas admits.

"He isn't supposed to be here," she stammers. "He isn't supposed to come here. Not here. This isn't supposed to happen here." She can't catch her breath—everything is too loud, too hot. The fire feels like a furnace at her back. She tugs on the neckline of her shirt, trying to breathe.

"He's gone," Thomas soothes, though there's an edge of confusion to the words. "I won't let him back in. I can adjust the security settings, make sure that even with a tandem Line—"

"You don't understand! This is *hers*, it's *hers*." She hides her face in her hands, willing the shaking to stop. He tries to put his arms around her, but she throws him off, gasping for breath.

"What's wrong?" Thomas cries. "What is it?"

"I can't breathe," she whispers. It's the loudest sound she can make. "Jesus, I can't *breathe*." She runs out of the room, which suddenly feels suffocating and small. The storm outside is in full swing and she falls to her knees in the dirt, letting the wind lash her, letting the rain wash it all away. She feels somehow that she has failed Calista; that she has let her memory be drawn into all this conflict. Ruined it somehow. "I'm sorry," she whispers. She tries to toggle off the heat sensors on her stim-pack but whatever Thomas has done has frozen her controls; the rain is freezing cold. She shudders, grateful to blame her trembling on something other than yet another panic attack. *Not here. They aren't supposed to find me here.*

After a minute Thomas follows her outside. He sits on the ground next to her, heedless of the muck and the cold.

"I'm sorry," Gracie whispers again.

"I didn't know..." Thomas says, and Gracie isn't sure how much of anything he knows, but the way he looks at her feels like he understands.

"It doesn't usually happen here," she says. There's no need to wipe tears from her eyes—the storm takes care of that.

"Can I help?" Thomas asks. After a long pause Gracie sidles closer, and he puts a tentative arm around her shoulders. When she leans in, he draws his grip tighter, clutching her against his side and wrapping the other arm around her, too. He runs a soft finger across the dragon scratches, and the pain vanishes.

"I missed you," Gracie whispers.

"I missed you, too," he says. "Like a heartbeat. You have no idea..."

She tilts her head up and he catches the gesture, kisses her gently. She's still trembling from the cold, but he's hiked his body temperature, and it's almost like snuggling against a heat lamp. The sensation of his lips on hers, so warm and gentle, is amazing.

When she pulls away and leans her head on his shoulder, drops of rain sizzle against his heat.

"Thomas...aren't you worried at all? That they're going to hurt you?"

"Not really," he admits. "They haven't found a way yet."

"That doesn't mean they won't."

"Are you scared for me?" he teases.

"Yes," she says, earnestly, and the smile fades from his lips—though not from his eyes.

"Then I'll be more careful."

"Really?"

"I just want..." He sighs and leans his head against hers, looking out across the rain-drenched garden. "I want this to be the kind of world you would be proud to live in. The rest of it—it's secondary."

"I like what you did with the social media hacks. It's like that idea we were talking about—the utopias."

"You gave me the idea."

"No—that was all you."

There's a short pause. He strokes her arm, dipping his chin against her hair. "You didn't like something."

She shrugs, knocking her head accidentally against his chin. "Sorry," she laughs, and he smiles.

"Good thing I can't bite my tongue off," he complains, laughing. When they finally settle back into a comfortable pose, or as comfortable as they can get in the wind and the rain, he nudges her to keep going.

She scrunches up her face. "The...censors."

"They were bad people."

"It scared me," she admits. "I think it scared a lot of people, and fear...that's what makes people hurt things. I don't want anyone to hurt you."

"I'm really not sure they can," he says, with a glimmer of curiosity.

"...Thomas?"

"I hate it when you say my name that way. It means you're going to ask something I won't like."

"What did you mean—when you told my dad that you weren't his invention?"

"Will you come build your utopia with me tomorrow? I want to have at least a hundred done before I start allowing interconnectivity."

She laughs and shakes her head. "You know, I think I would have been disappointed if you'd actually answered me. I might not have believed it was you."

"Just let us have a little while," he whispers. "I know you need to know. I know...I need to tell you. But I don't want to let this go. Okay? Just...a little while."

"Okay," she whispers. "Just a little while."

And she kisses him and lets herself put the mystery down...

For just a little while.

CHAPTER TWENTY-THREE

At school on Monday morning Gracie hovers by her locker, trying to kill enough time that she won't run into Khaiam. His date was last night, and she isn't sure if she can handle another emotional confrontation in the same twenty-four hour period. She fell asleep in Thomas' arms last night and woke up with the shape of her Line imprinted on her forehead.

When she came downstairs for breakfast her father was standing in the kitchen, making notes on a tablet as he ate cereal like it was a frustrating distraction. When they saw each other they both froze, staring across the ever-widening gulf. She didn't want to be the first to speak, but as always, her resolve was not as strong as his.

"So are you taking my Line away?"

"I should."

"Are you?"

"I should send you to live with your grandparents."

"Are you?"

"He's a goddamn terrorist!" Maxwell yelled. He slammed the bowl against the counter, shattering it. Gracie jumped back, but not before a slim white shard sliced a hard line across her upper arm. Her mother flew into the room, yelling.

"*Aie! Ustedes dos! Sinceramente, no sé qué esperas que haga con esto.* It's seven o'clock in the goddamn morning, can we have *five minutes* of fucking peace?" When Maxwell started to speak, she slammed her hand down on the counter. "No! Enough! Okay? Enough, both of you! Honestly, you would look in the mirror and not know yourselves as each other. Graciela, get your bag, I'm driving you to school."

So Gracie had left her parents arguing quietly and gone upstairs to get her bag. It wasn't until she was at school that she realized she had missed breakfast, but by then anxiety had robbed her of an appetite anyway.

"Hey Gracie." She jumps, caught unawares, and relaxes when she turns to see Angela.

I actually prefer Graciela, she thinks. She isn't sure why she can't speak the words out loud. "Hey."

"Ouch—what happened?" Angela points at Graciela's arm; she looks down in surprise. She'd forgotten about the cut —her jacket had been covering it on the drive over, but when she hung that up in the locker, her t-shirt left it exposed. It looks nasty. She rubs a finger over it as Thomas had done with the dragon scratch, and for half a second, she's surprised that it's still there.

"Oh—uh." She blinks, distracted and trying to find her way back to the conversation. "My dad broke a cereal bowl, and it went everywhere."

"Shrapnel. You could completely call it your war wound."

Graciela snorts. "Yeah, that's just my banger lifestyle."

"Who's a banger?"

Graciela winces and turns to see Khaiam jogging up to them. So close. Though maybe this is a good thing—she can use Angela as a buffer. "Rock on," she says, flashing her bloody arm at him.

"Ew, gross. What did you do?"

"Pottery mishap. How was your weekend?" She's proud of how smooth she sounds, like it's no big deal. *How was your weekend? Did you move on and forget me? I fell apart, over and over, and you weren't there.* But that isn't fair. How can he be there when she keeps him in the dark?

"It was good. Bella and I went to the movies—saw that new one where you get to be secret agents. She stabbed me in the back five times."

Angela snickers as Graciela closes her locker, and the three of them start walking to class together. "That sounds like a *terrible* date," Angela says. "Who stabs a guy they're trying to impress?"

"I like a girl with character," Khaiam says with a shrug and a grin.

"Calista sure had that," Angela agrees. There's a short, choked silence, and then she gets a stricken look on her face. "Oh, God, was that completely uncool of me? I didn't mean to completely make a thing."

"No, no, it's fine." Khaiam puts an arm around Angela and squeezes. He always has been good at setting people back on course. No wonder everyone is half in love with him. "You're right, she did. It's nice to hear her name sometimes."

"Yeah," Graciela murmurs, through the tight knot in her sternum. "It's nice."

————

At lunch Khaiam corners her again, this time without Angela to provide a buffer. "You, me, art history. I am going to make you pass this test if it kills me."

"After school? I can't."

He takes her books; she gives him a weird look, and he points at her arm, which makes her smile and acquiesce. She wonders when they started being able to communicate like this, with gestures and familiarity. She wonders if they were already starting to become friends, before, and it was just so overshadowed by their love for her that neither of them noticed.

"Are you...going out with Angela?" he asks. He tries to make it casual, but he's glancing at her out of the corner of his eye. She shoves him with her good arm.

"No. I'm...um..." She could tell him. About Thomas. But what if he didn't understand? "She's really nice. I think I'm just kinda straight."

"You must be such a disappointment to your parents," he says with a sigh, and she laughs.

"Shut up. That's only funny if it's not true."

"Oh, please. Your parents adore you."

"Says the guy whose parents have an altar to him in the living room."

"It's not an altar! It's a few trophies. Wait, why I am defending myself? Of course my parents adore me, I'm adorable." He grins widely and she laughs again, shaking her head.

"You're adorkable."

"I'll take it. So, what are you up to?"

"I'm...uh...gonna go talk to Paul, actually."

"Calis—Dr. Armstrong?" Khaiam corrects himself.

"Yeah. This...weird thing happened." She decides in a split second to tell him. Maybe not everything—she isn't ready to hear if he doesn't think she should be dating Thomas, if he doesn't take it seriously, or treat him like a person. But she can tell him the rest. "Dad told me I could go

Diving because I was worried about Thomas—well, you know, everything that he's been doing. But it turned out it was just a ruse so *my dad* could talk to Thomas, and it was the weirdest thing ever. He—Thomas, not my dad—he said that he was an invention, but he wasn't my dad's invention. And Dad seemed really confused."

"The mystery deepens," Khaiam says, sounding genuinely intrigued.

"All this time I thought there was some big secret Dad hasn't been telling me. But I think maybe he hasn't told me because he doesn't know."

"But you think Dr. Armstrong does?"

"Maybe. It's worth a try. I just—I hate not knowing. I feel like—I'm gonna get blindsided."

"Want me to come?"

"To the lab?" Graciela asks in surprise.

"Why not?"

"Uh—I—yeah. Okay. Sure—thanks."

"You know...sometimes you act like you're surprised I'm your friend." Khaiam hands her back her books as they reach her locker. She takes them, biting her lip for a moment as she decides what she wants to say in response.

"I guess...sometimes I am."

———

The two friends leave school together and take a bus down to the lab. It's a long trip, and Khaiam insists on going over art history flashcards, much to Graciela's dismay. Finally, she puts her hands over her ears in despair.

"Can we talk about something else? Anything else. How's Bella?"

"Ouch. Talking about Bella is preferable to art history?"

"You're right. Let's go back to art history."

"Wait, no, that's the insulting one."

"I'm kidding. I'm mostly kidding. ...She just doesn't seem like your type."

Khaiam shrugs. "I don't have a type. I like people."

"You do," Graciela acknowledges. "You're really good at that."

"Liking people?"

"Trust me. It's a skill."

"So, what's our plan?" he asks. "Good cop, bad cop?"

"No. Please no."

"I can do bad cop!" He twists his features into a dark grimace and leans into her personal space. "I said do you want trouble, huh, punk?" he snarls in a truly horrible gangster accent.

"If you don't watch it, I'm going to fire you as my sidekick," she warns.

"Why am I the sidekick?"

"Sorry, I don't make the rules."

"But actually," he says after a smiling pause. "What are you going to ask him?"

"I'm thinking I try the whole 'Thomas told me everything' line and see if that works."

"Nice."

"Thanks. I don't really have a Plan B, though."

"Try crying?"

"You are so sexist."

"Fine, *I'll* try crying."

"Deal."

"Oh, crap, this is our stop!" Khaiam hits the button but he's a second too late. They get off at the next stop and walk back four blocks. The weather is good; autumn is turning to winter, but it isn't raining, and it's warm enough Graciela has her jacket unbuttoned. The two make their way through the rolling hills of the tech campus and up to the main doors, where Graciela shows her ID to get them through security. They both have problems with their tablets passing the check (thanks to hacks Graciela has done on both of them over the last year) and end up leaving them at security rather than going through the whole process of having them vetted against corporate espionage.

"Shit. I mean, shoot. I mean, I thought of a problem," Graciela hisses as they walk down the long white hallway towards the lab.

"What?"

"My dad."

"...Will be at work," Khaiam says. "How did you not think of that?!"

"How did *you* not think of it?" she counters.

"Um—I could pull the fire alarm?"

"What? No! Jeez." Gracie takes out her phone and pulls up a program to anonymize the call, then clicks through to another layer and brings up a hack to dummy the signal so it seems to come from a specific number. Khaiam watches over her shoulder, amazed.

"What does that do? How did you do that? Why do you even *have* that?"

Graciela shrugs. "I like to play with programming." She dials her father's number, and when he picks up, she puts on a smooth southern drawl. "Yes, hello, is this Mr. Neumann? Oh, I'm sorry, Dr. Neumann," she smoothly corrects when he barks his title at her. She winks at Khaiam. "Well, it's the darndest thing, I don't know how in Creation it happened, but I am afraid I have you double-booked for your cleaning next week. Is there *any* chance you could come by today? You would just be saving my bacon. Now? Oh, you are such a dear. We'll see you in about half an hour? Thank you, sugar." She hangs up and curtseys. "And that is how it's done."

Khaiam grabs her and drags her into a nearby lab as the door to her father's lab opens and he comes out. They hide just under the window, trembling, as his footsteps echo past them and down the hall.

"And that's how it's done," Khaiam whispers, doing one of his soccer victory dances. Graciela grins.

"Well, you just saved my bacon," she says in her southern accent.

"You should be an actor. It's eerie. Also, I think you go to the same dentist I do."

"Dr. Danvers?"

"Yeah!"

"Weird!"

"After you?" Khaiam opens the door and they both exit back into the hall, straightening their clothes as if they just hid in an exhaust vent instead of a mostly empty lab kept immaculately dust-free because the facility houses sensitive electronics.

Graciela leads the way, taking a deep breath before opening the door. Finally, after all these months—her questions will be answered.

The lab is busy and full of unfamiliar faces. Men in suits seem to be cataloguing bits of equipment, while people in lab coats take photographs of the equations scattered around the room. She recognizes a few of them as lab techs who work with her father when he needs extra help for an update launch, but most are strangers.

"What the hell?" Khaiam whispers. All eyes are on them, standing in the doorway like idiots.

"What the hell," Graciela agrees.

"Graciela—Khaiam," Paul says with real surprise. "What are you *doing* here?"

Most of the people go back to work at that acknowledgement, though a few still have their eyes on the teenagers. One woman takes out a phone to make a call—Graciela feels paranoid thinking it might be about them, but there is something eerie in the calm action happening around them, and she cannot shake the feeling that they've made a terrible mistake.

"We want to talk to you," Graciela says.

"Your father isn't here—he just stepped out."

"I know—we're here to talk to *you*."

"I'm really very busy." He glances over his shoulder like something might jump from the nonexistent shadows. *Lie*, Graciela thinks.

"It won't take long."

His fingers sketch twitchy patterns in the air, but he bobs his head in agreement. "Fine, fine." He ushers them through the chaos and into one of the testing rooms. It's designed to have little to no sensory input, so they can test reactions to the Waves without outside interference. As soon as he closes the door they're wrapped in silence.

"What are those people doing?" Graciela asks. She knows it isn't what she's here to learn, but she can't help but feel the need to know. "Who are they?"

"It's fine, nothing to worry about." *Lie.* Though it's so obvious it practically isn't worth noting.

"Fine." She crosses her arms and squares her shoulders, taking more comfort than she expected to at Khaiam's quiet presence at her back. "It isn't why we're here, anyway. We're here because of Thomas."

Paul looks like a cornered rabbit. His eyes slide to Khaiam and back to her; he runs a hand through his hair, sending it into wicks and whorls. "I really think you should be talking to your father—"

"I talked to Thomas," Graciela says. "He told me everything."

Paul's intake of breath is sharp enough it might be characterized as a gasp. He stares at her, then at Khaiam, searching their faces for something. "I..." He stammers. "I don't know what you're talking about. You need to leave." He takes a large step towards the door but Khaiam moves to block him.

"You obviously do," Khaiam says.

"You shouldn't be here. The Department of Defense—your father—you need to leave," Paul says again. There's a desperate pull to his shoulders. *He's cracking. This is it. My answers.*

"You need to admit the truth!" Graciela snaps. She takes a step towards Paul, and the older man retreats. The power should feel good, but instead it leaves a terrible taste in Graciela's mouth. This man taught her how to ride a bicycle; he said it was a tragedy that her parents hadn't taught her and took both girls out for a day of scraped knees and windswept hair. It was the day she fell in love with speed.

"You don't know what you're saying—you don't—" He buries his face in his hands, scrubbing as if he can clear the air and make the teenagers disappear. When he lifts his head and they're both still present he gives them a begging look. "What...did it tell you?"

Dammit, just say it. "*He* told us everything."

"That *thing* is not a person!" Paul snarls. Graciela takes a step back, shocked at the look of animosity on a face so made for kindness. "It is a menace and a danger, and if you had *any sense* you would stay the hell away from it! You hear me? You stay the hell away from it!"

Graciela doesn't realize she's stepping away until her

back hits Khaiam's shoulder; he reaches out and takes her hand.

"What *happened* between you two?" Khaiam asks.

"Go home," Paul says, and his shoulders seem to deflate; the anger is gone as quickly as it appeared, and he is just Paul, a half-broken man who has lost the spark that made him more. "Just go home."

Khaiam turns as if he might leave, but Graciela squeezes his hand, forestalling him. "I can't do that. You act like I could walk away from all this, but it's too late. You think I'm in danger? Then *that's on you*. If something happens to me, it's because of *your* lies. Can you live with that?"

His eyes lift to meet hers, and Graciela can almost see his thoughts playing out, a time-lapse video of clouds moving through a blue sky. He cannot bear for her to hurt, even now; more for the memory of his daughter than for her, but the love is still there, buried somewhere under the grief. And the guilt? There seems to be that in spades.

He sighs and closes his eyes. "So help me God," he whispers. And then he opens his eyes, and opens his mouth to speak—

The door flies open, hitting Khaiam in the back and knocking him a few steps forward. His shoulder hits Graciela and she turns to face this new threat. Standing in the doorway are the two men in suits who came to the house over the weekend. The one who smiled at her does so again; and again, there is nothing kind in the gesture.

"Graciela Neumann? I'm going to need you to come with me."

"What the hell do you think you're doing?" Paul demands. Khaiam is half between her and them, but they expertly maneuver between the two friends.

"Who are you?" she asks. Everything is in chaos. One of

them is replying to Paul, spitting out jargon about the Home-land Security Act while the other grips her upper arm and practically pulls her off her feet.

"We're with the Department of Defense. We have a few questions for you. If you'll just come this way?"

Suddenly the room is full of people, and Khaiam's hand is ripped out of hers as someone steps between Paul and Gracie, holding him back with one hand as he yells—first at them, and then her name as she stumbles out of the lab.

"Hold on—wait—" she stammers, but no one is listening. A second woman in a suit has her by the other arm, and she is too bewildered to quite understand what's happening except that Khaiam has started shouting her name, and someone is holding him back, and everyone in the lab seems to be shouting or shoving, and she still can't quite process what's happening.

"This way," one of them says to her, in the soothing tone an adult who doesn't have children thinks is appropriate for a kid at any age.

Graciela feels a shiver of fear, and then over that a grim determination. She will not be pushed, she will not be led. She is Mallory, she is Desponia, she *does* know how to be brave and strong and wild and free. With a snarl she snaps her shoulder forward, throwing all of her weight against one arm and letting one of her legs drop out from under her.

It doesn't even faze them. They haul her up a bit higher, carrying her easily between them until she regains her feet; neither of their grips so much as twitch.

"Khaiam!" she screams, twisting in their arms now, panic lending her strength. "Paul!"

"Please calm down, Ms. Neumann," the man on her right says. He sounds bored and a little aggrieved. She can almost imagine his next words: *I don't get paid enough for this shit.*

"Let me go! What do you think you're doing?"

"You're being taken in for questioning, pursuant to Article Five of the Homeland Security Act. There's no reason to be alarmed."

"I want my parents—don't my parents have to be here?"

"Your parents will be notified in due course." They've reached the lobby. The security guard glances up at them and frowns—Graciela barely resists the urge to scream for help. She doesn't think it would do much good.

"Don't you have to show me a badge?" she asks, clutching desperately at straws.

"Here." The woman on her left flicks her suit jacket aside to show off a laminated badge with a logo and her name. Graciela doesn't recognize the logo, wouldn't know a fake from the real thing.

"Oh...kay."

"Our car is just right here."

They lead her down the sculpted lawn to the curb. She's expecting a black sedan, something with tinted windows and bars between the driver and passenger, but the agents take her to a relatively normal blue four-door car. There's one of those retro stickers on the back with a picture of a stick family, as if to advertise who might be in the car.

"I just—" She glances back over her shoulder, but there's no sign of pursuit. The other agents must have delayed Khaiam and Paul enough that they haven't made it out of the building—if they're even following.

"Now, Graciela. No one wants trouble." The male agent opens the back door and gives her a pointed look.

Reluctantly, outmatched and out of options, she gets into the car.

CHAPTER TWENTY-FOUR_

She isn't sure if the cold in the room is some kind of interrogation tactic, or if she has frozen so completely that even the air is still. It seems impossible that she has not had a panic attack, but now that there's actually something to fear, she finds it difficult to feel anything at all.

The agents drove her through the city and out to a suburb she didn't recognize. The guard at the gate let them through with only a visual ID, and they left the car out front so they could lead her directly inside. The setup seemed a lot like a police station, with a bored-looking man at the front desk and a bunch of individual desks scattered around one large room. Just past the main bullpen, there were a series of side doors. One opened into this room, where they unceremoniously deposited her. They took her purse and phone, patted down her pockets, and then left her there without a word.

She has no idea how long she has been sitting here, staring at the ceiling tiles. There is no clock in the room, and without the ubiquitous presence of Surfaces at every hand, time is hard to measure. The only things in the room besides herself are three chairs, one table, and a giant one-way mirror.

She would never have described herself as claustrophobic, but the total lack of outside stimuli is starting to affect her. Counting dots on the ceiling helps break the monotony, but she does not know how long this calm veneer will last.

It sounds like a gunshot when the door finally opens. The same two agents enter the room. The man has taken off his suit jacket and tie; he's carrying a few manila folders and a handful of paper. *Paper* files. Graciela channels Desponia and resists the urge to scowl. She sits back in her chair, trying to tip it onto two legs to show just how little she cares; but it's bolted down, so she settles for slouching instead. One arm falls at her side while she balances the other elbow on the chair's arm, a picture of cool indifference.

"You seem to have calmed down," the woman remarks dryly. Both adults take seats across from her.

"What do you want?" Gracelia asks. She toys with her fingernails, pushing the edges of the skin back with her thumbnail. Eye contact is for people who care. Desponia has no skin in this game, and Gracelia can play at the same.

"Tell us about the AI." The man opens one of the folders and slides it across the table. It's full of artists' renderings of Thomas—with his fiery hair, with his boy-next-door looks, with his night-black skin. One or two of the images are screencaps of Dives, but most are drawings, probably witness accounts. None of them capture him quite right—but his dancing eyes would no doubt be impossible to reproduce in this way. Thomas is made to be in motion.

"Looks like you're more than caught up," she says.

"Let's start with what we don't know," the man continues. "Your father's research seems inconclusive on the nature of its origin. Can you fill us in?"

"The great mystery of life," she says, but secretly she is shocked. So not even the Department of Defense understands how Thomas came to be created? Is that the secret Paul is keeping—even from Maxwell? "I only got a B+ in my quantum computing class. Your guess is as good as mine." Then she grins. "Well. Probably not *quite* as good as mine. Do you even need a college degree to be a secret agent?"

"This is not a game," the woman snaps, and Graciela feels some of her confidence trickle away. Why is it so hard to keep hold of herself, of the version of herself she wants to be? She grips tighter, doubles down against the lump in her throat.

"So I'm guessing you're the bad cop?" she asks.

"You're damn right I'm the bad cop. And I am out of goddamn patience." She slams her hand on the table. Graciela jumps.

Her response, though coated in snark, is quiet. "That didn't take long."

"How do we find it?"

Graciela shrugs. "Have you tried being younger and a hell of a lot nicer? Works for me."

"He shows up every time you Dive, doesn't he." She doesn't phrase it as a question, but Graciela answers it anyway.

"Not every time," Graciela hedges. But her eyes dart back and forth between the agents, and everyone knows she just made a mistake.

"Good," the man says. "You're going to help us catch him."

"Like hell I am!" She doesn't need Desponia now; Graciela has enough fire for herself. She leans across the table, intensity in the lines of her body. "You have no jurisdiction over him. He's not an American citizen. There aren't even regulations that cover his existence."

"I can assure you that we are working well within our

mandate. The AI is a direct threat to U.S. citizens, and it will be contained and destroyed."

She sits back, rocked. "You're talking about *killing* someone."

"Please. It's a piece of technology," the woman says.

"A broken, incredibly dangerous piece of technology," the man seconds.

"You don't know what you're talking about." Gracie squeezes her eyes furiously closed, wishing she had the words. If she could only speak eloquently enough...would it make a difference? Could she save him? She opens her eyes, knowing she at least has to try. "Thomas is a completely autonomous person. If you had an interaction with him—you couldn't tell the difference between his version of life and ours. He's...*Thomas.*"

"Even assuming you're right, and that he is some new kind of life," his voice implies this is a very big *if*, "he's still undertaking terrorist actions. We have a responsibility to stop that."

"Since when is hacking *terrorism?* Giving people stim-packs and removing parental controls doesn't hurt anyone."

"And locking people offline? Or worse, locking them *online?*" the woman says.

"You can't be locked online, the Line can always be externally removed," Gracie says with a dismissive roll of her eyes. *Luddite.*

"If you won't agree to help us—" the woman starts, and Gracie talks over her even as the woman continues.

"I won't."

"—then we will proceed without your cooperation."

"What does *that* mean?"

The man takes over. "Think this decision through very carefully, Graciela. You could be charged with conspiracy to commit terrorism, or hindering a federal investigation, both of which are serious crimes. I know you have a very bright—"

Again, Gracie interrupts. "You don't know me at all. You don't know anything about me."

"I don't need to know you to know that you don't want to waste the best years of your life in federal prison."

She lets the last of Desponia fall away as she draws her knees up to her chest, resting her heels against the edge of the chair. She wraps her arms around her legs. "I want a lawyer or I want my parents. You can't just keep me here." She presses her face against her knees.

"Your parents are being notified—the office seems to be having difficulty finding their contact information, but I'm sure they'll get through soon. And in the meantime, you have something we need, and no one is leaving this room until we get it."

Gracie doesn't answer, just grips her knees harder and presses her face more firmly against her knees.

"There's no point in hiding and pretending this will go away. It won't," the woman says.

Gracie closes her eyes. She pictures herself in the Waves, on the rolling purple hill where she kissed Thomas under the Seussian sky. The leaves laugh as the wind rustles them; she can almost hear the sound.

"This is your last chance to be on the right side of this issue, Graciela." The man is trying to make his voice warm, but it doesn't suit him. *You should both be the bad cop,* she thinks, and fights down a hysterical giggle.

"Enough," the woman says. "We don't have all day." She makes a gesture at something, and the man gestures back. Gracie can't see them, of course, but she can hear the rustle of fabric. The man stands and exits the room, while the woman comes around the table towards Gracie. She ignores her until she feels the woman's hand on her wrist. By the time she raises her head, it's too late to stop the handcuff from snapping shut.

"Are we going somewhere?"

"You could say that." The woman yanks Gracie's hand, hard, and slides the still empty handcuff under a bar in the table.

"What the hell are you doing?" Gracie asks, coming to her feet. The agent transfers her grip from Gracie to the empty handcuff and makes a grab for Gracie's free wrist. She pulls it away and tries to take a step back, but she's hampered by her pinioned wrist. The struggle, though savage, is brief. Gracie almost punches the woman in an attempt to break free, and both of them are heaving for breath by the time the second cuff snicks into place. "Let go of me! What are you doing?"

The woman steps back, taking a deep breath and brushing hair out of her face. "You had more than ample opportunity to cooperate."

Gracie wrenches against the cuffs but succeeds in nothing but hurting her wrists. She slides the cuffs back and forth along the bar, but it grants little range of motion; even standing is awkward. "So what, you're trying to intimidate me into confessing? Good job, you scared the shit out of a teenage girl!"

"Well, it is appropriate," the woman says. "Since you're the rabbit."

"I'm the—what?"

The door opens and the male agent walks in again, carrying a Line.

"Ah," says the agent. "And there's the snare."

Gracie hauls on the cuffs again, even knowing it's futile,

as a sense of real terror begins to eat through the fog of her emotions. "Stop it. Let me go."

"Sit your ass down before you fall over," the man suggests, and he stalks closer with the Line in his hands. Gracie backs up as far as she can, and as he nears her sphere of motion, she lashes out with one foot, half-shrieking. The woman swears and sprints around the table, making a grab for her, but Gracie drops practically to the floor, panic giving her strength and purpose.

"Get off me!" she screams even as the woman grabs her by the shoulders. She kicks again, mostly flailing now, as the man grabs her around the back of the neck and hauls her close. His expression is grim, and she bucks and convulses in desperation. The woman's grip slips; Gracie falls backwards, her trajectory arrested by the metallic grip of her restraints. The momentum yanks her forward and she slams her head against the table.

She sees stars, hears a whine as the world goes dark and bright again. The weight of the Line on her temple is almost soothing in its familiarity, but she knows something is wrong and can't quite place what. Her body is dragging on her arms, the world is disappearing and sliding away, her head is pounding, her stomach churning, and there is sand under her hands.

Sand?

She staggers to her feet, bringing up a hand to shield her face. She is standing in a small, punishingly bright room. She can stretch out both arms and touch the walls, which are smooth and white and rise endlessly into the air. It's cold enough that she can see her breath, and when she spins in place there is nothing to see but the walls. A tiny square tube, somewhere in the Waves.

She pulls up the Dive menu to find she's in a generic

avatar, and all the options are grayed out. She's never seen anything like it—this is far beyond Thomas's ability to stop people from disconnecting. She has no tools of any kind—no ability to send a ping, no connect or disconnect functions, no access. She is cut off.

She feels panic building and tries to fight it, but her heart-beat and increased breathing whisper that she is losing. There is nothing to focus on, no distractions nearby. She presses both hands against one of the walls, shuddering, and tries to think of a calming exercise, anything.

"Did you think Thomas was the only one who could trap people in a Dive?" The voice belongs to the female agent, comes from everywhere at once. Gracie grabs onto those words, trying to run them over and over through her head, but her breathing is too fast, her thoughts too jumbled. She presses her forehead against the wall and tries to take a deep breath. *Don't breathe until she speaks again,* she thinks. *Don't breathe.*

Her lungs burn.

There's a flare of colored light, which slips from the top of her own head and disappears up into the white void. A flare. After a long pause, the flare goes off again. This time she raises her head and watches; the flare is made of tiny glowing pictures. Her eyes, her hands, her laugh. *A snare. A rabbit. Don't come, Thomas.*

If she can fall unconscious, the connection will break. Even dreams slip from the Waves. The burning is stronger, and she doesn't know if she can do it. *Don't breathe,* she thinks and holds a picture of Thomas in her mind. She sinks to the ground, curling up with her chest pressed tight against her knees and her forehead almost touching the ground. There are stars behind her eyes. Her throat burns and her head feels full. There is an almost overwhelming need to breathe, or cough. *Don't breathe,* she thinks, and imagines she can hear his voice calling her name.

The world starts to drift. She doesn't know if she is strong enough. She feels a hand on her shoulder and thinks, for a second, she did it. She's dreaming, and her father is here to pick her up and rock her to sleep.

But when she turns her head it isn't her father—it's Thomas. "No!" she gasps, and then draws in a huge breath, coughing, and the burning gets worse before it gets better as Thomas wraps an arm around her shoulders.

She feels a sharp tug on some metaphysical level, and then Thomas glares and draws her in closer. The feeling dissipates, even as there is a crank and a click and a ceiling tile slaming into place a few inches above their heads, trapping them both in total darkness.

"It's a trap, Thomas, they're trying to kill you," Graciela whispers, clinging to him with the desperation of the panic still writhing under her skin. She cannot see his face but there is an intense concentration in his voice when he answers.

"They're trying to disconnect you from the system so they can trash the entire server."

"Will that work?"

There is something strange about his voice, almost emotionless, as he answers. "They've shut down the firewall I used to access the server. All they have to do is turn off the router and server, and then destroy the physical copies."

"No, no, no, no. Oh God, Thomas, Thomas." She presses her face into his neck, sobbing, and feels another tug against her *self,* a sucking that seems to emanate from somewhere in her heart. "What do we do? There has to be something— they'll pull my Line if they can't disconnect me through the interface! Thomas—"

He kisses her, a sweet soft thing; in the complete dark he almost misses her lips. "Don't cry, Graciela," he whispers. "Neither of us are really here."

"What?" she asks, and then there is terrible pain, and the world smashes into pieces and bricks, and she screams, and she is falling, and she does not hit the ground.

CHAPTER TWENTY-FIVE_

She tastes light, sees colors. Her body shrieks and spasms, bruises blooming on her collarbone, below her elbow. The pain is intense, nausea rocking on the heels of vertigo, and she loses her lunch on the shoes of the agent still crouched in front of her, removing her Line. She's experienced the Bends more times than most Divers, but she's never had her Line forcibly removed. She understands now the headlines she mocked about people being treated for trauma after escaping from one of Thomas'... Her thoughts lurch to a halt. Thomas!

She tries to scream but her teeth are still clenched; every muscle feels engaged. Her wrists are burning, one of them bleeding from the force of her convulsions and the metal of the handcuffs. As the tremors smooth into twitches, she starts to shake anew, this time from the tears running down her face.

"You can't," she gasps, "you can't."

"It's already done." The man takes out a key, unlocks her cuffs. She does not have the strength to catch herself, knocks her head again as she falls to the ground. He tries to catch her, but he moves too slowly, and then awkwardly holds her shoulders for a second before letting her go. She curls up on the ground, sobbing, not sure whether the inability to move her limbs stems from her muscles or her heart.

She cannot break again. There will be no pieces left.

She does not know how long she lies there. People go; people come. Someone tries to speak to her; someone shakes her shoulder. She closes her eyes and refuses, tunnels into the deep dark where solitude is an inevitability. *Neither of us are here*, she thinks, and she lets herself drift to the place where they are still together.

Someone says her name, touches her forehead. Someone picks her up, and she thinks this must be the dream she had, her father carrying her through empty halls. Her head is pillowed on his arm and she is a child again, before she learned there was no such thing as safe. He stayed too late at the lab and she fell asleep on his desk; he carries her into the house and tucks her safely into bed.

"*Sweet dreams,*" he whispers, and a heart machine beeps slowly in time.

"*You aren't really here,*" her mother sings, the lullaby soft as her touch. Light rises and falls, and people speak and whisper and shout and stroke her cheek, but all she sees is a little girl in a bright blue dress.

"*Look at me, Daddy!*" she shrieks, and spins and spins under a glitching sky. "*I'm not really here!*"

The stars come out, dance above her through hazy dark waves. Thomas brushes his fingers across her forehead and whispers her name, and she closes her eyes and smiles. "*Thomas,*" she whispers, and his lips brush against hers.

"*Graciela, Graciela. Come back to me.*"

"*I'm not here,*" she whispers, and she feels his fingers strong in her hair, the touch of his palm against her chest.

"Graciela," he whispers again, "open your eyes."

She does. She is sitting in a dark bubble at the bottom of the sea. Above her, jellyfish drift like slow-moving stars, luminescent in the murky dark. The light is soft and blue, Thomas's voice gently muted. The only sound is her heart, their breath. Peaceful. She smiles and traces the lines of his face in her mind. He's wearing the same avatar he had on when she gave him the truth of his name, and his dark skin almost disappears in the low light.

"I love you," she whispers. His whole face brightens, and she traces it now with her fingertips, memorizing the curves and planes. "I should have told you when—" her voice cracks, breaks. "Why didn't I tell you?" She buries her face in her hands, willing the dream to crack, too, to break apart and leave her drifting.

Instead, Thomas touches her hands, soothing. "You're telling me now."

"You're gone," she whispers.

"Graciela—I'm right here. You're okay. Graciela—open your menu."

"My—" She starts to ask what, but thinking of her menu has caused her to flick her fingers unconsciously, bringing up the admin menu from her standard Line.

There's a menu. She's Diving. Somehow she's—

She stares at Thomas. At his smile, too perfect for a memory. At the jellyfish, too beautiful for her imagination. At the admin menu—*God, an admin menu, so pedestrian.* She flicks through her options, sorts through code and brings up a seashell. It manifests in the palm of her trembling hand, smooth and white and ridged, one tiny chip on the edge to add realism to the illusion. She isn't dreaming.

"Thomas?" she asks, her voice beyond cracked, and when he grins, she throws her arms around his neck, wishing she wasn't crying again, grateful when the arms that wrap around her are solid and real. "Thomas, God, I don't understand, they killed you, the firewall—"

"I dipped a toe."

"What?" She pulls back, slides a hand across her face to wipe away the flood's debris.

"When I got that ping from you, it didn't seem right. You always send notifications through the chat program, and...no offense, but they're not exactly sophisticated. You also have this adorable belief that I have nothing better to do and I'll definitely see it the first time." His words are flippant but he's still holding her close. She's sitting in the cradle of his legs, and he keeps one hand around her shoulders like he's afraid she'll disappear if they lose touch entirely.

"You always do," Graciela points out, and then kisses him, and then hits him. "I thought you were dead!"

"But I'm not."

"So you knew it wasn't me."

"I suspected. And then you were behind a firewall—so I dipped in a toe. I copied my data—created a Manifestation that I could have reintegrated if it turned out there was no problem."

"You—wait—what? You can *copy* yourself?"

He shrugs. "Sort of. Not really. It's like we were talking about—copy and paste instead of cut and paste. Missing the formula."

"A manifestation of your brain pattern at the moment you create it," Graciela says, wonder in her voice. "How is that even possible?"

"That's how your father got Manifestations," Thomas says, confused that she doesn't know that. She waves the words away.

"No, obviously, but you shouldn't even *have* brain patterns, not technically. How is that even possible?"

He grins. "You'd think you would get tired of marveling at my awesome powers."

"Never," Graciela promises and kisses him again. He returns the kiss, pulling her close like he's afraid she'll drift away.

"I'm sorry," he whispers. "I couldn't... I won't ever let something like that happen to you again."

She touches his chest, wondering if there's a heartbeat there, if he would miss it if it went away. "You can't protect me out there."

"I will find a way," he whispers, and his voice is a glimpse of that other side, the darkness that he does so well at hiding. "I will never let them take you from me."

"Speaking of..." She flicks up her admin menu again and toggles on public browsing. A square appears at the bottom right of her vision, showing a hospital bed. Khaiam is hovering anxiously over her, staring at her face for signs of motion. "Oh my God! I'm in the hospital?"

"Oh. Uh." Thomas shrugs, embarrassed. "Yeah. You were out of it. I even... I tried to get Maxwell to let me talk to you, but he's an asshole."

"Thomas."

"So I asked Khaiam, and he snuck you in a Line."

"He looks really worried." She kisses Thomas again, and then pauses, really looking at him, staring into his eyes. She's stopped asking herself why they seem so familiar—now they belong to no one but him. "I should probably go... I should talk to him, let him know I'm okay. And I don't want him to get in trouble with my parents if they come back and see he's snuck me a Line. They might confiscate it."

Thomas nods, reluctant to let her go. She runs a hand

down his arm, ending with curling their fingers together. "I meant what I said, Graciela. I will find a way."

She kisses him, and wonders if this fire will consume her.

"I meant what I said," she says. "I love you."

She is still holding his hand as she presses the disconnect, and the world de-rezzes and slips away in blue fire. The last thing she sees is Thomas' eyes, intense and dark, devouring every second of her presence in his world.

———

Coming back into her body feels like a punishment. Her eyes are burning like she hasn't blinked in hours, and the whole-body ache is profound and omnipresent. She has a headache worse than the time she got hungover from drinking too much mead at the Armstrongs' Christmas party, and her wrists are bandaged and stiff.

She moans and tries to make a complaining joke, but all that comes out is a croak.

"Gracie!" Khaiam surges forward, grabbing one of her hands and then instantly letting go when she winces in pain. "Oh, shit, I'm sorry. Does that hurt?"

"Everything hurts," she croaks. "Water?"

"Oh, uh, yeah." He quickly disengages the Line and hides it under her pillow, then grabs a cup of water and straw off the bed. He helps her drink with ease—it isn't the first time he's ministered to a girl in a hospital bed, Gracie knows. These are the moments of bravery no one acknowledges— that he came here, despite the memories.

"Thank you," Graciela says, doubting he will know how many layers the words contain.

He brushes hair out of her face and clears his throat like he's chasing away tears. "You scared the toast out of me."

"I scared myself," she admits. "How long have I been out?"

"Four days."

"*Four days?*" she dumbly repeats. "Four...Jesus."

"See, I told you you scared me more," he jokes, but his eyes are serious, the fear still lingering. He sits next to her, looking like he's trying to find a part of her to cling to that won't be weird or painful. She takes his hand, hiding the wince the movement evokes, and he squeezes the tips of her fingers, mindful to stay away from her wrist this time.

"Thank you. For bringing me the Line."

"That was easy—getting rid of your parents was the hard part."

"What did you say?"

He laughs ruefully. "I don't know, I think I was babbling. Have you noticed I'm a terrible liar? I just said something about wanting to talk to you privately, kind of acted like an embarrassed teenage boy who can't handle emotions."

She chuckles, but the motion hurts, and her smile quickly drifts away. "I am so sorry—I didn't mean to..." What? How does she explain, or even excuse, four days of drifting through her own thoughts? *I didn't mean to leave you,* is what she should say. *I just couldn't bear any more pain.*

"I know," Khaiam says, and she thinks maybe he does; maybe he reads the unspoken words in her eyes. Maybe, after all this time, he knows her better than she thinks.

"I'm sorry if I was weird about Bella," she says, abruptly.

He looks caught off-guard, but instantly jumps into soothing mode. "You don't need to worry about any of—" he starts, but she cuts him off.

"I was scared. It was stupid."

"Scared of what?"

She hesitates, wondering how to say the words in a way

that won't make her sound like an idiot. "Do you ever... For a long time I thought... I guess I was just..." She laughs and rubs a hand across her face, scrubbing some of the sleep from the corners of her eyes. "Speaking of teenagers who can't handle emotions..."

"You always have been worse at that than me," he says with a gleeful grin.

"Stop making me laugh. It hurts."

"Everything hurts," he says, and then seems to regret the allusion to greater things. He clears his throat and scratches his head. "You know, after...you know. I was worried that you would get bored of hanging out with me."

Gracie almost sits up, stopping herself at the last minute when the pain in her core muscles reminds her that she's still an invalid. "Are you kidding?"

He shrugs. "I thought you felt sorry for me."

"You thought *I* felt sorry for *you*? Are you completely delusional?"

"Hey, opening up emotionally here, you're supposed to be nice to me," he jokes. He squeezes her hand once and then lets it go, picking up the cup and helping her have another sip of water. "You..." He clears his throat. "You and Calista were always so close. I felt a little like an intruder. I guess I was a little afraid you were going to dump me once you thought I could handle it."

"I feel like I've stumbled through a mirror into an alternate dimension where I'm the desperately popular one who everyone loves and who's good at everything."

He gives her a look, but he's smiling. "I'm not desperately popular."

"And everyone loves you. And you're good at everything. Even Mrs. Dimas likes you, and she hates everyone."

"Thanks." He dips his head down, embarrassed.

"I was scared that if you started dating Bella and you weren't sad and broken like me, you wouldn't want to spend time with me anymore," Graciela blurts. Khaiam glares over his sharp intake of breath.

"You aren't broken."

"I mean—kinda, though."

"No more than any of us," he allows with another of his patented Fadel smiles. "Look, let's make a pact, okay? No more being insecure idiots who don't trust that people like us just for who we are. Deal?"

"Deal," Graciela says, and shakes his hand.

"Should I go tell your parents that you're awake?"

"Oh. Right. Parents. That would probably the responsible, mature thing to do."

"Which is why you didn't think of it," he teases as he stands. He sticks his head out the door; apparently her parents are in the hallway, because half a second later they're in the room. Her mother kisses her and murmurs endless platitudes in Spanish, while her father takes the seat Khaiam vacated and squeezes her hand.

She wonders how easy it is to forgive someone when we're afraid we might lose them, and how hard when we think we won't.

"How are you? Does it hurt?" Carmela asks in Spanish.

"*Sí*, everything hurts, but it isn't so bad," Graciela promises. Khaiam hovers in the doorway, looking unsure about whether to stay or go, and Graciela cocks her head to indicate he can stay.

"You had us so worried. Khaiam, dear, will you go get a nurse and tell them she's awake?"

"Sure, Mrs. Sandoval," he says, and turns away before he catches her exasperated look.

"Honestly, how hard is it to remember?" she asks,

brushing hair out of Gracie's face even though it doesn't really need adjusting.

"He's a little distracted," Graciela points out. "He probably hasn't been back to the hospital, since..."

"How's your head?" Maxwell asks.

"Fine. Do I have a concussion?"

"A minor one," Carmela says. "They don't think there was any damage. We're suing the Department of Defense."

"Can you *do* that?" she asks in surprise.

"You're damn right we can," Maxwell says, and Gracie feels sorry for whoever is on the other end of that anger.

"They were trying to kill him," she whispers.

"Who?" Carmela asks.

"Thomas. *Dios mio, Mama.*"

"Yes, well, they failed," Maxwell says. "And I made a successful argument in front of the governor that the technology is too valuable to destroy. We've still had no luck replicating it. If we can't study how and why Thomas works, we may never be able to create another intelligence quite like him."

"Nice to hear you've been hovering over my bedside," Graciela dryly answers.

"You must be feeling better if you're already capable of sarcasm," her mother says.

"My sarcasm bone wasn't one of the broken ones," she answers.

"You don't have any broken bones," her father says.

"It was just...exhaustion," her mother says, trading looks with her father. "But..."

"Let me guess. You want me to go and see Dr. Zhao."

"Well. Yes, we do. We've been trying to give you time, but maybe that hasn't been the best solution to the problem. We should have been more proactive."

"Fine."

"We also think..." She trades looks with her husband, who gives a subtle nod. "That our initial instinct was right. Clearly, through his actions or through his orbit, Thomas is dangerous right now. It would be best if you stayed away from him."

"Are you fucking kidding me?" Gracie sits up, ignoring the intense pain in her muscles at the motion. "I'm not here because of *Thomas*. I'm here because of asshole DOD special agents with James Bond complexes."

"Graciela! That kind of language is entirely inappropriate. You are *here* because you were caught in the crossfire between unscrupulous people and the AI. The thing about important people is that they are rarely the ones who get hurt —it is the people next to them who suffer the consequences."

Maxwell's gaze drops at that, and Graciela wonders if he considers himself to blame; if Carmela's comment is not just about Thomas, but about the father who has allowed his family to get caught up in all this.

"You want to know where I am because of Thomas?" Graciela pulls the Line out from under her pillow and holds it out, not caring if the intensity of her grip crushes it to dust. "I'm *here*. I'm *alive*. Thomas is the only thing that makes the world I'm in better than the one I can live in in my memories." She is proud of the dryness of her eyes; she hopes, for at least a little while, that she is done with tears. "Or at least he was. He helped me see all the things I have—the people I have," she says, thinking of Khaiam and letting herself find her smile.

"*Mija*." Her mother sits on the edge of the bed, but her attempt at a soothing voice just sounds strained. "I'm glad you feel that Thomas has helped you. But don't you think it might be time to take a step back? His future is very uncertain, and—"

"*Mama.* I'm not arguing anymore. And I know that doesn't feel fair, and I know that you're scared for me—and I am, too. I don't want to be here," her wave takes in the hospital bed, the IV patch on her arm, the heart monitor wirelessly transmitting every steady beat, "any more than you want to see me here. But none of this is Thomas's fault. And he doesn't have anyone else to protect him." It takes all of her energy not to glance at her father when she says those words, but she still sees him stiffen out of the corner of her eye.

"And who is protecting you?" her mother asks.

"I am," she promises. "I will be careful."

"I don't like it," Carmela says.

"Are you still protecting him from me?" Maxwell asks.

"I don't know," Gracie says, lying back and closing her eyes. "I guess we'll just have to see."

CHAPTER TWENTY-SIX_

THEY LET HER OUT OF THE HOSPITAL A FEW HOURS later. Bed rest and a whirlpool bath are all she needs to soothe the muscle pain, and the wrists will heal on their own. The concussion brings with it a long list of requirements, but they mostly boil down to "be gentle with yourself." No physical exercise, no sudden movements, and no staring at Surfaces or screens for too long.

The very first day she's back, only an hour or so after she gets home, her mother knocks on the door. "Gracie? There's a girl here to see you—Angela? Should I tell her you're too tired?"

"No!" Gracie smiles to take the sting out of the interjection. "No, thanks, she can come in."

There's a pause, probably as Carmela goes and retrieves the other girl from the foyer, and then Angela comes in. She's holding a card and looks a little intimidated, though by what Graciela isn't sure. "A short visit, alright?" Carmela chides. "You don't want to wear yourself out."

"Okay, Mom," Graciela says, but she's already smiling at Angela, who comes over and sits beside her bed.

"I got everyone to sign it," she says shyly, holding out a card.

Graciela takes it. There's a cartoon cheerleader on the front, holding pom poms and saying, *You can do it!* Inside it says, *Get better soon!* "Paper card. That's so retro," she says appreciatively.

"I know you're all into the tech stuff, but...I thought you might like it?" It's a question, so Graciela answers it.

"I love it. Thanks." She winces as she tries to stretch an arm out to put the card on the side table, and Angela jumps in to help.

"What, um... Are you okay?"

"Just a bit bruised. What did they...say happened?"

"Just that you had an accident." Angela takes in Graciela's taped wrists, her bruised skin. "Gracie," she blurts, "you know I really like you, right? And I know you don't like me but—"

"I do like you," Graciela interrupts.

"I know, but I mean..." She coughs awkwardly, scratches the back of her head. "I guess what I'm trying to say is, I completely would try to help, you know, make you be happy. If I knew how."

"Um...Angela?"

"Yeah?"

"Do you think I tried to commit suicide?"

Angela stares at her. "Um. Did you...not?"

"No!" Graciela covers the bandage on her wrist and winces. "But I can see why you'd think that." And then she thinks about the past few months. The panic attacks. The tears. The breakdowns in school. She wonders briefly why she never *has* considered it, feels suddenly and intensely grateful as she realizes how much worse things could have gotten. "I really get why you would think that," she allows.

"So—but—what happened?"

"Uh." Graciela laughs. "Well. That's kind of a complicated story... You know the AI?"

"I'm not completely at a loss," Angela protests.

"Well, I sort of got into some trouble about it. The DOD—"

"What's that?"

"Department of Defense. Anyway, I'm fine now."

"I don't get it."

"I know. I'm not explaining very well."

"But you're really okay?"

"Angela—thank you."

The other girl blushes and ducks her head down. "I didn't do anything."

"It was really brave to ask me to the dance. I'm sorry I bailed early—I had a really good time. I guess I've been...kind of wrapped up in my own stuff lately. Things are so complicated...it's hard to see past that, you know?"

"Not really," she admits. "The most complicated thing in my life is completely Bella."

Graciela laughs, then holds her ribs as the pain drifts through. "Yeah. Well. These last few weeks... I've been doing a lot better, and a big part of that is being friends with you."

"Really?" Angela brightens, glowing under the praise. "So, I did help?"

"You did. You so did."

"Oh. Then, good. Oh! Did you hear Bella and Khaiam are going to the movies on the weekend, but then Todd got really jealous and *he* said—" Angela chatters on and Gracie smiles, enjoying every second. There's something soothing about the world Angela inhabits—the one, if Graciela is honest with herself, she used to be part of. She isn't anymore, and she isn't sure she wants to pretend that things are still the way they used to be. But it's nice to go back and visit—if only for a little while.

———

Angela brings homework as well as the card, so the next day Graciela has tons to catch up on, and her mother sits by her bedside and helps her answer questions so she doesn't have to stare at the tablet or read too many long passages. It's the most time they've spent together in the last year, though neither of them talks about much other than the task at hand. Maxwell spends most of his time at work; on top of the DOD lawsuit, he's also fighting with his funders about workflow priorities, though he won't discuss the details.

Graciela is delighted to see that her network feed is full of get-well wishes from classmates. She had no idea there were so many people who would even notice that she was gone, let alone take the time to ping her. Angela comes by and drops off flowers, and Khaiam stops by every day after school, just to say hi and keep her up to date on what's happening in her absence. Her mother has okayed her taking the rest of the week off, and she'll return to classes on Monday morning.

She and Thomas meet every day, sometimes two or three times. He's concentrating his efforts on creating the utopian playgrounds they discussed; maintaining the sandbox effect while he isn't there is proving to be a challenge, since the Dive Interface wasn't intended to allow advanced modifications while online. She talks him through some of the more complicated aspects of the technology; his understanding, and lack thereof, is fascinating. In the same way that everyone knows how to breathe, but only a pulmonary specialist can explain *how* breathing works, Thomas can do things Graciela can only imagine, but has no idea how he's accomplishing it. Together, they manage to create a truly breathtaking algorithm for internal edit control. Graciela almost runs downstairs to show it to her father, knowing how amazed he would be...but the wall between them feels insurmountable, and she doesn't know quite how to make the first step.

Instead, she creates a world she thinks he would like; a gift, perhaps, for a future when they are more in sync. In her world emotions *are* physics; strong thoughts have consequences. Thomas teases her, trying to make her angry to see what will happen, but all she feels is love, which chases the clouds away and brings birdsong flitting through the air. The streets are wide and paved, with the sloping roofs of an alpine village, and every wall and cobblestone tells a story. Memories, so no one and nothing is ever forgotten.

Thomas's world is mostly incorporeal, a stream of data that breaks you down into electricity and impulse. Kissing there feels like falling into a fast river, battered between the rocks of the rapids but borne ever forward, breathless and giddy. The sensation of not having physical form is dizzying, but Graciela likes it. She tells him about falling in love with speed, about Calista and Paul and the borrowed bicycle. Thomas grows very quiet and seems about to speak, but instead wraps his arms around her and tells her stories of the Waves. The heroes who are rising to his call, the changes that are coming, slow and seeping, perfect zero. Unavoidable.

On Saturday Khaiam comes over for a movie night, but instead they end up talking for hours, the TV playing quietly and unwatched in the background.

"Do you think the Mars colony will ever decide they want to come home?" Graciela asks at one point. She's curled up in a chair, toying with the yellowing bruises on her right wrist. Her muscles are mostly healed, though she still wakes up from nightmares where she is trapped, a rabbit in a snare, screaming at Thomas as a forest fire descends down a wooded slope.

"I wouldn't. They're basically in charge of establishing a new society from the ground up. That's completely exciting," Khaiam says.

"It's a lot of responsibility. What if they get it wrong?"

"What would you change? If you could fix one thing?"

"Fix how? I mean, I don't know if you can change human nature, and that's the thing that needs the most work." Graciela tosses Khaiam the bag of popcorn.

"I don't know if I would want to change human nature." He upends the bag into his mouth and chews, musing, before finishing his thought. "You never know what's all interconnected. What if you get rid of greed and then realize you accidentally ditched... I don't know, compassion."

"You can't have compassion without greed? You're gonna have to show your work on that one."

"Well...compassion is caring about other people. Greed is caring about yourself—but, too much. So maybe if you're incapable, completely, of over-caring about yourself, you wouldn't be able to be really selfless." He taps the Surface near his arm and drags it into motion capture mode, flicking his fingers to skip through the channels.

"Hmm. Maybe. People like to claim you can't appreciate light without darkness, but... I don't think I'm on board."

"No?"

"We were happy, weren't we? Before we ever knew what it was like not to be."

"Yeah. I guess we were."

"What's that?" Graciela touches his arm, stopping his quick flicking. It's international news, the evening edition. A ticker tape on the bottom announces live coverage of a breaking story in Madagascar. The screen is split in two, with a teary-eyed reporter is standing in front of a concrete building on one side of the divide; on the other, a middle-aged woman sits in a meadow glade, clearly a Dive rendition. The woman is crying, her audio slightly garbled by the intensity of her emotion.

"—I don't know how much longer," she's saying, "and don't be scared for me, Mommy loves you, just close your eyes. Marcel, if you're watching you make them close their eyes, I love you so much. I love you."

The audio switches back to the reporter. "We're trying to get her family on the Line now. Emergency services have surrounded the building, but the placement of the bomb makes it very difficult for agents to reach the device without risking setting it off. So far, no demands have been made, but—"

"Oh my God." Graciela covers her mouth with one hand, horrified, and Khaiam reaches out to take the other.

"Is she inside the building?"

"I think so."

The audio has switched back to the woman, who is trying to regain her composure as she makes a list of all the people she wants to send her love to, all the things she hasn't said. "Francine, I forgive you. What a stupid thing to argue about. Everyone, if you're fighting with someone you used to love—stop. It doesn't mean anything. It just doesn't mean *anything*."

"Mrs. Perez, do you have eyes on what's happening in the building?" the reporter asks.

"Y-yes," the woman stammers. "Sort of. I'm in one of the offices upstairs, but I can hear shouts from the lobby. I saw at least six men in masks and guns—"

There's a flare of blue light on the Dive side of the screen, and a man rezzes into place behind the woman. The reporter perks up, pointing at the version of it she must be seeing, which is down and a little to her right. "Mrs. Perez, is that your husband?"

"Thomas," Graciela gasps.

"Seriously?" Khaiam leans forward, straining to make out details. Sure enough, the person is Thomas, wearing Johnnie's face from Urban Noir. He flicks his fingers at the camera, but he's distracted, and the feed doesn't quite disappear; it grows a little hazy, though, and the audio is garbled.

"We seem to be experiencing technical difficulties," the reporter says. "We're working to get the feed back up and running, if you'll just bear with us a moment." Meanwhile, Thomas is saying something to the woman. She clutches his arm and nods desperately. He asks her a question; his attention on her is intense, laser-focused. She nods again and closes her eyes. She grips each of his arms and he holds them, staring at her like he could burn an image of her onto his eyes. He speaks to her, calming, perhaps reassuring.

There's a sharp, loud sound, and then the audio snaps back into place, though the video remains hazy. "Don't be afraid," Thomas is saying. "Okay, I'm going to go on three. Okay? One—"

One side of the screen rocks with a terrible explosion. The reporter ducks, her swearing covered by an automatic censorship program as she stumbles across the moving ground. Behind her, the building has been reduced to a heap of rubble. Nothing moves. Nothing could have survived.

In the Waves, Thomas holds the arms of the woman. She hasn't de-rezzed. Somehow she is still there, and Thomas is staring at her with raw triumph in his eyes.

"Antoinette?" he asks. "How are you?"

For half a second her face remains blank, and then it

crumples back into tears. "Tell my family that I love them," she pleads.

"Antoinette. You're safe. Do you understand?"

"Francine, I forgive you. What a stupid thing to argue about," she says. Her voice is desperate, a perfect parroting of her earlier words. It looks like Thomas has made a Manifestation of her, but from the look of frustration and rage on his face, that was not his intention. "Everyone, if you're fighting with someone you used to love—" Her image freezes, staring plaintively at the camera, and then the feed goes black.

"I'm sorry, we've lost contact," the reporter says. Her voice is trembling, though she stands steady now on the street; thick smoke rises behind her, and dust is starting to fill the air. "We're trying to reestablish the link now—ambulances are on hand, but it seems unlikely that anyone has survived this devastation. Again, I am on the scene of a terr—"

Khaiam waves the TV into silence. "Jesus."

But Graciela's mind is far away, racing through possibilities and permutations. "Khaiam."

"What?"

"He created a Manifestation."

"Yeah, I mean—should that even be possible?"

"Theoretically. Your Line scans your brainwave patterns and allows it to interact with the system, so those scans are accessible. Uploading it that quickly, in real time, would take insane processing power, but Thomas has already shown he has that. It's the same technology Dad used to make Manifestations in the first place. He was trying to create artificial intelligence by copying people into the Waves, but it didn't work."

"But why would Thomas be trying to create another AI

using your Dad's failed methodology? Why wouldn't he be using the method that *worked*?"

"I think he is," she gasps, horrified. "I have to go."

"What? Go where? What did you just figure out?"

Graciela is already on her feet, grabbing her purse, checking to make sure she has her phone and her Line. "I'll be back in about an hour."

"Are you kidding? No way, I'm coming with you." He leaps to his feet, but she grabs hold of his upper arm.

"I need to do this on my own."

"Gracie—you and Thomas."

She winces, adjusts the strap of her purse even though she doesn't need to. "Yeah."

"Is there—I mean..."

"Yeah," she says. "It kind of... I didn't really expect it. But yeah, we're... I don't know, whatever we are."

"But he's..." Khaiam hesitates, clearly unwilling to say what he's thinking, but it's obvious on his face.

"Not you, too."

"No," he promises. "It's just... I'm just surprised."

"He's real, Khaiam," she whispers. "I know—God, if I'm right maybe I've been more right than I knew, all along. And I need to know, and I don't think I'll be able to convince Paul to tell me the truth if you're there."

"Remember what happened *last* time you tried to get Dr. Armstrong to tell you the truth?"

"That was different."

"You promised you would be careful."

"I am. Khaiam—I can't keep living with these secrets."

"Fine. Let me at least come with you to the lab. I'll wait outside."

"Are you sure?"

Instead of answering, he opens the door. She squeezes his hand, and they walk out together.

———

It's late enough that she's pretty sure Paul will be at home rather than at the lab, so they take the local commuter bus; it isn't hard, but the trip is strange, strained; every detail seems full of portent. The ads that flash their hollow smiles as they pass the windows; the Surfaces that flicker and trigger and go dormant again with their approach and departure; even the stormy sky, threatening a rare deluge and making the night seem darker than it is. Pathetic fallacy, she reminds herself, but the world seems poised on the brink. She and Khaiam exchange only a handful of words, both of them too keyed up for much more. There's a coffee shop at the end of the block, and Graciela convinces Khaiam to wait there while she goes on alone.

She takes the walkway up to the house like the steps to the gallows. She cannot stop hearing what Thomas said, all those words she was too blind to see the truth of.

"What if you don't just copy the information in someone's brain—what if you cut the entire swath of their brain pattern out and paste it into the Waves?"

"But that would kill them."

"And bring them back to life here."

She rings the bell. There's a long pause before Mrs. Armstrong opens it. She looks momentarily lost, as if the sight of Graciela on her doorstep has transported her back—to a time when her daughter was alive, most likely.

"Gracie? What on Earth—it's after eleven!" she says, but she instantly steps back to let her in.

"I'm sorry to bother you. I just needed to talk to Paul quickly?"

"He's in his lab. Where's your ride?" she asks, peering out the door.

"I took the bus."

"I don't think your mother would like that," she says, frowning.

"It's fine, Mrs. Armstrong."

"Why don't I give her a call—"

"It's fine, Mrs. Armstrong," Graciela says again, more forcefully. "Thank you." She pushes past her and down the hall, finding her way with the ease of old memories, though it's been many months since she was here. Her steps echo on the hardwood floor, and she feels a charged solemnity descend. It feels like a panic attack is approaching but she knows it's something more, something cleaner. Truth.

She opens the door of the lab. Paul stands by a blackboard, ostensibly making calculations but really just staring into space. He only looks over half-heartedly; double-takes when he sees her, something in her expression triggering a warning.

"Gracie?" he asks. "What on Earth are you doing here?"

"What did you do to him?" she asks. She knows the answer now, but she has to hear it; cannot quite believe what her brain is already piecing together. *Why don't you tell them my real name?*

"To Maxwell?" he asks, glancing around the room.

"To Thomas."

"We've been over this, Gracie, and I think it would be best if I called your father." He drops the whiteboard marker, paces across the room.

"What did you do to him!" she screams. He is caught off-guard, shocked by her vehemence, by a side of her he's never seen. He has known her since she was three years old—has never seen her angry, not once.

"This has nothing to do with you," he says, unwilling to make eye contact. He picks up his tablet, holding it like a barrier between them.

"At the launch, he wanted you to tell us his real name."

"Gracie—go home!" Paul snaps. He has found his inner parent, a brace of steel, but the pain in his eyes is a weakness in the armor, and Gracie slams into it.

"He hates you," she says, and Paul takes a step back as if shot. "Even saying your name makes him shudder."

"Stop," Paul gasps. He takes a step away as she stalks closer, almost trips over a chair and rights it, fumbling. "Gracie—you have to leave this," he insists. "Just let him go—just leave him alone, just let it go. Please, Gracie. You need to stop."

"I don't know how to stop." She stares at the whiteboard where he was working, picking out words and numbers as isolated units before her eyes focus and she scans the whole. She recognizes some of the formula, but it's been altered—it's her father's work into brainwave copying. It's proof.

"I've never kissed anyone," Thomas said, as if for him that wasn't the same thing.

"Jesus Christ," she whispers. She feels her legs growing weak—reaches out but there's nothing to hold on to. Everything is shifting. She wants to be sick, swallows bile. Paul sees what she's looking at and runs over, but they both know it's too late. He grabs a cloth, throws it over the board as she staggers back. "I thought I was wrong... I wanted to be wrong..."

"It's—it's nothing, it's—"

But it's far too late. Gracie hears herself make a noise, some desperate negation, stumbles away from Paul. He is changed, suddenly, this jovial sweet man from her childhood, this sinister creature with blood on his hands.

"God," she gasps. "Oh God, Paul. *Who did you kill?*"

Tears are streaming down his face, and he's shaking his head, shaking, shaking. "It isn't like that, it wasn't like that, you don't understand, I thought...I could save her. I thought I could save her."

"Her?" she whispers. And suddenly...it makes sense.

She swipes her hand against the Surface on the wall, brings up her desktop. A flick and two swipes pull up her photo folder. She finds the picture she's looking for, swipes it larger, and larger again. She can hear Paul sobbing as the wall fills with a pair of eyes so brown they're almost black, with dancing lights in their depths. She lets out a sigh, releasing pain she hadn't even known she was clinging to, a sense of rightness settling over her heart. She turns; Paul has curled up against the floor, his head on the hardwood.

"Calista?" she whispers. "You saved her?"

"No," he sobs, "no, no, I tried, I tried, I tried."

"But you did," she presses. "That's how—that's—Thomas."

"That thing is not my daughter!" he screams. She has never heard a sound like it; feels her heart grow smaller just being in the same room as it. The agony of guilt, the clawing pain of failure, the hollow emptiness of knowing you can never go back.

"Then what is he?" she whispers. But Paul doesn't answer—she isn't sure he can. She wonders if a person can come back from that kind of destruction; thinks there will always be holes between the pieces where Calista used to be.

She staggers to her feet. The lab is eerie, the silence sounding louder against the backdrop of his tears. She realizes it's the first time she's seen a grown man cry, wonders if something is breaking in her, too. If there's a hopeless kind of growing-up you can never come back from.

She walks out of the lab. Mrs. Armstrong is standing in front of the door, staring in fear and growing awareness. Graciela looks at her, not knowing what to say, not knowing how to fix the things that have broken. Finally, she says nothing; walks away instead, down the hall and out onto the front porch.

The storm has broken—rain pounds against the cold white walk, turning the garden into mud. She walks out into it, feels the immediacy of it and closes her eyes, tilts her face into the deluge. What does Paul mean? If Thomas is Calista...and all this time...and this pain... She wanders onto the grass, sits down at the base of a tree where she and Calista used to play as children. They made a potion that they swore made the tree grow a foot in just a day, and Paul told them how proud he was, and what great scientists they would be.

Paul. Calista. Thomas.

Her clothes are soaked through in seconds. She rifles through her purse, pulls out her Line with trembling hands. She presses it to her forehead, heedless of the rain, knowing she has started down this path and she cannot stop. Suddenly she is angry, furious. The secrets they have kept have cut her, broken her, made her bleed. How dare they? How could they have born her pain?

Her Homepage rezzes into view. For some reason, maybe thanks to Thomas's hacking, her clothes are soaked here, too. She turns the switch on her flare, watching the raw rush of data, and lets the fury build into fire.

CHAPTER TWENTY-SEVEN

THOMAS STEPS OUT OF THE TREES WITH A BOUNCE IN HIS step. His hair is black and straight, his clothes androgynous. His face is the closest she has seen it to the beauty of the creature at the launch, the farthest from the Thomas she has come to love. He waves a hand, brings the sun out, but Gracie knocks it back behind the clouds and he lets it go, squelching through the dirt to her side. He has his hands in his pockets, and when he catches sight of her expression, his own grows wary.

"Why didn't you tell me?" she whispers when he's close enough to hear.

"Tell you—?"

"*Why didn't you tell me!*" she screams.

He ducks his head, squeezes his eyes shut. "Paul finally told you."

"All these months...*goddamn you!* All these months I've been dying without you! How could you do that to me?"

He's at her side in a heartbeat. The muscles in his jaw tremble and his hands hover, desperately wanting to offer some solace he isn't sure he can give. "I didn't—I wasn't sure you would understand."

"I *cried* for you. I-I—" She makes a gasping noise that isn't quite words, fights through it. The cursed tears are in her eyes again. It always seems to come back to tears. "I missed you so much the world came apart. I couldn't—god*damn* you, I couldn't even breathe, couldn't—how—and you were...*here*, all along, you were...you..." She's sobbing and she hates it and he's reaching for her, and she hits his chest, sobbing, and he wraps his arms around her and she hits him again, folds against him, clings to him. All those empty nights, all that grief she thought could never leave her pours out, and she sobs until she can't breathe, until he looks afraid, until the anger feels tempered by the joy of him, *here*, and not lost to her, not gone.

She catches her breath, leans back against the cottage so her face is protected from the pounding rain. She clings to herself, the only sure thing left in the world.

"Paul doesn't think it's you," she says.

"But you do?"

"I don't know how I didn't see it right away." Because she's looking back, now, with the clarity of memory, and every moment where she remarked how familiar he seemed makes sense; and every joke he made, or the easy way they laughed together, makes sense; and every smile they shared, and the way they fit together like puzzle pieces, makes sense.

He sits on the ground, and gradually she sinks down to sit beside him. He traces flowers in the dirt, and she recognizes the shape as something Calista used to draw. She wonders how many urges like that he's had to fight, how much of himself he's been holding back.

"Why doesn't he think it's you?" she asks.

"Because...of this." He waves a hand at himself. "I was his

little girl. And then...I was here, and...and..." His voice is dreamy, remembering the stunning joy of freedom unasked. "It was like all the chains on my body snapped and broke. I could be...anyone." There's a ghost of a smile on his lips, which is battered by the next memory, killed in the end.

"But you never told me..." Gracie says.

He looks up at her, and she has no doubt she's looking at Calista: not a copy of her, not a mixture of her and something else. Calista. "I loved you," he says with an eloquent shrug. "And it all felt wrapped up together, like I couldn't tell you a part without telling you all of it, and I just...didn't see the point. In living through pain I could never fix."

"I'm sorry," she whispers. "I'm so sorry I never knew."

"You know now," he says. The vulnerability in his eyes evokes quiet nights, curled up in their pajamas under the covers, sharing the secrets of where their lives would go. And she had no idea that this secret lay between them, and now, knowing... She can't imagine how it took her so long to fall in love.

"I know now," she agrees, and she kisses him as the rain falls. He wraps an arm around her waist, draws the kiss deeper, desperate, his body shaking between them, steaming in the cold rain. She isn't sure if he's crying, isn't sure if she is, but feels wounds she thought were bone-deep starting to heal. *Nothing is indelible*, she thinks, and for the first time, the thought makes her smile.

"You're really okay?" he asks.

"I don't know what okay means anymore," she says. "But I know that I love you. I don't know—exactly where we... we..." she blinks, coughs, holds a hand to her throat.

"Graciela?" he asks. Holds her shoulders between his hands, as if he can keep her there, but they both know what's coming. She coughs and the world explodes into pixels, shatters, and she curls onto her side, retching against the wet grass.

———

Her father throws a blanket over her shoulders, drags her to her feet. "Are you insane?" he yells. "You're going to catch hypothermia!"

"And you just pulled my Line!" she yells, teeth chattering. "Remember, how I ended up in the hospital?" But Graciela knows in her heart it was stupid—she's frozen solid, can't stop the shaking.

"I told you to stay away from it!" he yells back. "I warned you it was dangerous!"

"Did you know?" she demands.

"Inside. Now." He points at the house, but she doesn't budge.

"Did you know? Did you know the AI is Calista? That you didn't invent anything!"

He gives her a strange look, and she realizes he has no idea. She wonders how he could be so blind, and then she sees the thoughts flickering behind his eyes, and she watches them die, one by one, and understands her father a little better. "That's nonsense," he snaps. "You're delirious." He grabs her arm, propels her towards the door, and she is borne along.

"Would you *listen* to me? Paul altered your research into copying brainwave patterns—he uploaded Calista, that's who Thomas is."

"I don't know where you got this insane idea, but that's what it is," he tells her. "It's barely worth a response."

"It's *true*," she snaps. "Ask Paul!"

"Brainwave scans create Mannies with poorer functionality than regular programmed Mannies. They're incapable of adaptation."

"This wasn't a scan. It was an upload. *Dad.*" She drags him to a stop, steps away from the front door. "He didn't copy and paste—he cut and paste."

"Inside. Now." He pushes her through the door, shuts it behind them both. Paul is standing in the hallway, crying, in the middle of an animated conversation with his wife, but they both stop as the door opens. The sight of it stalls Maxwell's forward momentum. "Jesus, Paul," he says, at a loss for more.

"It's Calista. Paul—you didn't do anything wrong. You didn't lose her. It's Calista," Graciela insists, but he's shaking his head and he won't hear the words.

"Jesus," Maxwell says again. "What the hell did you do?"

"I had to save her," Paul whispers. He and Maxwell share a look, decades passing between them, knowledge Gracie will never have. "I had to try."

"You stay the hell away from that AI," her father says, rounding on her, and the vehemence startles her backwards.

"Why would I do that?"

"Because it's *dangerous!*" he yells. "You think you're playing some kind of game, some teenaged fantasy, but you aren't! Whatever Paul did, wherever the AI came from, it is not Calista! It is not your friend!"

"What the hell is *wrong* with you both?" she cries. "What are you so damn afraid of?"

"It changed her—Gracie, whatever she became in the Waves—she's not the person you knew," Paul insists.

"Why?" Graciela demands. "Because he's a man?"

"Yes!" Paul snaps.

"Open your eyes!" she screams. "He's your son! He loves you and you're killing him!"

"Enough!" Maxwell hollers over the fight. "Enough," he says again, more calmly, as Paul and Graciela both subside like chastised children. "Gracie—you are forbidden from Diving. You are forbidden from seeing the AI. You will stay out of this until we have...sorted it, until we...figure this out. Do you understand?"

"I understand. Better than you think," she says. She spins and runs down the hall, past her father, hearing his scream, into the lab and through it, through the door into the testing room beyond. She slams it closed, keys the lock, and grabs the experimental Line on the arm of the chair. The room is linked to a screen projector, and she keys that up. She thinks maybe, if she can force them to see Thomas as she does, if she can just make them *understand*, maybe she can fix this.

She hears banging on the door; the door rattles in its frame. Will they go so far as to break it down? She picks up the sensor, places it against her temple. The banging is louder now, the door trembling. She sinks back against the reclining chair and Dives.

The modified Line brings her into a site she's never seen. It's a bleached desert full of reddish rocks, the air wet and hot in her lungs. The atmosphere presses down on her, sapping her strength, and she feels the sting and bite of insects that dart towards her and away too quickly to swat. Small red marks appear almost instantly on her skin, and she staggers when she takes a step forward. Paul must be testing stim-packs to see what ranges of exposure do to the body on the other side of the Line. She's wearing a neutral skin, masculine, but she can't see her face to know if it's Paul or her father. The legs feel strange, jerky, and she brings up the menu and searches for a means of reaching Thomas. She's surprised to see what looks like a tandem Dive line set up, but the person it's attached to is just a fuzzy shape. She grabs it and tugs, hoping for the best.

There's a terrible noise, a booming all around her. At first she thinks it's something she's done, but it comes to her that the sound she's hearing is feedback from the real world. She doesn't know how to adjust the settings on the Line, searches for a private/public browsing menu, but there's nothing there. She drags at her collar, trying to clear her airway, and wonders how quickly a person can die from heat like this. She sinks to her knees, but she can't find an address bar. The site is probably partitioned to make sure other Divers don't wander into it; she can't hack her way out, not from inside. And if she disconnects, hacks out, and re-Dives, will it be too late?

"What did you do to her?" Thomas yells, and she swivels in surprise. He's standing behind her, a mirage in the shimmering heat. His skin drips with water, keeping him cool but steaming in the blazing air. His hair is spiked into upside-down waterfalls, pouring into a cloud of rain around him.

"Thom...as..." she breathes, swaying. He goes still for a moment, studying her, and then in a heartbeat, he's at her side.

"Graciela?" he asks, as she falls into his arms.

He picks her up, holding her close against his chest, and the world shifts around them into the perfect blue of the raw Waves. She feels her skin burning, sloughing off, feels a new person growing inside the lavender coolness of his arms, tastes her father screaming, screaming, and then they are standing in the perfect blackness of the sky. All around them, stars and galaxies twinkle, and the air is so still no sound can travel. He sets her down and she's afraid she might fall, but somehow she floats there in the blank spaces between the stars.

"Graciela?" he asks again, and his voice comes to her like a thought, appearing directly in her mind without the inconvenience of traveling through air. She nods, catches her breath. Her skin is sunburnt and raw, her lungs still burning, though the cool emptiness she drinks in feels like aloe vera against the pain. She feels a shift as Thomas lays her own avatar onto the borrowed Line, wipes away the face that used to live there. She's surprised how slight the difference is; wonders what it would be like to wander through life wearing someone else's face.

"What happened?"

"I told Dad everything, and Paul admitted the truth, but they're still trying to argue that it isn't you. We're set up with a projection canvas. I just need—I need them to see what I do."

"I think your father is working with the Department of Defense."

"What? After what they did to me—he wouldn't."

"He asked to meet me on Urban Noir, but when I showed up there was just a bunch of Empties in suits. Shot me about eighty-two times. It felt weird, but nothing happened. I think the site tried to boot me offline but there was no connection to follow, so I just didn't go anywhere."

"Thank God." She tries to stand but her shaky limbs don't want to lift her, and he joins her instead. They find each other's arms, bury their heads against each other. "I don't know what to do," she murmurs. "I don't know who to fight, how to make this okay. They're so determined to keep us away from each other—"

"We'll find a way," he promises, and she knows it's not a vow that he can keep. She clings tighter, as if she senses she is reaching a point where he might disappear through her fingers like mist.

"If I don't come back—" she says, but he shakes his head, shakes her by doing so. They are connected now, tied together, irrevocably.

"Don't say that."

"If I don't come back," she insists, "you know how much I love you, right?"

"I can't do this without you," he whispers. His voice is cracking, light bleeding in her mind, and she wishes it could always be like this; so quiet, so still, his voice inside of her, a part of her that can never be taken away.

"Don't ever let them make you think you aren't real," she demands, tears in her eyes. She feels a shudder run through her body; knows the moment is near. She clings tighter, knowing this goodbye could be for a long time, vowing it won't be forever, vowing she will come back to him, no matter what, no matter how they try to keep them apart. She will always come back.

She coughs, feels her body convulse.

"No!" Thomas screams, and he grabs her, *holds* her, and the shudder passes across her, consumes her, and she jerks away from herself, but Thomas's hold on her arms is iron, and she screams as fire fills her muscles, fills the sky. She feels something rip, tear, *give*, and she tumbles into the starry sky, heaving, breathing in the silence, and the world is crisp and clear, present like it has never been before, and it has opened around her into something unfamiliar, crisp and cutting like diamond.

She can see the lines of code in the world around her— knows if she dipped a finger through them she could rewrite them or wipe them away. She can *hear* the Waves, a steady drumming in her bones, an awareness of the millions of people Surfing and Diving all around her. Just beyond the subtle skin of the site, she sees the raw data of uncharted

Waves, the spaces in between, the roots of the universe. She feels her connection to it; feels, too, the sudden sharp lack of the world beyond. Her menu is gone. No dropdown functions, no messaging system for pinging outside sources, no basic programming set. She is cut off. Adrift. *Uploaded.*

She screams.

She bangs against the ground, but there is nothing solid to touch; tears desperate holes through the horizon, but there is no lab behind it, no father's waiting arms. She spins, runs, but there is nowhere to go, stops and starts and knows that she is still screaming and that she might never stop.

Thomas follows her, tries to catch her arms, suffers her panicked blows and tries to cover it all with soothing noises. "It's okay, it's okay, Graciela, it's okay."

"No—no, no, what did you do? Oh, God, what did you DO!" she screams. She smashes her fists against his chest, knocks him back from her. She is lost; panic overwhelms her, with no direction to extinguish the energy burning through her veins.

"You're safe now! They can never control you, Graciela, you're free. It's okay—you're free."

"I'm not free—I'm DEAD!" she screams. She doesn't seem to process the words until she hears herself speak them; gasps and staggers away. Turns to stare into the endless horizon, the holes she's torn dripping with blue light, unManifested code. "I'm dead," she whispers. "Oh God...you...you killed me." She turns to face him, uncomprehending, a depthless terror in her eyes. "You killed me," she whispers again.

"But you're right here," he insists. Tries to take a step towards her, stops as if hitting a wall as she flinches away. "You said it yourself—Graciela," he begs, tears in his voice. She imagines she can feel his salt-stained words in her mind, moving through her skull like liquid. "You said that I was real. So if I'm real—and you're just like me—how can you be anything less than you were a second ago?"

"I'll never grow up," she whispers. Her voice is discordant, hollow. She speaks as if by rote, staring at him and somehow at nothing, unfocused. "Never go to university, never disappoint my parents with my mediocre grades. I'll never hold my child in my arms, never cry when it skins its knee for the first time. I'll never...I'll never...I'll..."

"But you can do all that here," Thomas promises, his voice thick and wet with unshed tears. He reaches his hands out towards her, imploring, his feet rooted in place. "You said this place was real. You said it yourself. I...I thought you would be happy."

Her face twists, darkens with rage, her pain focusing on this, the only thing in the world—the only real thing left in her world. *"You killed me!"* Graciela screams, and her voice is a hurricane, a tornado, a whirlpool. He cries out, grabs his head, but the sound goes on and on, an endless barrage, and he staggers back once, again, and she follows, battering his defenses, pushing him away, again, further, until he falls through a hole in the site. She closes the door behind him, barring him out, though she is aware of his presence like a spot of light in the back of her mind. She will never be without him—will never be alone again.

She sinks to her knees and cries, sobs, as galaxies wheel around her, the endless majesty of the universe, the immutable path of the years.

EPILOGUE_

He sits at his desk, staring out at the winter landscape on the other side of the glass. The trees are heavy with snow—just another thing to get used to in New England. He likes the seasons, likes the feeling of time progressing. Nothing ever felt real in California.

The teacher dismisses the class, consults the attendance sheet. "Mister...Fadel? Could you stay behind?"

He swings his backpack over one shoulder, approaches the front with trepidation. This is the first time one of his university teachers has so much as said his name—he likes the feeling of obscurity brought about by a class of two hundred, hoped he could disappear in this ancient institution.

"Yeah?" he asks.

"I'm not sure you entirely understood the assignment," the teacher says. She holds the essay out to him, and since it seems like he's supposed to take it, he does.

"I didn't?" he asks.

"I asked you to write an essay about modern reimaginings of the Persephone myth," the teacher reminds.

"Yeah," he says. The teacher sighs.

"So—this is a short story. About some kind of ghost in the machine."

"But—it's—you know, a Persephone and Hades story. But modern."

"How is this a Persephone story?"

"Well—she loved him. But to be with him...she had to go to the land of the dead. You know, to die. And she didn't want to. Like how Hades tricked Persephone into eating the seeds. Thomas, you know...killed her. And I thought—all the stories talk about the part where Persephone gets dragged down there, right? And they talk about Demeter saving her so she only has to spend half the year there. But they don't talk about...what it's like. For Persephone. What it would be like, to be there, every day. To be trapped in that place...with the guy she loved. Except he's also the guy who killed her. And she's all alone if she doesn't forgive him, but how can she..."

The teacher sighs, the long-suffering sigh of an academic who doesn't feel they should have to deal directly with first-year students. "Yes. It's a very tragic story—Despoina and Thomas, king and queen of the Waves, forever in love, forever locked in hatred. It's also a short story."

"Yeah?"

"I asked for an essay. A comparative essay."

"...Oh."

"Take it back—rewrite it by Friday, and I'll regrade it. Feel free to use this myth as your modern example, but make clear contrasts with the original story. Okay?"

"Sure," Khaiam agrees. "Thanks." He slings his backpack more securely over his shoulder, starts to walk away.

"Mr. Fadel?" the teacher asks.

He stops, turns back. "Yeah?"

"The story—it was well-written. It felt almost like...you

knew these people. But there's no truth to it, is there? All these rumors you hear?"

"About people dying and being uploaded to the Waves?" he asks. He remembers his girlfriend, the way she would stare at you, so solemn, just before she would burst into laughter; remembers his best friend, the gentle crinkle of her nose when she was upset with you. He feels the knot of pain in his chest, the place forever empty; thinks of the Line sitting untouched on his desk in the dorm. "No," he lies. "It's just a sad story."

ACKNOWLEDGMENTS_

This book started from a simple idea: a single line in a beautiful poem, *I come to you on wire wings*. So many thanks to Dave Strauss, who wrote me that poem a lifetime ago, and spawned the dream that eventually turned into this book.

Thanks of course to the Parliament House team, whose trust and vision was crucial to letting this project finally see the light. This story is incredibly close to my heart, perhaps the most of anything I've written, and seeing it finally in print is a life's dream.

As always, a thousand thanks to be my beta readers: Kali, who gave her name to Calista; Hollis, who gave me the biggest confidence boost of my career when she told me I had made her cry; and Mom, who for once didn't tell me the story was too sad, even though it probably was.

Wren Handman is a novelist, fiction writer, and screenwriter from Vancouver, Canada. She writes a wide range of stories, from adult fantasy (*Command the Tides*) to young adult paranormal (*In Restless Dreams*). All of her stories are connected by one thing: the magical blended with the everyday, because she secretly wishes magic was real. And who's to say it isn't? You can find Wren spending way too much time on Facebook, while she isn't crafting, reading, or getting too excited about how much she loves things.

GRACIELA STILL NEEDS YOU_

Did you enjoy Wire Wings? *Reviews keep books alive . . .*

Graciela *needs your help! Help her by leaving your review on either* GoodReads *or the digital storefront of your choosing.*

She thanks you!

www.ingramcontent.com/pod-product-compliance
Lightning Source LLC
Chambersburg PA
CBHW050824190726
48286CB00007B/1985